SPECIAL AGENT

Angels & Imperfection Book 2

DAN ARNOLD

Special Agent
by Dan Arnold

Paperback Edition

CKN Christian Publishing
An Imprint of Wolfpack Publishing

6032 Wheat Penny Avenue
Las Vegas, NV 89122

Paperback ISBN: 978-1-64734-688-1
Ebook ISBN: 978-1-64734-687-4
Library of Congress Control Number: 2020936899

SPECIAL AGENT

DEDICATION

To Lora
Here we go again!

To my family
Thank you for challenging me, encouraging me
and being my biggest fans.

FOREWORD

Wolves are by nature stealthy. Sometimes they are masters of deception.

The sheep are by nature gullible. They will believe almost anything.

The Shepherds are appointed to stand between the sheep and the wolves.

CHAPTER 1

My assistant Christine Valakova, wearing a charcoal grey pantsuit with an emerald green blouse which matched her eyes, was sitting at her desk in the outer office/reception area when the phone rang.

"Tucker Investigations, how may I direct your call?"

She listened for a moment and then she replied, "Yes ma'am, please hold,"

She punched the intercom button.

"John, line two. It's your lady friend, the attorney from next door."

From the safety of my walnut paneled office, I could just imagine Christine's face; fairly certain she was rolling her eyes. Christine has never liked Ms. Doyle. Referring to her as my "lady friend" had been meant to annoy me, which it did.

"Good morning, this is John."

"John, this is Melody."

Doyle, Doyle and Starnes, the law firm that occupied the suite next to ours, had recently become the only other tenant on this floor. I was loosely on retainer as their primary investigator. I say loosely, because they didn't need a full time investigator, and I wouldn't have worked for them on a full time basis.

Melody Doyle was an attorney, a partner, and the

rather attractive daughter of Clarence Doyle III, the founder and senior partner in the firm. I was aware Melody had a crush on me.

"Good morning, Melody. What can we do for you today?"

"Oh, baby, the things you could do for me!"

Melody had never been shy, but this was ridiculously unprofessional.

"What's the reason for your call this morning, Ms. Doyle?"

"Come on, John, you're no fun. Can't you ever think about anything other than business? Everything is always business with you. Don't you want to play with me?"

"Melody, can you get to the point?"

"Oh, that's better, baby. The point is I want you."

"I'm sorry I thought this was a business matter. Isn't that the reason you called?"

"I suppose it's one of the reasons, John."

I could virtually feel her pouting through the phone at my ear.

"OK. Can we talk about that?"

"Oh well, fine then. We have a client who was injured on the job. He was nearly killed when a load of badly stacked bricks fell on him as he was working to construct a retaining wall. He suffered numerous broken bones, including a crippling spinal injury, and he has a traumatic brain injury that will leave him impaired for the rest of his life. We feel the injuries were caused by gross negligence and an unsafe working environment. We believe the employer knew of the danger and ignored it. Worse, we believe he instructed the employees to ignore the danger, and he threatened to fire anyone who would not work under those conditions."

"How may we assist you in investigating the incident?"

"John, you are so frustrating. Do you have to be so formal? Loosen up, baby!"

"Ms. Doyle, Can we keep this professional? What do you want us to do?"

She sighed loudly into the phone.

"It seems we need you to find a witness. The employees are mostly illegal immigrants from south of the border. Our client will testify, as best he can, but we need additional witnesses. Most of the other employees have disappeared. The ones we have located and interviewed refuse to cooperate. They are afraid of deportation, and they're afraid of their employer. Not just afraid for their jobs, but actually afraid for their personal safety."

"Construction sites are usually required to abide by OSHA and other State and local safety requirements. How could the employer have failed to be in compliance?" I asked.

"Evidently this company does mostly smallish projects in rural areas using illegal immigrant labor. The jobs are finished quickly before any OSHA inspector even knows they're going to happen. More often than not, there isn't even a permit pulled."

"You say most of the employees disappeared. How is the company going to stay in business and meet its commitments?"

"These are illegals, John. There's no shortage of available labor. The ones who've disappeared have already been replaced."

"OK, Melody, give Christine all the information you have on the company, as well as the names of the employees who would have knowledge of this or other past incidents. We'll take it from there. Please stay on the line and I'll transfer you over to Christine."

"I'd rather play with you."

"Yeah, uhh, you mentioned that already. Let's stick to business, OK?"

"I said I'd rather play with you. Why don't you come over and play?"

"What in the world?" I thought.

I put her on hold and punched the intercom button.

"Christine, Ms. Doyle has some information for you related to a case we'll be investigating. I'll put her through on line two."

After I punched the button to send her back to Christine, I considered the strangeness of our conversation.

Melody Doyle had come on a bit strong a time or two before this, but it had not been as deliberately unprofessional or interfered with business in the way this conversation had.

I was glad she'd called me on the telephone and not actually shown up in person.

What was going on with her?

CHAPTER 2

My next appointment put me on the highway. As I often do when I have long distances to drive, I rented a car. This was an economical choice because I could recoup the expense from my client, while driving an anonymous new car with better gas mileage than my big diesel pick up.

It's a little less than a four hour drive from Tyler, Texas to Magnolia, Arkansas. Whether you go east on I-20, through Shreveport, Louisiana and then go north, or if you go into Arkansas by way of Texarkana, it takes about the same amount of time to get there.

I'd headed east on I-20 that morning, driving into a major thunderstorm just as I was approaching Shreveport. It was the same storm that hit East Texas earlier in the morning. I drove with lightening crashing and thunder booming all around me. In the worst of the rain, visibility was cut down to a few yards, and traffic crawled for about twelve miles. I left the interstate at Minden, Louisiana, driving north in a steady rain toward Magnolia. The road wandered through forests primeval and bucolic farmland.

The rain slacked up and the worst of the storm had just passed through when I arrived at my destination. Fifteen years had passed since my last visit to Magnolia.

As I drove around on the rain scrubbed streets, I noticed how generally run-down things were.

Some years back, on my first visit to Magnolia, I'd still been in the Navy and was invited to a team mate's family home for Thanksgiving weekend.

That team mate was now the County Sheriff for Columbia County, Arkansas. I'd seen several election posters with his name on them from the moment I entered the county, and about an equal number for some other guy who wanted his job. The signs suggested Buddy was in the middle of a re-election campaign. I dropped in on him at his office.

"John, is that really you? I can't believe it. What's it been, ten, twelve years?"

"I suppose so, Buddy. You got transferred to San Diego while I was in Walter Reed."

"Yeah, that Pakistan op was a hairy deal. At the time, I didn't think you had a chance of pulling through. I can't believe you're upright and walking. I'm glad to see you're fully recovered now. You don't even look a day older. What's your secret?"

"Clean living."

He laughed.

Wilson Boudreaux "Buddy" Livesque (call sign - Live Screw), was a party animal back in the day. Now he was a bastion of the community. A kind of beefy guy, at first glance you might think he was overweight. Maybe he was, a little, but most of that weight was still solid muscle. His once sandy brown hair was now nearly all silvery gray. He'd always had the same twinkle in his eyes, rosy cheeks and a bright red nose. Although Buddy didn't have the beard or the red suit, the overall effect sort of brought to mind images of Santa Clause. As much as he reminded people of Santa, when we were sent on missions together, the enemy had never enjoyed the presents that "Live Screw" brought them.

"Buddy, I couldn't help noticing things are looking a little frayed around the edges here in Magnolia. I don't remember it this way."

"Well, the last big oil boom ended almost forty years ago. That oil income gradually faded away. Little by little the town has been fading away as well. If it wasn't for the college, the timber industry, poultry farms, brine plants and hunting, we'd be in worse shape than we are. Magnolia is still a great place to live and work, but finding work has gotten pretty tough."

"I noticed people wandering around with no real purpose. Some of them looked like zombies. Have you got a drug problem here?"

"Not any worse than anywhere else, I guess. Sure, it's a lot worse now than it used to be. People have to make a living somehow, and drugs can be profitable. When the economy collapsed, a lot of people moved back into this area from places like Detroit and Chicago. They have family here, so in a sense, they were coming home, but some of them brought their problems with them. For too many, coming back here meant more unemployment. With all these people moving back, it seems there aren't enough jobs to support the growing population. Most of the skilled labor force moved away to wherever the work is. Some of the unskilled people figure it's easier to make meth out in the deep woods, than it is to find a job."

I wasn't surprised. The same thing was happening all over the country.

"Tell me about yourself, John. What have you been up to?" Buddy asked.

"Well, after I left the Navy, I went to work for the Department of Homeland Security for a few years. I got tired of working for Uncle Sam and decided to go private. These days, I have a small detective agency in Tyler, Texas. I'm in the people business. Private investigation is all about people and their problems. At Tucker Investigations we serve big corporate clients with security or insurance fraud issues and we serve individuals and families with their more personal issues."

Buddy considered my answer for a moment.

"I know what PI's do, John. What brings you into my neck of the woods?"

"I'm here on business, Buddy. I'm looking for a guy by the name of Diondro Taylor. He has family around here, somewhere."

"Are you a skip tracer?"

"No, he isn't wanted for revocation of bail and I'm not a bounty hunter."

"OK, what's the deal?"

"About a month ago, a woman by the name of Amanda Sawyer was assaulted in a grocery store parking lot in Tyler. She was forced into her own car at gun point and told to drive away. A young black man observed the assault and attacked the 'perp' through an open car window as the vehicle was pulling away. He got ahold of the guy's gun hand and took the gun away from him without a shot being fired. Mrs. Sawyer was able to stop the car and escape. The guy who dived through the car window to help her was Diondro Taylor."

"Good for him!"

"Well, yes and no. Like most metropolitan areas of the country, Tyler has an inner city gang problem. In this case, the guy with the handgun is the most prominent member of one of the street gangs in Tyler. His name is Hector Lopez, known as 'el vibora'. He was arrested on the scene. For stepping up and interfering with the gangbanger, Diondro is marked for death. He left town in a hurry. I'm pretty sure he came here."

"Do they need Diondro to go back to Tyler and testify?"

"That's part of it. Diondro would be a useful witness, but he isn't essential. The store has cameras on the parking lot. There's excellent video of the whole thing. The gangbanger is going away for sure. This is his fifth arrest as an adult. He has multiple drug possession and assault convictions going way back. Because he's violated his parole, he'll go down on multiple charges this time. He has a long date with prison, no matter what. The point is; I've been hired to find Diondro because the victim's family wants to make sure he's safe and gets rewarded for his action."

"Huh. This is the first time I've heard of that!"

"Well, there's also a weird wrinkle."

"Of course, there is. What else is new?"

"The gang also hired someone to find Diondro. If they find him before I do, I have to assume they have a different reward in mind."

Buddy shook his head.

"Please tell me you are not about to turn my county into a war zone."

I shrugged.

"I have no such intention. My plan is to find Diondro and make sure he stays safe. If he will testify, I'll take him back to Tyler for the trial. If he won't testify, I'll get him set up somewhere where he isn't known. Either way, I've been instructed to arrange for his college tuition."

Buddy took a deep breath and let it out slowly.

"OK, what can I do to help?"

"Do you know his family?"

"Maybe, maybe not. There are several Taylors in the county and I don't know them all. I'll check with a couple of my deputies though. We'll find someone who knows the right family. Is there anything you can tell me to help narrow it down?"

I told him what I knew and what I didn't know.

"Well, it's lunch time. I want you to come home with me. Josie will be thrilled to see you after all these years."

Military families often form strong bonds. Perhaps none are stronger than those formed among members of an elite Special Forces combat unit like the Green Beret, Delta Force or the SEAL teams. The bonds between such men are tight, and the families become close. Wives support each other when the husbands are away. Even when they are off duty, the men tend to hang out together. Single guys like me get adopted into the larger family formed by the group. Naturally, the wives and girlfriends try to set us up with their friends. Josie tried to do that for me, but because of my mission on this planet, I was in no position to get serious with any of the available women.

I was pleased the years hadn't changed the friendship between Buddy and me. It was as if I'd just been off on a deployment for the last dozen years.

"Hey, Josie, look what the cat dragged in!"

Josie was not the same volatile and semi-wild child she'd been when she and Buddy first married. She'd grown into a more substantial, mature and Godly woman. Maybe thickened a little around the waist with the years, but she was instantly recognizable.

"Well, as I live and breathe, if it isn't 'Old Mother' Tucker!" Josie said, wrapping me in a hug.

There is nothing the least bit reserved, genteel, or refined about the behavior among the special operators of a SEAL team. Buddy was called "Live Screw" as his call sign, because of the way his last name is spelled. His name is Livesque, pronounced "Liv-eck," but the spelling was just too easy to make fun of.

I'd earned my call sign because I was the guy who always took care of my buddies when they forgot some important detail, suffered an injury, or were just too drunk to take care of themselves. It happened a lot in those days. My call sign became part of a rhyme; "Old Mother Tucker, is a bad moth-er******."

I hadn't heard anyone call me that in about a dozen years. Well, the last part had been used some, but not my nom du guerre.

In this war, I've been known by many names.

We spent lunch catching up and remembering some wild times we'd shared and the friends who'd fallen.

"Hey, is that a picture of Buddy, Jr.? The last time I saw him he was what, maybe five or six?"

Buddy's face clouded a little."

"Yeah, John, that's Wilson Livesque, Jr. We all call him "Bud." He graduates from High School tomorrow night. I'll bet he remembers you. If you're still in town, would you like to come to the graduation?"

"Yes, I would, I'd like it a lot."

After lunch, while Buddy made some phone calls, I helped Josie clean up.

"Josie, I thought something was bothering Buddy when we were talking about Wilson, Jr. Is everything all right with him?"

"Well, yes and no, John, Buddy is so proud of him he could bust. Did he tell you Bud has been accepted to Annapolis?"

"Wilson, Jr. is going to the U.S. Naval Academy?"

"Um hum. He'll be the first commissioned officer in the Livesque family. You know Buddy's family is a Navy family going back three generations."

"Yeah, I know. Wow, that's terrific! You said yes and no, what's the problem?"

"Some of Bud's friends are a bit wild. They're drinking and running around. Bud has fallen in with them. About a week ago, Bud was with them in a car when it got pulled over. The driver was arrested for DUI."

"I guess it's kind of typical for some high school

seniors. I can see how y'all would be disappointed Bud would choose that course."

"It's even worse, John. There's been some bad blood between them over this. Buddy is the County Sheriff, and he's up for re-election. He feels like Bud's behavior is a slap in the face and disrespectful of his position in the community. He's also worried that before the summer is over, Bud will screw up his admission to Annapolis, somehow.

"I'm sorry to hear that. Why do you think Bud is behaving this way?"

She shrugged.

"I don't know, John. I guess it isn't much different from the way we behaved at that age, back before we became Christians."

CHAPTER 3

When Buddy came back into the kitchen, he had news.

"John, I think we've identified the family you're looking for. Some are Taylors and some are Carlisle's. They're longtime residents of the county, going back to the end of the civil war. They have about three hundred acres of timberland they lease to hunters. They get their income from timber sales and the hunting leases. There are half a dozen homes, mostly trailers they live in, at the end of County Road 3802, right on the edge of LaSalle Bayou. That's about fifteen miles south of town.

"Thanks, Buddy. If you'll give me an address, I'll set my GPS navigation and head on over there."

"Uh, I don't think that's the way we want to approach this."

"... Why not?"

"I have a deputy who's married to one of the Carlisle girls. She'd be a cousin to Diondro Taylor. I think we might want to go at this kind of sideways. My deputy or his wife should probably be the ones to make the inquiries."

"Why is that?"

"These folks kind of keep to themselves, and they are extremely distrustful of outsiders. If you go driving in there asking about Diondro, they'll most likely tell you they've never heard of him and be otherwise generally uncooperative."

"Can we give them a phone call and set up an appointment?"

Buddy chuckled.

"John, you're thinking like a business man. These folks don't do things that way."

"What do you mean?"

"Most of them won't even answer a phone call unless they recognize the number. They don't like getting phone calls from sales people or bill collectors. If you call them, they probably won't answer the phone. If they do answer it, as soon as they hear your voice, they'll turn ignorant and you'll get nowhere."

I nodded. I've had some experience with that.

"You let me handle it. If Diondro is over there with them, I'll find out about it. Then we can figure out how we want to approach the family."

I didn't like it, but I realized Buddy was right. I figured if the Taylors and Carlisles were that distrustful of outsiders, Diondro would be safe right where he was — for a little while.

"I'll tell you what, John; you come back over to the Sheriff's office. I'll introduce you to my deputy who's married to the Carlisle girl, and we'll do some strategizing."

I nodded.

"OK, let's do it your way."

The deputy was a black man, about twenty-five years of age. He stood just over six feet tall, with an athletic build and a shaved head that shone like polished bronze. His uniform was crisp and tailored. It figured. Buddy would expect and accept no less from his men.

"John, meet Jermaine Jackson, no relation to the singer. Jermaine, this is John Wesley Tucker. John and I were in the Navy together."

We shook hands.

"The Sheriff told me some of this, Mr. Tucker. As I understand it, you want to locate a black male, nineteen years of age, by the name of Diondro Taylor. He would be one of my wife's cousins. That about right?"

"Yes, it is, Deputy Jackson. Diondro isn't in trouble, or at least not in trouble with the law. He's something of a hero, actually. He saved a lady in Tyler from being abducted by a gangbanger down there. The street gang wants him dead. So, I believe Diondro came here to hide out for a while."

He nodded.

"Uh huh, call me Jermaine, Mr. Tucker. Why you here?"

"Please, call me John, Jermaine. I'm here because the family of the woman Diondro saved, as a reward for his heroism, wants to pay for Diondro's college education. I also want to make sure he stays safe. I've learned the gang hired someone to find Diondro. They mean to kill him."

"Why they want to kill him? He the only witness?"

"They want to kill him because the guy Diondro jumped was the leader of the pack. They intend to send the message, 'don't mess with us'. There are other witnesses, but only Diondro messed with them. He's the one they have to kill."

"You locate Diondro, you planning to take him back to Texas?"

"I don't know. That'll be up to Diondro. It would be helpful if he would testify in the case, but it isn't essential."

"Why you think Diondro came to Columbia County?"

"I've been in communication with his mother, who lives in the town of Chapel Hill, just outside Tyler. She wouldn't tell me where Diondro is, but she indicated he was with family somewhere out of state. I did some investigating and figured this was the place."

Jermaine considered all this for a moment.

"Alright, I'll talk to my wife. I don't know him myself. I can't promise anything, know what I'm sayin'?"

"Sure, Jermaine, thank you."

"Uh huh. It may take some time. Where you staying at?"

"I figure I'll get a motel room, probably at the Holiday Inn."

"No, you won't," Buddy interjected. "He'll be staying with us, Jermaine. You can reach him at my house."

I could see there would be no point in arguing about it. I gave Jermaine my cell phone number so he wouldn't have to disturb Buddy when he called me.

Buddy had some official business to attend to. So, since I had a little time on my hands, I set out to do some research. At the book store on the Southern Arkansas University campus I bought a plat map showing all of the PLSS Sections in each Township and Range in the county. It showed each section with names attached to individual tracts of land. It also had all of the county roads on it.

It was a little complicated to figure out where CR 3802 was because of not knowing exactly which Township and Range it was in, but once I found it, I was able to get a general idea of the layout of the Taylor/Carlisle land. On a hunch I went to the local Wal-Mart, and sure enough, they had a county atlas for sale. Not only did the atlas show all the roads, it also showed other points of interest like the bayous, lakes and rivers, which were not clearly indicated in the plat map. With my air card functioning as a Wi-Fi hotspot, I used my laptop to access Google Earth. Once I typed in the appropriate data, I had an excellent satellite image of the property in question. I was able to zoom in and out on the various buildings, logging roads and fence lines, etc. that made up the Taylor/Carlisle property. I printed off the most useful images on my portable printer. This gave me very useful and comprehensive mapping and visual images of the entire area where Diondro might be holed up. All of that had only taken a couple of hours. The next step was to do some actual reconnaissance of the area.

Southwest Arkansas is heavily forested, much like East Texas. North America's southern forests know no state boundaries. They stretch from Virginia in the East, to Texas in the west, and spread across most of the southeastern U.S. In that part of Arkansas timber is the primary industry, in conjunction with oil and gas drilling.

Within two miles of the city limits, I was deep in the back woods. I drove south out of Magnolia on a State highway for about five miles, turning onto a smaller black top road. I drove past where CR 3802 branched off, noticing, that just as I had found in my research, 3802 was a dirt road. A little farther on, I turned left on the next blacktop road. I drove for about two miles before the road crossed over LaSalle Bayou. On the other side of a bridge, I stopped and got out of the car to have a look at the bayou.

I was here because I'd learned the Taylor/Carlisle land had this paved county road as a southern boundary. From here, the family homes were less than a mile away, as the crow flies. From the other side of the bridge, a person could hike over there through the woods and not have to cross the bayou. It wouldn't be an easy hike because here the forest wasn't plantation pines, but mixed native timber, thick with brush and vines. There were greenbrier vines, poison oak, Devil's Club, honey locust and other plants that could put a hurt on you. It was more like a jungle than a woodland park. In several places, all the thick brush and vines made it virtually impenetrable.

From where I was standing, both the bayou and a stretch of woods were between me and the place where Diondro was most likely located.

At this point, LaSalle Bayou was only about thirty feet wide. The water was dark and muddy, like tea with just a touch of milk, or weak hot chocolate. As is common in most bayous in this part of the world, the water was probably only a few feet deep, even in the deepest parts. There were cypress trees lining both banks. Spanish moss hung down like living tinsel, and the cypress knees jutted up out of the water, here and there. This was the time of year when the water level in the bayou would be at its highest point. Later in the summer, there would be much less water, leaving the cypress knees looking like miniature mountains, towering above muddy plains.

Watching the water, I saw an occasional swirl on the surface, evidence of the gar, catfish, bass, bream and other aquatic life inhabiting these southern waters. Although I couldn't see them, I knew alligators and water moccasins were also keeping a wary eye on me from their nearby hiding places

I was sweating profusely now in the afternoon heat and humidity which naturally follows the thunderstorms. The air was as stagnant as the water of the bayou. I was somewhere beyond uncomfortable. When I got back in the rental car, I turned up the AC to high, and drove on more slowly. I was looking for a feature I'd seen on the satellite image. I found it about a quarter of a mile farther on.

CHAPTER 4

Because hunting, fishing and other outdoor actizities are such a big part of the culture and the economy in that area, there was a really nice sporting goods store in Magnolia, Arkansas. On the way back into town, I stopped and bought a few items I thought might come in handy.

I drove back to the Sheriff's office and met up with Buddy, just as he was getting ready to head home. I followed him as he drove his official Chevy Tahoe through Magnolia and out into a pretty new subdivision on the eastern edge of town.

I noticed a dark grey Toyota sedan seemed to be following us. It stayed behind us on every turn. It could've been a coincidence, but I don't believe in coincidence. As we turned into the subdivision, the Toyota kept on going down the road. It had Texas license plates, not unusual this close to Texas, but not typical either.

We had just gotten to the house when Wilson Livesque, Jr. came driving up in his pickup.

Buddy looked at his watch as Bud approached us on the porch.

"Getting home from school a little late aren't you? It's nearly six O'clock."

Bud shrugged, as he attempted to go past us into the house.

"Hang on a minute, Bud. I want you to say hello to John Wesley Tucker. You remember him don't you?"

Bud stopped and looked me over.

"Say, are you "Old Mother" Tucker?"

I grinned.

"As ever was."

Bud shook my hand with a firm grip.

"I was just a kid back in Virginia the last time I saw you. Over the years, my dad has talked about you a lot."

"Yeah, what have you heard?"

"Oh, you know… my dad's war stories mostly. The things he can talk about. I thought you got killed or something."

"Naw, just shot up a little. I would've died, if your dad hadn't gotten me to the chopper. Say, I've heard about you, too."

"Really, what have you heard?"

"Oh, you know just the usual stuff. You're an honor student, Captain of the football team (sorry about the state championship), your father's pride and joy, and one other thing. Let me see… what was it? Oh yeah, now I remember, you're going to Annapolis!"

Bud glanced at his dad.

"Uh, yeah, I guess. Where did you hear all that?"

"Your dad can't stop talking about how proud of you he is."

Bud glanced at Buddy again.

"Huh, you could have fooled me."

Buddy stiffened up.

"I have to say, I'm pretty impressed. You've grown into a fine young man. I can see why your dad is so proud of you."

"Well… thank you, sir."

"You can call me John."

"Yes, sir… uh, I mean, John."

Bud went on into the house.

Buddy stopped me on the porch.

"I never said any of those things about Bud. How did you know?"

"Josie told me. If you don't mind my saying so, Buddy, you should have told me yourself, but even more importantly... you should have told Bud."

He nodded.

"Yeah, you're right. I just have a hard time with stuff like that."

"You don't have a hard time showing your disappointment."

"Is it that obvious?"

"I noticed it. I expect Bud notices it every day."

I left Buddy on the porch to think about it.

That night, I took everyone out to dinner at a pretty good Mexican restaurant. Since there were only four of us, we took my rental car.

When we walked out of the restaurant, I scanned the parking lot and the street. I was sort of looking for a dark grey Toyota.

"Are you expecting trouble?" Buddy asked me quietly.

I shrugged.

"Yeah, I'm the same way," he said.

"I thought maybe I was being followed, earlier today."

"Good grief! You men sure make a girl feel safe. Being married to a cop, I've gotten to where I take notice of everything around me, too," Josie said.

"Situational awareness is a good habit to develop." Buddy nodded.

"No harm in that," he agreed.

"Better safe than sorry," Bud chimed in.

Buddy scowled at him.

"A stitch in time saves nine." I added, with a wink.

"He who laughs last, laughs best," Bud said.

"You can't teach an old dog, new tricks," Buddy chuckled.

"You can with the right incentive," Josie said, batting her eyes at Buddy."

"Oh, yuck!" Bud observed.

We all laughed.

Later that evening Buddy and I sat and talked, alone in his home office.

"I expect Jermaine has had a chance to talk to his wife by now. Chances are some phone calls have been made and we'll learn something useful in the morning."

"I'm about ninety percent sure Diondro is here."

"Yeah, about that… look, I don't want there to be any trouble. Folks around here don't interfere in each other's business. As long as no crime has been committed, the Sheriff's Department stays out of it. I don't have to be involved. I'd like to keep it that way."

"I can't promise you anything. I'm telling you, Diondro is in real danger. If I can find him, so can whoever else is looking for him. If they get to him before I do, he'll be killed. Do you want to deal with that?"

"No, I don't. I just want you to know where I stand in this."

"Where exactly do you stand in this?"

Buddy was thoughtful for a moment. Then he grinned.

"I stand with you, John. You remember what we used to say on the teams? 'Whenever, wherever, whatever, we stand together.' I've got your six."

I grinned back.

"I already knew the answer. I just wanted to make sure you knew it too."

Buddy chuckled.

"Just like old times, huh?"

"We won't have a whole SEAL team with us in this thing, though."

"I sure hope we won't need one." Buddy said, with a shake of his head.

"You were busy this afternoon, so I did some recon of the area. I also have satellite imagery of the land, access roads, and topography around the property where I believe Diondro is."

"You seem extremely concerned for his safety."

I nodded in affirmative.

"I am, more concerned by the minute. I'm not the only person looking for him. Whoever they are, they mean to kill him. I don't know who's coming for him, how many there are, or how good they are, but we need to plan and prepare for contingencies."

"Like I said, just like old times, huh?"

"Let's hope not."

CHAPTER 5

In the old days, we would've done some mission specific training. We would do some dry runs in scenarios and locations designed to most closely replicate the situations we might face in the actual execution of the mission.

In the old days, we'd been part of a complete team of highly skilled operators. We had the full resources of the United States Navy providing logistics and support.

This was not the old days. This was not an overseas mission that would almost certainly involve combat with hostiles. In this case, there was every possibility we could avoid direct conflict, especially anything approaching armed combat.

Buddy and I both understood this, but "Live Screw" and "Old Mother" were trained to consider and prepare for any eventuality. We still thought in terms of infiltration and exfiltration. We thought in terms of plans A, B and C, ready to adjust for changing or unforeseen circumstances. We thought about managing aspects of the fallout from the action.

The first thing to be accomplished was to verify the location and make contact with the subject. Plan "A" would be to simply meet with him and take him to a secure location without any drama.

"Plan "B" involved accomplishing the goal of plan "A", while dealing with a nonviolent level of drama.

Plan "C" included an armed confrontation with an unknown number of combatants.

We wanted to avoid plan "C".

The next morning as I was driving to Buddy's office, I noticed the dark grey Toyota was behind me again. My cell phone buzzed in my pocket.

"Hello."

"John, this is Gary. I had a little talk with a guy by the name of Kevin Watkins yesterday. He's the foreman for the construction company."

"How did it go?"

Gary is one of my part time operatives. He's a career fireman, and his shift duties leave him with time to do some work for me. He's a big guy and a country boy. He can fit into any situation where ordinary working men might be seen. He tends to be a bit blunt, and he's never politically correct. Usually he just does surveillance, as his schedule permits, but occasionally he gets to play in the game.

"Watkins is a hard case, or at least he likes to think he is. Long story short, I did the thing where I posed as a guy looking for work. We hit it off pretty good. My experience in construction helped. He's considering hiring me as a crew chief. Naturally, I failed to mention I'm a fireman."

"Good job, Gary. It sounds like our plan may work."

"We'll see; maybe yes and maybe no. If not, I'll go to tracking those Mexican guys who split. I expect they're still around here. They're probably just doing day labor wherever they can find it."

"OK, but don't bother looking for them until we see how the new job opportunity works out. I'd still rather have you on the inside to see how the operation works. If you do get hired, I'll work on finding the missing former employees myself. We'll go at it from both the inside and the outside. It could mean you'll be tied up for several days though. It could be a week or more. How long can you do this, until it seriously interferes with your firefighter duties?"

"Yeah, well, I've been meaning to talk to you about that. I have twenty years on the job. I think I'm ready to retire. Could you use me full time?"

It caught me off guard.

"Oh, gee, Gary, I don't know. I don't think I could afford to pay you full time."

"Alright then, I'll let you know how it shakes out."

He hung up.

When I swung in to park at the Sheriff's office, the Toyota kept on going. I got a look at the driver. He was a big black guy with a shaved head. I was thinking he might have been Jermaine Jackson. I was almost surprised to find Jermaine, already waiting for me in Buddy's office.

"Good morning, Jermaine."

"Mornin', Mr. Tucker," Jermaine nodded.

"You can call me John, Jermaine"

"Yes sir."

"Jermaine was just starting to tell me about his conversation with his wife," Buddy said.

I nodded at Jermaine.

"Jasmine, that's my wife, she say she talked to her Aunt, Clarice Carlisle. Clarice say your man Diondro is there, alright. He came up here cause he scared, like you say."

I nodded again.

"She say she'll talk to him. She give him your number. Maybe he call you."

"OK. That's good enough for now."

I looked at Buddy.

"How do you want to handle this?" he asked.

"I'll wait to hear from Diondro. Because I'm being

followed, I won't go anywhere near there, until he calls me."

"You sure someone's following you?"

"Yeah, same guy followed me here again this morning."

"Maybe they don't know Diondro Taylor is up here."

"They might not. If I left town and headed home, they might think he wasn't here and follow me all the way back to Tyler."

"Is that what you're gonna do?" Jermaine asked.

I shook my head.

"We can't take that chance. Just because I left town, it wouldn't mean Diondro wasn't here. It would only suggest I hadn't found him. If they do know he's here, they'll kill him the first chance they get."

"But if you do stay here, won't it suggest you have found him?"

"Not if they continue to follow me."

"Why is that?" Jermaine asked.

"... Because I have another reason to be in town, having nothing to do with Diondro."

"What reason?"

"I'm here for Bud's high school graduation tonight."

Buddy grinned at that.

"You know, that gives me an idea."

We started doing some planning.

Later, in the afternoon, I got the call from Diondro.

"Good afternoon..."

"You, Mr. John Tucker?"

"Yes, I am."

"Mr. Tucker, my name is Diondro Taylor. I hear you want to talk to me."

"Yes, I do Diondro, Thank you for calling me."

He didn't say anything.

"The reason I wanted to talk to you, Diondro, is to tell you Mr. and Mrs. Sawyer want to pay for your college tuition. They will pay your full tuition for up to four years, to any school you can get into."

He was silent for a moment.

"I got to go back to Tyler?"

"No, Diondro. There are no strings attached. You can go to school anywhere that will accept you."

"… But, what about the trial?"

"It would be good if you wanted to testify, but there are no strings. You will get to go to college for free, either way."

He was quiet again.

"It's just that… What I mean is… I would testify, but I heard those dudes mean to kill me."

I took a moment to consider my response.

"Yeah, that's true, Diondro. The leader of the gang is the guy you jumped. He has it in for you, personally. They're looking for you, right now."

"I figured I'd be safer up here."

"Diondro, I found you. They'll find you, too."

He was quiet again.

"I don't know what I should do."

"Diondro, I intend to provide you with my personal protection until this thing is resolved."

"Why?"

"You need my help."

"I got family around me, up here."

"Diondro, do you want them to have to fight off some stone killers. Do you really think they could?"

He thought about it for a moment.

"No, they're pretty old, mostly."

"All I can do is promise you, I'll keep you safe, whatever you decide to do."

"Could you keep me safe in Tyler?"

"Yes, I can."

"… Even through the trial?"

"If you come to Tyler, we can have the help of the

police department."

"… Can't count on them."

"You can count on me."

He was quiet again for a while.

"I've heard of you. You're the dude who found those missing girls. My mom says she asked around about you, and people say you're solid."

"I do what I can. I won't lie to you. I can keep you safe."

"I gotta think about it. I'll call you back, later."

"Sure, that's fine. Call me back whenever you're ready."

CHAPTER 6

We were taking two cars to the graduation, primarily so whoever had me under surveillance would have a chance to follow me to the assembly hall at the SAU campus, where the ceremony was being held.

Buddy, Josie and Bud had left a little early so that Bud could be on time, and be where he was supposed to be in the assembly of graduating seniors. Josie had promised to save me a seat.

I became aware of the tail within about a mile of the house. He had probably been following me since I left Buddy's house, but I couldn't detect him for sure until he had been with me for a little ways. He had been smart enough to put a couple of cars between us.

I made a phone call.

When I pulled into the giant parking lot at the SAU campus, the dark grey Toyota was three cars behind me. I took my time getting out of my car, so the driver of the Toyota would be able to find a parking space and still see me as I headed into the assembly hall building.

We figured whoever was following me would see this graduation crowd as a perfect place for me to meet up with Diondro. This meant my tail would have to stick close to me, which is exactly what he did.

When I entered the building, there were two sheriff's deputies providing security at the entrance. I didn't see them stop my tail, but he didn't follow me into the assembly hall.

I saw Josie waving to me from her seat on the front row, and I made my way to her through the gathering crowd. We sat and chatted until Buddy joined us.

"John, you're not going to believe who the guy is that's been tailing you."

"I guess you didn't have any trouble stopping him?"

"No, he was pretty cooperative."

"Yeah, I would expect that from a cop."

"How did you know?"

"I figure the Texas plates on his car are an indication he's not just any cop, but a cop from Tyler, Texas."

"You've known this all along?"

"No, but I had started to suspect something of the sort. It just makes sense, a cop hiring out as a P.I. He would know me from my involvement with the Tyler PD. I'm well known in Tyler. Cops know how to follow people. He probably followed me to the rental car place, and from there it would be easy for him to follow me here to Magnolia. "

"We had to let him go with just a warning. He has a badge and a license and he hasn't broken any laws."

"I understand. Did you get him to tell you who he's working for?"

"No. He clammed up on that subject. He said it was the point of "private" investigation. I sure don't like the idea of a police officer working for a street gang."

"How hard did you lean on him?"

Buddy shrugged.

"... As hard as I could and still stay within the constraints of the law."

"Yeah, he would know your limitations. What is his name?"

"His name is Kirby Wilson and his badge says "Sergeant." I'm sorry, John. I did the best I could. I ignored the notion of professional courtesy. I gave him my best impression of a back woods Arkansas, country sheriff. You know, 'Y'all get on out of town now, boy! Ya hear?'... That sort of thing. I don't think it worked very well though."

I laughed.

"Fair enough, thanks, Buddy."

The lights blinked, the band struck up a tune, and the graduation started.

When they finally called out Wilson Livesque Jr., and Bud started across the stage, Buddy jumped to his feet and whistled. Bud saw him and grinned. Buddy pointed at Bud, standing there in the auditorium right in front of all those people watching, he just stood and pointed at Bud.

Bud was not the least bit embarrassed. As he marched across the stage, he pointed right back at Buddy.

I looked at Josie and saw the tears start. No surprise there.

As Buddy sat down, I was a little surprised to see he was looking a little misty eyed himself.

CHAPTER 7

After the graduation ceremony, Bud joined us and we took some pictures with him in his cap and gown.

Bud was excited and looking forward to partying with his friends.

"I'm heading out with Scott and Bill. Don't wait up. I expect we'll be out late."

Buddy frowned and started to say something, but I interrupted him.

"Hang on a second, Bud. I have a graduation present for you."

"Oh, you don't need to do that…"

"I insist, the problem is, I left it back at the house. How about you ride back to your house with me? Besides, I have something I want to talk to you about."

"Can I just get it later? Scott and Bill are pretty much ready to go now."

"You know where they're headed don't you?"

"Well, yeah, I do."

"Ride back to the house with me, you can take your truck and meet up with them, later. Chances are the house is pretty much on the way to where they're going, isn't it?"

"Yeah, I guess."

"Don't be rude, son. It won't delay your plans much. If Mr. Tucker wants to give you a graduation present, you should be thankful and gracious. Ride back to the house with him," Buddy said.

"OK, I'll just tell them to go on. I'll be right back."

Bud disappeared into the crowd.

"He was right, John; you shouldn't have gotten him anything."

I looked at Josie.

"This is a gift that will keep on giving. I have to do it."

"Well, thanks, John. It's very thoughtful of you. We'll see you back at the house," Buddy said.

He and Josie greeted several people and eventually blended into the throng of people that were leaving the building.

It was several minutes before Bud made his way back to where I waited. I saw him stop and chat up a couple of the girls. Several men slapped him on the back or stopped him long enough to shake his hand and wish him well. I could see he was a pretty popular kid.

"OK, Mr. Tucker, can we make this quick?" Bud asked, as he came up beside me.

"It won't take much time at all."

"Bud, are you a Christian?"

I was driving, so my attention was somewhat diverted, hopefully making the question a little less confrontational.

"Uh, well yeah, sort of, I mean, I go to church and stuff."

"Do you understand the difference? Do you know what it actually means to be a follower of Christ?"

"Yeah, I guess."

"So, I'll ask you again, are you a Christian?"

Bud looked out the passenger side window and mumbled.

"No, I suppose not."

I let it sit for a moment.

"Any special reason why not?"

"Well, not really. I believe in God and I know Jesus died for our sins, but..."

I let him flounder.

"I'll bet you're too busy having fun to make that kind of a life commitment."

"Yeah, that's it. I guess I'll probably do it later on."

I nodded.

"I knew your parents, back before they became Christians."

"What was that like?"

"Oh, we were in the Navy. We were clandestine operators and we were often in harm's way. We lived life on the edge. There were some wild parties and your folks were as wild as anybody you can possibly imagine."

"I can't imagine it at all."

I smiled. Kids never can imagine what their parents were like when they were younger.

"Oh yeah, let me tell you! They were wild, but they were not happy. They thought they were having a good time, but there was a great deal of misery along the way. They were lost and struggling to find their way from day to day. Just like most people are, lost and hoping for something better."

"What happened to change them?"

"They were searching. They wanted more than that kind of life has to offer."

"Well, back then, you were SEALs. You were in danger a lot. You could have been killed at any time. I guess it would make a person kind of scared and more open to the whole God thing."

"Everyone is facing death, Bud. Our days are numbered. Some will die today or tomorrow, even tonight. When or how we die is not what matters. What matters is how we live.

God requires righteousness to get into heaven. Not our own righteousness, but that which He gives us. The wages of sin is death. The gift of God is eternal life, by Jesus' sacrifice, but only for those who accept His gift. A gift isn't really yours, if you don't accept it. Are you a righteous person? If you were to die tomorrow, why should God let you into heaven?"

He didn't answer.

"Sometimes people think they have time. They think they'll wait till the end of their life, to accept the gift of salvation and make the commitment."

"Yeah, I guess so."

We were approaching an intersection and there were many flashing red and blue lights ahead. Traffic was backed up and slowly crawling forward. Cops were directing traffic around a huge fire truck that nearly blocked the intersection. We could see a jackknifed eighteen wheeler off on the far side of the intersection. Behind the fire truck, there was a huge plume of smoke. Firemen still held hoses and foam had been sprayed in the intersection and on something smoldering on the other side of the fire truck.

I saw Buddy's Tahoe pulled over at the side of the street. Buddy was standing beside the vehicle with Josie wrapped in his arms. Buddy's lights were flashing in countermeasure to the rest of the flashing lights. I pulled in behind them and hit my emergency flashers.

Bud and I got out of my rental car.

"Mom, what's wrong? Are you OK?" Bud asked.

"Oh, Bud..."

"What is it, what's happened?"

"Bud, its Scott and Bill, they're both dead. They ran the red light right in front of us and an eighteen wheeler hit the car. I'm so sorry." Buddy said.

"Thank God you weren't with them! Oh, I shouldn't have said that." Josie cried.

"Easy, baby, it's OK. We know what you mean." Buddy said.

Bud stood there shocked.

"Are you sure? I mean maybe it wasn't Scott's car."

"I'm sorry, Bud. I had a good look at the car when they went flying past us. It happened practically right in front of us. The fire was too intense for me to get close, I tried, son. Several people stopped to help, but we just couldn't get to them. They never had a chance."

We made it back to the house much later than had been planned.

Bud was pretty shaken up.

"Maybe if I had been with them, this wouldn't have happened." He said.

"If you had been with them, you would still be with them now, in the morgue." Buddy observed.

"Oh this is so horrible! They had just graduated. They had their whole lives ahead of them." Josie said.

"John, if you hadn't taken Bud with you…"

"Timing is everything."

"Yes, it is… did you know this was going to happen?"

I shook my head.

"No, I only knew Bud was supposed to come with me."

"How… how could you know that?" Bud asked.

I looked him in the eye.

"God speaks to me."

"No way, no way, man! If that's true then your God just let my friends die."

We were all silent for a moment.

"Or are you saying God killed them to get my attention?"

"Bud, this was not an act of God. Not in the sense you're suggesting. He knew the choices that would be made tonight. He knew what the consequences of those choices would be. He allowed me to intercede on your behalf."

"And he just let them die? Why didn't you intercede for them?"

"They are sheep of another pasture."

"What the hell is that supposed to mean?"

"God has plans for you, Bud. He is calling you and He directed me to this time and place. He allowed me to give you this opportunity. This is my graduation gift, but I'm just the delivery boy. The gift is from God."

"My friends are dead! What kind of gift is that?"

"It is the gift of life. You and you alone must choose what you will do with it."

"Dad, do you believe this shit?"

"Bud, you're upset. This is the most horrible thing that has ever happened in your life, up to this point. You're alive and they're dead. I know how it feels. I know how shocking it is and how unfair it all seems. Do I believe this is a gift and an opportunity? Yes, I do, Bud. I sure do."

"I too, Bud, Honey, I believe it is a gift. It's a gift we don't deserve, just as all of God's gifts are undeserved. I'm grateful and heartsick at the same time. I'm so sorry Scott ran the red light. I'm so sorry Scott and Bill died, but I'm also happy you weren't with them," Josie said.

"I, I just can't believe it…"

"It takes time to deal with all of the questions. It takes time to recover from the grief. Time is part of the gift God has given you."

"Stop it! Stop all the God talk. I don't want to hear it."

I nodded.

"I'm going to bed. Good night y'all"

CHAPTER 8

The next morning As Buddy and I were having breakfast and discussing the events of the previous evening, my phone rang.

"Mr. Tucker? It's me, Diondro Taylor. I'd like to talk to you."

"Hey, Diondro, how are you?"

"Fine, I guess, can we talk?"

"Sure, go ahead."

"Uh... no, I mean I want to meet you and talk about this stuff."

"OK, when and where?"

Buddy was watching me intently.

"Can you come here?"

"Sure, but I don't know exactly where you are. Don't tell me. Let me ask you a question... Are you with your family?"

"Yes, if you're coming from town, you just head..."

"Hang on. I know where they live and how to get there. Don't tell me over the phone. Just tell me which one is the house where you are staying. I mean is it the third one on the right or the second on the left? You know, like that." I interrupted.

"Oh, OK. I'll be at the last house on the end of the road. You know where it is?"

"I do. What time do you want me to come there?"

"Can you come now?"

"Yes, Diondro, I can. It will take me about thirty minutes to get there though. Is that alright?"

"Yeah, come on. I'll be waiting."

I looked at Buddy.

He nodded.

"Well, Watson, it appears the game is afoot."

"Yes it is, Sherlock. God willing, I should be able to get him to leave with me today. Hopefully without any encounters with whomever the street gang sent to kill him."

"Whomever, really, Sherlock you said whomever? If the goal is simply to get him out of there, I could still place him in protective custody."

"No, Buddy, we talked about that. You can't spend Columbia County resources on an out of state citizen who has committed no crime, at least not for very long. Meanwhile everyone would know exactly where he was."

"Have you given any more thought to me going along with you?"

I shook my head.

"If the County Sheriff shows up out there, it could get complicated."

"Not if I'm there in an un-official capacity."

If Buddy knew what I knew, he would understand why the Sheriff would be the last person they would want to see out there.

"Diondro and his family are expecting me to show up alone. I don't want to scare them into doing something stupid."

"I'm not that scary, John."

I grinned at him and held my hand up with my thumb and forefinger about an inch apart.

"Yeah, you are... a little bit."

He chuckled.

"Are you really thinking their phone might be bugged, or mine? Or maybe somehow your cell phone signal is being monitored?"

I shrugged.

"Not likely, but I like to be careful."

"There has to be a reason you don't want me to go with you. Is there something you haven't told me?"

I was afraid he would ask that question.

"It's hard to slip something past you, isn't it?"

He narrowed his eyes at me as he made a rolling gesture with his hand.

"Well, when I did my little recon run out there the other day, I made an unexpected discovery."

"And that was...?"

"You know how you told me the Taylors and Carlisles get their income from timber sales and hunting leases?"

He shrugged.

"I found another source of revenue."

"Oh no..."

I nodded.

"Yep, I had seen on the satellite image an old logging road that goes out to the county road on the other side of LaSalle Bayou. It appeared to have had enough traffic on it to stay open and in good repair, but there is about thirty yards of brush and saplings growing up right at the end of it, where it ought to join the county road. All that brush forms a screen and prevents people from driving in there from the county road. It seemed odd at the time, but I figured to check it out as a possible emergency escape route."

Buddy managed to look both worried and eager at the same time.

"I found the road alright, after I worked my way through the brush and saplings. I found out why the old road shows so much sign of use. I was walking along the logging road when I came to about a half an acre of very healthy pot plants."

Buddy shook his head.

"The feds fly around looking for commercial marijuana production. I expect a half acre of pot plants would be hidden from aerial view by the thick forest all around it."

I nodded in agreement

"Yes, and it isn't the only patch of pot."

"Well, how much is there?"

"As near as I can estimate, hidden in the woods along the edge of LaSalle Bayou, there may be as many as eight or ten plots of about half an acre each. All together it may be four to six acres of total marijuana production, scattered over about twenty five acres in surface area. The Taylors and Carlisles appear to be pretty successful pot farmers."

"Oh brother...! At about one thousand dollars per plant and a hundred or more plants per half acre... it adds up to a fortune." Buddy calculated.

"Yeah, so you see having the County Sheriff on their property in any capacity would probably make them a little edgy."

"How is it the hunters who lease the land for hunting haven't found the weed?" Buddy asked.

"When do they hunt?"

"Pretty much in the fall and winter, mostly deer and ducks in the season."

"The marijuana crops would have been harvested by then."

"Yeah, but the hunters come out at various other times during the year to scout, do trail maintenance, plow feed plots and put up the blinds. They also hunt hogs, wild turkey, rabbits and squirrels and what not, depending on the season."

I considered the possibilities.

"I guess they are either told some areas are off limits - it is only about twenty five acres out of the whole three hundred acres, or they are controlled in some other way. During a year when some of the timber will be harvested, maybe they don't grow pot. They didn't seem to have any of it in the pine plantation portions of the three hundred acres. It was only in the thick native timber areas, along the edge of the bayou down at the nearest point to the county road. At least that's the way it looked to me, as I studied the satellite images in more detail."

"So they could grow and harvest it and use the logging road to slip it out to the county road, without attracting any attention."

"Right, and if people come to visit them where they live, the bayou is between them and the 'farm' just a few hundred yards away."

"This is a huge problem, John. I'm going to have to shut them down. Commercial production and shipping across state lines is a serious Federal violation. I'll have to get Treasury and the ATF involved, maybe even the DEA and FBI."

"Yes, but it will have to wait until I can get Diondro out of there. He had nothing to do with the farming operation. He probably doesn't even know it's going on."

"Oh, man, this is a cluster..."

"Yeah, and I'll tell you this, I've never seen or heard of a pot farming operation that didn't have armed guards. I was plenty worried when I realized what I had stumbled into. I saw a couple of armed men, but they didn't see me. They had a rifle and a shotgun, and all I had with me was my handgun. I backed out of there, real careful like. It was only by the grace of God I didn't get myself shot."

Buddy heard this and it added fuel to the fire.

"This is the worst thing I can imagine. I'll have to make multiple arrests. Kids will grow up without their parents..."

"Try to look on the bright side; this is bound to be good for your re-election campaign."

"I can't worry about the campaign. This will have a huge impact on the community. Nothing good will come of it. I wish they hadn't done this."

"There is another thing you have to consider..."

"What's that?"

"Does Jermaine's wife know about the pot farming? Does Jermaine know?"

"I'll have a talk with Jermaine. I may have to bring in the state police."

"Cross that bridge when you come to it. I've been invited to go in there. I'll keep my eyes open and I'll tell you what I learn in the process."

"Do you think you are still the only one who knows where Diondro is?"

I shook my head, indicating a negative response.

"By now, Sergeant Wilson has had plenty of time to get a lead on the location of the Taylor place. I'm just hoping whoever he has notified will be behind me by at least four hours.

Buddy was thoughtful for a moment, and then he made a decision.

"OK. You go on. This has gotten even more complicated, so you'll need to be double-extra careful. We'll still go with plan A. I'll be close by, like we had already arranged. Call me if you need any help."

CHAPTER 9

As I drove south out of Magnolia, I noted I was not being followed. It suggested three possibilities. Maybe Sergeant Kirby Wilson of the Tyler Police Department had taken the warning from Buddy seriously and pulled out of the deal. Perhaps he had already figured out where Diondro was, had phoned it in and had headed for home. Or, he had given up and figured he was barking up the wrong tree. Diondro was somewhere else, and I had just come up here for Bud's graduation.

Whatever the actual situation, I was glad Sergeant Kirby Wilson wouldn't be further involved.

After I had gone on to my room the previous evening, I had called my friend in the Tyler Police Department and alerted him to Wilson's involvement. Detective Lieutenant Anthony Escalante was not pleased.

"So, what you're telling me is Wilson is working for the street punks who want to kill Diondro Taylor. I guess it's legal, John, but it sure is low and I don't like it. Do you think he knows who hired him to investigate Diondro's whereabouts?"

"I would know, Tony. Wouldn't you know who

had hired you?"

"Yes, absolutely I would. I was just trying to jus-
tify his motives."

"His motive is money. A man who would do
something like this for a day rate, can't be trusted,
Tony. He will do just about anything for a buck, if
he thinks he can get away with it."

"I see that, John, I'll pass it along to his super-
visors, but I can't promise anything. The name is
vaguely familiar. I'm sure I've met him on the job. I
wonder why he has the time to follow you around
in Arkansas. I'll make sure he gets checked out by
Internal Affairs, but if he hasn't broken any law or
violated any police regulations..."

"I understand, Tony. I only called to give you a
"heads up" for future reference. It's just some useful
information to have."

"It is, but it also makes me pretty angry. A member of this department would be willing to see a kid
killed - not to mention it puts you in danger."

"I can take care of myself."

"Yeah, I know you can, but this shouldn't have
happened. Our job is to serve and protect..."

As I turned off of the black top road onto the dirt
road designated CR 3802, I was considering all the
possibilities. I had dressed for a day in the woods,
and prepared as best I could for any of the various
scenarios Buddy and I had discussed, but it all came
down to this. I could see the first couple of the old,
single wide, mobile homes ahead. There was one on
each side of the road.

As I drove past the mobile homes, two pickup
trucks, one from each side of the road, pulled out
of the dirt yards and blocked the road behind me.
Clearly, this was a practiced maneuver and it did
not bode well. This was a dead end road. I couldn't
go back out the way I came in and nobody could

follow me in. It might be a good thing, or a very bad thing. It was interesting they had done it in a way that would ensure I saw them do it.

I passed other mobile homes and a couple of houses looking like they were about a hundred years old, weathered and run down. There were dogs running loose at most of the residences, and pit bulls on chains in front of a couple of them. Here and there, I would see a person standing by the side of the road, watching me go by.

About a mile farther down, at the end of the road, there was a big circular turn around area with half a dozen buildings scattered around the edge. The satellite images had shown these, but it hadn't been entirely clear what the buildings were. Now that I was approaching them, I could see they were a couple of mobile homes and houses with sheds and storage buildings between and behind them. They all appeared to be dilapidated or otherwise in various states of disrepair.

There were several cars and pickup trucks parked in the area.

More interesting was the group of people milling about.

There were half a dozen young black men shooting hoops on a make shift dirt basketball court. They varied in age from about twelve to about twenty. Watching from porches and leaning against cars and trucks, there were another eight or ten older people, mostly men with an old woman to be seen here or there.

The young men ignored me as I drove up, but three of the older men were clearly there to meet me. I was relieved to see there were no guns in evidence.

I parked my car near the row of mailboxes attached to a steel post and took a moment to assess the situation.

It kind of looked as though I had driven up to a family reunion, without the food and fun. Also, unlike a family reunion, there were no young women or young children anywhere to be seen. In fact, other than the basketball players, there was not anyone in evidence between the age of about twenty and sixty.

I stepped out of the car and approached the three older men who were waiting for me.

"Good morning. I'm John Wesley Tucker. I believe Diondro Taylor is expecting me..." I reached out to shake hands with the first man in the group.

It was like taking hold of a dead fish. A warm dead fish, but lifeless and limp, all the same. It was the same way with each of the three men, and not one of them would look me in the eye.

They might have been brothers and I suspected they probably were. Each man was about five feet nine inches tall and had the hard, stringy look of men who have lived their lives outdoors. They were black men with heads in various stages of balding, the remaining hair now white and close cropped. They each had a little facial hair in evidence. One had side-burns another had two patches of white beard, growing on each side of his chin. The oldest man had a white moustache and a soul patch. All three wore overalls, over faded T-shirts. They had the look of farmers. These were old men who had seen the world change a lot, since they had been boys back in the nineteen forties or fifties,

The oldest man spoke up. He appeared to be about 80, but he could have been older or younger.

"Uh huh. He be 'long, directly. He my sister's-daughter's, boy. You come on inside."

I was wearing a long sleeve camouflage shirt; it was too warm to be comfortable in it.

"Yes sir, thank you. I believe the day is starting to heat up already."

He turned without reply and led me up onto the porch of the nearest house, as the two other men fell in behind me.

The house we stepped into was not the same house inside, as it was outside. Outside it was faded and warped lumber with peeling paint. Inside, it was clean and tidy, freshly painted and had all the latest updates. There were new appliances evident in the kitchen, the furniture was tasteful and expensive, and there was a big screen TV, playing loudly in a giant entertainment center that took up a whole wall. There was a ceiling fan circulating the cool air from the air conditioner.

"Sit," the older man said, pointing at a huge, brown leather couch.

He sat down in a big, matching recliner and began to rock. The other two men stood just inside the door.

I sat on the couch, as I had been directed to do. The blaring TV was annoying.

The old man sat and rocked and studied me for a few moments. Then he spoke.

"Why you here?"

"Diondro asked me to come and talk to him."

"Hmm hmmm. Why you don't leave him be?"

"Do you know what happened in Tyler?"

"I knows all bout that. That's Tyler, not here. I axed you why you here?"

"Could we turn off the TV?"

He stared at me, but he wouldn't look me in the eye. After a moment, he picked up the remote and turned the television off.

"You is trouble. You a cop?"

"No, I'm not a cop and Diondro is not in any trouble."

"He say different."

I nodded.

"He isn't in any trouble with the law, but there are some people looking for him to do him harm. I'm just trying to help him."

He studied me some more, with eyes that drooped

and seemed watery. He still managed to avoid eye contact.

"We don't need no troubles."

"No sir, but I think having Diondro here will bring you trouble."

He closed his eyes and rocked for a moment. Then he nodded.

"It brought you here, you is trouble, sho nuff."

He opened his eyes and looked toward the door.

"Go fetch Diondro."

CHAPTER 10

When Diondro Taylor entered the living room, I recognized him as being one of the boys who had been playing basketball on the hard packed dirt of the yard out front. He was about six feet tall and he had some short dreadlocks, just starting.

I stood to greet him.

"Diondro, I'm John Wesley Tucker."

We shook hands. Diondro's handshake was firm and he looked me in the eye.

"Pleased to meet you, sir, thank you for coming out here."

We both sat down on opposite ends of the couch.

"I'll get right to the point. As you know, I have been hired to find you and tell you the Sawyer's intend to provide up to four years of college tuition for you, to any school where you can gain admittance. In addition, I'm prepared to provide you with protection from the people who seek to do you harm, until this matter is resolved. Do you have any questions?"

"Well, uh, yeah. How is it gonna get resolved? I mean these guys are out to get me, if I go back to Tyler. So, what will change that?"

I nodded. It was a good question.

"You are in danger, right here, right now. By now they have found out where you're hiding, more or less the same way I did. I believe they have sent someone to kill you, here in Arkansas."

The old man made a face when he heard me say that.

Diondro started to speak, but I held up my hand to stop him.

"We need to move you right away. I can keep you safe. I also have a plan to put a stop to this. Once Isaac Washington gets put away, some of the incentive to harm you will be gone. I intend to remove any further incentive once he gets sentenced."

Diondro considered his options for a moment.

"OK, but where will you take me?"

"Where would you like to go?"

"I want to go home."

"You can and you will, eventually. In the meantime where would you like to go?"

"I want to go back and testify against the punk. If I do, can you keep me safe?"

I realized Diondro was asking me these questions for the benefit of the three men, who were watching, especially the old man in charge.

I nodded.

"Yes, I can and I will. I have some resources available to ensure that outcome."

Diondro looked over at the old man.

"What do you think, Uncle Andrew?"

Diondro's Great Uncle Andrew considered it for a moment.

"You most a man now. You gots to do what you gots to do. We be tryin' to keep you safe, but..."

"But you are not equipped to deal with hired killers." I interjected.

"Yassah, that's a part."

I looked at Diondro.

"Diondro, how did you get up here? Do you have a car?"

"No sir, I took the bus to Texarkana and Uncle Andrew picked me up and brought me over here."

"Go pack a bag. We are leaving right now."

"I'm packed. I'll go get my bag."

When he had left the room, I faced the old man.

"Another part of the problem is you have a marijuana farming operation going here, and you don't want a lot of attention brought out to the farm."

Andrew jumped, startled at my remark. "Where you hear that at?" The old man asked.

"What were you thinking? The feds are going to swoop in here and wipe you out. Some of you, maybe even everyone in this family, will go to prison."

"I axed you, how you know 'bout that?"

"I know about it. The Columbia County Sheriff knows about it, and pretty soon everyone in this part of the country will know all about it. Why did you do this?"

The old man shook his head.

"I knowed it was wrong to do."

"Then... why?" Diondro asked, coming back into the room. He had overheard part of the conversation.

"We is poor, Diondro. We needs things. Johnny come down from Detroit. He July's boy..." he nodded toward one of the men by the door."... and he say we ought to do this. He say he got contacts up there. He move what we grow." Last year we just grew a little, maybe an acre all together and he sold it. This year we be growing more. We don't like it, but... we is poor."

I looked the old man in the eye.

"Let me guess... Johnny is up in Detroit, right?"

"Hmm hmmm, that's right."

"So, he won't be here when the feds kick down your door."

The old man shrugged.

"And Johnny won't be going to prison with you, unless they can catch him in the act of distribution. Now let me ask you this... Does Johnny sell the weed and then send you a portion of the proceeds?"

"Hmm hmmm."

"So you grow it, harvest it and transport it to Detroit?"

He nodded.

"Do you take it to Johnny?"

"Naw, sir. He got a storage building up there, where we leave it at."

"You don't even see Johnny?"

"We sees him, sometimes."

I shook my head.

"Let me tell you this; you've got one chance. Destroy the crop, right away. Go to the Sheriff and tell him the whole story. Invite him to come out here and inspect the property. Promise him it won't happen again and give him permission to inspect, anytime he wants to. That's your only hope. Good bye, sir."

The old man just shrugged again.

Diondro and I walked out to my car.

Most of the people who had been outside had wandered away.

Just as we started to get into the rental car, the radio in my shirt pocket crackled.

"Live Screw to Old Mother, come in Mother."

I pulled the short range radio from my pocket.

"Old Mother, go Live Screw."

"Bug out. I repeat, bug out."

"Roger that, Live Screw. Bug out now. Go to Plan Baker, repeat Plan Baker. Old Mother out."

"Roger that, Old Mother. Plan Baker. Live Screw out."

CHAPTER 11

I grabbed Diondro's bag and pushed him toward the house.

"Go back in the house, go right now."

"Is it them federals coming?" The old man asked, from the front porch.

"No, it's someone coming for Diondro."

We heard gunfire coming from somewhere up the road.

The people who were still outside the house were all staring up toward where the sound of gunshots had come. We heard the sound of crunching metal from the same direction.

"Run!" I yelled. "Get out of sight; the shooters are coming on down here."

My announcement sent everyone running for cover.

I dashed to the trunk of the rental car and grabbed Buddy's Mossberg 12 gauge pump shotgun and a field pack, with a dark camouflage pattern. I dropped Diondro's bag into the trunk and slammed it shut.

As I sprinted toward the house, I saw a car hurtling down the road toward us, in a cloud of dust.

As I flew through the door of the house, the car was slewing to a stop.

Inside, I found the house was becoming an armed camp. Each of the old men now held a rifle or a shotgun.

I took a quick look out the window and saw four swarthy men with AK rifles and handguns getting out of the car.

I smashed the front window with the barrel of the Mossberg and blasted two quick shots over the top of the car. The men dived out of site behind the various vehicles still parked out front.

"Y'all need to just get back in your car and go away. The police will be here soon and you'll be trapped between us and them. If you don't leave now, some of you will die here today."

"Oh, si eso es cierto, but it will be you who will die, hombre. Send out the boy and we will take him and go away, maybe." The man spoke with a heavy Spanish accent.

I turned to the old man.

"They didn't plan on confronting armed resistance, but they aren't going to leave. They'll surround the house and shoot it to pieces. We need to clear out. If they plan to get away, they know that they have no more than five minutes to finish the job. The cops will be here in fifteen or twenty minutes."

I pointed toward the back of the building.

"Diondro, we're going out the back. Those men will need about one minute to plan how to get into position around the house. By then, we'd better be back in the woods."

I looked at Andrew.

"You need to get out of this house. I'll try to draw their fire and get them to follow us into the woods, but I don't know what will happen after that. If we lose them, they may come back here."

The old man nodded.

"Y'all git. We'll be alright. Stay away from them dope fields, we got guards there. They shoot you too, if they see you."

Diondro and I went through the kitchen and the

utility room, out onto a screened porch at the back of the house. From there we could see a shed right behind the house and beyond it the tree line, like the edge of a jungle.

"Diondro, we're headed for the bayou. You take off at a dead run and don't look back. Get into the trees and whatever happens, stay low and keep moving. Wait for me at the edge of the water."

He looked scared, but he nodded.

I keyed the radio.

"Old Mother to Live Screw, Charlie, Charlie, Charlie, extraction point, Delta. Over…"

"Live Screw to Old Mother, roger that, Plan Charlie, extraction point Delta."

I pushed Diondro ahead, and we both ran down the steps and out into the little yard behind the house. Diondro sprinted straight for the trees, but I took a moment to sling the pack over my shoulders and edge around the back corner of the house.

Sure enough, two of the gunmen, taking advantage of all available cover, were working their way off to this side of the house. They were running bent low and were not in a position to fire. They saw me just as I leveled the Mossberg at them. They both dived in opposite directions, and I didn't get a clear shot, so I took off running toward the trees.

Automatic AK 47 rifle shots hammered behind me and bark flew in my face, as I dove for cover in the brush under the trees.

"Hey! The cops will be here in a minute. You boys can't shoot worth a damn. Don't you think you should go?"

"Oh yes, we go, after we kill you and the boy." The man speaking with the Spanish accent was the same man who had spoken before.

There was the sound of breaking glass from the side of the house and a shotgun barrel emerged through the shattered window.

The men opened fire on the house, just as the shotgun fired.

I took the opportunity to head for the bayou.

From up the road, the sound of an approaching siren could be heard. I figured it had to be Buddy, coming to the rescue. It had not been part of the plan. He would be driving right into a fire fight. The four assassins would feel trapped and desperate.

I didn't like it, but my duty was to protect Diondro and get him to safety. Live Screw would know how to take care of himself.

As I ran through the strip of forest, I heard the chatter of an AR 15 and AK assault rifles, mixed with the occasional shotgun blast. I hoped Santa Clause A/K/A Live Screw, was bringing these gunmen some of his presents. It was a wide open gun battle.

I found Diondro at the edge of the water. I pulled a couple of camouflage boonie caps out of the pack and handed one to Diondro along with a camo T-shirt, indicating he should put it on over the sweaty white T-shirt he was wearing.

"In we go..." I said.

I started to wade out into the bayou.

"What? No sir! I'm not going in there. I can't swim."

"OK. The water is probably no more than chest deep on me, anywhere along here. On you it's only a little more than waist deep, shallower in most places. We won't have to swim. We'll just wade through it."

"Do we have to wade across it?"

"No, we're going to wade downstream toward the bridge on the county road."

"What? Why?"

It sounded like the gunfire was drawing nearer to us, as the gunmen fell back from the house, toward the bayou, firing at Buddy or whoever was shooting at them.

"They'll be on us any minute now, Diondro. Just shut up and follow my lead."

I set off into the water and began wading down-stream, moving as fast as I could, while feeling along the bottom carefully for fallen timber, pot holes, beaver cuts or anything else that might ruin the day. When I looked back at Diondro, his eyes were huge but he was right behind me. I was holding my shotgun up out of the water and had turned to speak to Diondro, when I saw movement near where we had gone into the bayou. We had only gone about twenty five yards downstream, but we were in the shade and near the knees of a big old Cypress tree

I held my finger up to get Diondro's attention and pointed back upstream. Diondro slowly turned and looked. A figure emerged from the reeds at the edge of the bayou. He looked across and then up-stream.

Diondro looked back at me and I slowly sank down in the water till just my eyes, boonie cap, and shotgun were above the waterline. Diondro sank down too, staring at me in terror. I was watching the gunman, down the barrel of the Mossberg.

The man was agitated and he barely even glanced down- stream. He didn't see us. He pushed out into the bayou and struggled to hurry across, constantly turning to look behind him, splashing and sloshing water everywhere. Ten seconds later he was lost to view as he crawled up the bank on the other side.

Diondro and I started to stand up, but then I heard someone nearby yelling.

"Hoy! Venir aquí me. Fueron asi!"

"¿A dónde se fueron?"

Two heavily armed men burst through the reeds where the other man had come out. Both of them jumped into the bayou without looking around at all. They splashed across the bayou as if their tails were on fire.

"Yeah, way to go, Live Screw, only three left in the fight." I thought.

As soon as they were out of sight, I started off downstream again, with Diondro stuck to me like glue. We only had a few hundred yards to go, as the crow flew, but it was by no means a straight or easy route. The bayou twisted and turned. Where it was narrow it was deeper and tree roots had been exposed. There was brush tangled here and there and we slipped and struggled over submerged limbs and other obstructions, constantly trying to move quietly. Twice, we flushed cottonmouth moccasins from their hiding places. I stepped on a big snapping turtle that lurched under my foot and gave me a scare.

We had only made it downstream about one hundred and fifty yards from our entry point, when we heard new gunfire, very close by. That would be the assassins meeting the guardians of the pot fields.

Another hundred yards farther along and I had hopes we would not be found. We were well hidden in the bayou and by now completely covered with mud, cobwebs, muck and debris. I stopped to rest. It was getting hot, and my pack had filled with water. I poured the warm, swampy water out and removed a bottle of water from the pack and handed it to Diondro. We shared the water. We were both too hot and miserable to talk.

We heard the sound of multiple sirens approaching the scene where we had escaped the shooting. Those would be the Sheriff's deputies and other emergency services arriving on the scene.

I considered going back the way we had come and decided it would be both easier and quicker to stick to the plan and go on down to the extraction point at the bridge.

That decision saved our lives.

We got moving again into somewhat deeper water. I heard a noise behind us and was startled to see a man jump into the bayou only about ten feet beyond where we had stopped to rest. He swung toward us and his eyes lit up as he raised his rifle.

"Les tengo! Ven pronto, Juan."

I shot him in the face with my Mossberg from no more than twenty five feet away. His head was destroyed before he could squeeze off a shot.

Right behind us there was the sound of an automatic rifle bolt being pulled, and then there was a crash in the brush beside us and another man appeared, blindly firing his AK assault rifle in our direction. Water erupted all around us. Diondro fell over backwards into the water, as I fired two aimed shots from the Mossberg. The gunman went down. I reached down into the bayou and fished around for Diondro. I felt him and grabbed a hold of Diondro's T-shirts and pulled him up above the water.

"Where are you hit?"

Diondro was snorting and spitting out bayou water.

"I'm not. I don't think I am. I got my feet tangled up in something and I fell."

"OK, stay low and keep moving downstream."

I thumbed fresh shells into the shotgun, as I scanned the bank and the woods, looking for the third man.

He was not to be seen.

Five minutes later we were approaching the spot where I had stopped the car and studied the bayou a couple of days before.

I had Diondro rest in a kind of bole at the base of a big Cypress tree, hidden behind a screen of cattail and low hanging Spanish moss, while I scouted the rest of the way.

I saw the bridge, but there was no sign of Buddy. I had stepped out into the open before I sensed I was being watched. I started to turn back toward Diondro, when I heard a rifle shot and felt the bullet whip close past my head. I was stuck out in the open, with no idea where the shot came from. Right in front of me, no more than ten yards away, a man holding an AK 47 fell forward, face first into the bayou. Part of his head had been blown away.

I turned back toward the bridge, looking for the shooter. I figured the indistinguishable lump I had barely noticed on the edge of the bridge was a man lying prone under some sort of camouflage cover, probably with a scoped rifle trained on me. It was nearly a hundred yards to the bridge and he was almost completely hidden and shielded by the edge of it. With my shotgun, I didn't have any hope of a shot on him, but he could easily shoot me with his rifle. The lump moved a little and the radio crackled in my pocket.

I jumped, startled. I had figured the radio would be useless after having been submerged in the water, more than once.

"Are you OK, Old Mother?"

I pulled the radio out.

"Roger that, Live Screw. Show me a sign."

The lump on the bridge rose up into a kneeling position and pointed his rifle barrel up. Live Screw, covered entirely in a ghillie suit, waved his radio above his head.

I waved back. Even without a spotter, Live Screw could shoot with amazing accuracy, out to about a thousand yards. In this heavily forested environment, he would never have opportunity or need, to shoot beyond a couple of hundred yards or so. At that range, with his specially modified rifle, he could easily shoot groups on an area smaller than the size of a dime, but the dime wouldn't survive the first shot. Neither had the man now floating face down on the edge of the bayou, a halo of dark red blood slowly mixing with the chocolate colored water.

"Come on out Diondro. We're safe now."

CHAPTER 12

Buddy continued to provide cover as we waded out of the bayou and up to where he had parked his Tahoe. As he joined us at the vehicle, he was shedding the layers of his ghillie suit, which he dropped into the cargo space. He put his specially designed Remington Model 700 sniper rifle into its hard case.

"It got real hot laying up there in the sun, waiting for you. I was half afraid somebody would come driving along and run over me, thinking I was a pile of moss or something."

"You could've waited in your truck with the air conditioning going." I said.

"Not once I heard all that shooting. It sounded like a pretty good running gun battle."

Diondro was staring at Buddy's sweat stained Sheriff's uniform. I realized it was time for introductions.

"Diondro, shake hands with the Sheriff of Columbia County, Sheriff Wilson Livesque. He just saved your life, and mine... again." I said

"My friends call me, Buddy." He said, shaking Diondro's hand.

As we drove back toward the Carlisle/Taylor

compound, I asked Buddy what all had happened, from his perspective.

"I'd just gotten into position at the turn off onto 3802 when this carload of heavily armed thugs drove by. They didn't see me in my ghillie suit, but I got a good look at them. That's when I called you on the radio. You were trapped down there at the end of the road and I couldn't help. Plan B was you would cross the bayou and head out fast on the old logging road. I was supposed to pick you up there, at the end of it. I had run back to where the unit was parked when you called in Plan C. I hauled tail to get to the extraction point at the bridge."

"Well then, who came down the road with their siren going and engaged the gunmen, while we bugged out?"

"It was Jermaine, in his unit. I had called him and told him what was going on. He was already on his way out here to confront his in-laws about the pot farming. He was pretty upset, and told me he and his wife had no idea anything like that was going on. They've only been married for two years, so they figured this pot thing must be something new."

"Yeah, that's true, Buddy. They just started growing it last year. A family member up in Detroit talked them into it. They're complete amateurs, and real ignorant amateurs, at that. They have taken all the risks and only gotten an insignificant fraction of the profits. They haven't made any real money. They will be real happy to be out of the dope business. Is Jermaine alright?"

Buddy looked over at me.

"I don't know, John. I've been busy watching out for you. We'll know more in a minute."

The scene down at the end of CR 3802 was orga-nized chaos. There were at least half a dozen police cars from various agencies with red and blue lights flashing. There were ambulances and fire trucks, all flashing their lights as well. We could see Jermaine's patrol car where it sat, all shot up, with the tires flattened.

Buddy immediately took control of the scene and began gathering information and giving orders while we remained seated in his Tahoe.

After about ten minutes, he came back to us and filled us in.

"Jermaine is OK. When he heard shots had been fired, he felt like he had to try to protect his in-laws. The 911 dispatcher had gotten several calls, but Jermaine was way ahead of any other available units. I had just left to meet you. The gunmen were firing on the house when he came down the road. As soon as the shooters saw him, they lit up his cruiser. He got out with his AR and for a minute the gunmen were taking fire from both him and the house. Jermaine managed to get one of them. The other three fell back into the woods. Jermaine followed them as far as the edge of the woods, but he was out-gunned, so he went back to the house."

"Is everybody alright?" Diondro asked.

"No, son, I'm sorry, there were three men in the house and they were all wounded or otherwise injured some. One of them was killed."

"Who died?"

"I'm told the name of the deceased is Andrew Taylor."

Diondro hung his head.

"We found the body of the guy Jermaine dropped. No ID. He looks Hispanic. There is no sign of the other three gunmen yet. Jermaine figures they went across the bayou. He and I both heard a lot of shooting over that way while I was waiting for you. I've sent deputies across to check it out."

He looked at me.

"How about you, do you have any idea what happened to the other three gunmen? I figure I shot one of them."

I nodded as I answered his question.

"Three of them crossed the bayou, and it sounded like they encountered the guys who were guarding the pot fields. I don't know what happened in that fight. A few minutes later, two of them jumped us. I dropped both of them in the bayou. You'll find the bodies floating about three hundred yards downstream from here. I'm pretty sure the man you shot was the fourth would-be assassin."

Diondro buried his face in his hands.

"This is all because of me. At least five people are dead and others hurt because of me." He said, miserably.

"No, son, you didn't cause this. Life is hard and it isn't fair. This is not your fault. You've done nothing wrong." Buddy said, looking Diondro in the eye.

"Y'all have risked your lives for me."

"That's what we do, Diondro, and it's the same thing you did for Mrs. Sawyer." I pointed out.

"How do you want to handle this, Buddy?"

"You and Diondro get in your car and head on back to Tyler. I'll take care of this mess."

"How, I mean what's going to happen here?"

Buddy was thoughtful for a moment.

"It appears from my preliminary investigation, four armed men attacked a local family. It may have been drug related. At least three of the gunmen were killed, as was a local man. The gunmen appeared to be Mexican. How does that sound?"

"It's a good start. The gunmen probably weren't Mexican though. I think they were from farther south of the border. They had probably done some guerilla fighting somewhere. They could be from Nicaragua, Panama, maybe even Columbia."

"How do you know?"

"The accent and the Spanish they spoke were not Mexican. They were familiar with their weapons, but not very well trained, and they were pretty comfortable in the bush."

"Huh, well, either way it suggests this whole thing is drug related. Maybe even a cartel. I wouldn't be surprised if my men don't find some marijuana growing back in the woods." Buddy winked.

"Y'all get out of here before the news people show up and start taking pictures and asking questions. I'll walk you over to your car, better leave the Mossberg here in my Tahoe."

"Thanks, Buddy. I knew I could count on you."

CHAPTER 13

We drove out past where the pickup trucks had blocked the road. One of them was still half parked in the road. The other truck had been backed up hurriedly and had smashed into the corner of the trailer house

At the head of the road, there was a Sheriff's department road block. There were other cars parked out there and a couple of photographers were taking pictures of everything in sight. There really was nothing to see, but the road intersection, trees, and the roadblock. They would need helicopters to get pictures of the property where the shootings occurred. I was pretty sure by this time phone calls were being made to get that very thing into the works. This would be a big story for the evening news."

I had Diondro duck down out of sight. I was still wearing my boonie hat and I put my sunglasses on, so if they did get pictures of me and the rental car, they would have some work to do, if they tried to figure out who I was.

Buddy had radioed ahead, and the deputies waved us on through the road block. We drove past the TV vans, just as they began arriving on the scene.

"OK, Diondro, you can sit up now."

We drove along in silence for a while, as we headed south toward the Louisiana line.

After a time, I looked over at Diondro, where he sat chewing his lip.

"We'll stop, get cleaned up and get some lunch in Shreveport or Bossier City, is that alright with you?

"Yes, sir."

"You seem worried, Diondro. What are you thinking about?"

"When is the trial?"

"In about three weeks."

"That's a long time to be hiding."

"Oh, I expect it will go by quickly enough."

"Where will I be?"

"I have a friend who lives in a gated community outside of Tyler. We'll keep you there most of the time and move you around when we need to. I'm going to give him a call now."

I hit the speed dial on my cell phone.

"Hey, J, W., How's it going?"

"Well, Tony, you'll probably learn some of the details from the evening news. The simple answer is I have Diondro Taylor with me. We're headed back to Tyler from Arkansas, and I'll need to get him situated. We'll be there in about four hours. We'll be providing him with around the clock protection from now until after the trial."

"What's the plan?"

"I'd like for him to be able to stay with you at night and whenever I'm too busy to have him with me. I'll bring him straight to you, now. I'll keep him with me and/or Christine at the office, when we can. We'll work out the details when we get there."

"OK. We'll keep him safe. Tell him I'm proud of him for having the courage to stand up for what's right."

"I'll tell him. There's something you should know.

Evidently, the individual we talked about last night called someone and told them where to find Diondro. They took a run at us. I'll fill in the details later, and you'll probably see it on the news."

As we drove up the on-ramp to I-20 headed west, I told Diondro what Tony had said about him.

"My friend Tony is impressed with your courage. So am I. I know you were pretty scared back there in the bayou. You were scared, but you did what had to be done. That's the very definition of courage, Diondro."

"Yeah? Maybe. I was plenty scared alright, but you were so calm, you seemed to know what you were doing. I had to trust you, I couldn't think about anything else."

"When we get into Shreveport, I'll get a motel room so we can both get cleaned up and change out of these wet clothes."

The motel clerk barely raised his eyebrows when he saw and smelled me. I had been driving for more than an hour, so at least I wasn't actually dripping bayou water onto his polished floor, but I was tracking mud across it. He didn't seem at all put off by my appearance. Even though I was standing there in soaking wet, mud and muck splattered, camo clothing, he just took my credit card and, after completing the registration, wished me a nice day.

Perhaps he thought I was someone leftover from the TV show "Duck Dynasty."

After getting cleaned up and grabbing a fast food lunch, we were again headed west. As we approached the Louisiana/Texas border, I asked Diondro a question.

"Diondro, are you a believer?"

"What do you mean?"

"I was asking if you're a Christian."

"Oh, uh no, I'm not, not really. My Grandmother was a religious person, but I don't have much use for it."

"Why is that?"

"I'm not superstitious. I don't believe in any of that mumbo jumbo."

"Is that what you think religions are?"

Diondro nodded in agreement.

"I figure as long as there have been people, there have always been religions. Some of them have died out or been forbidden, or whatever, others came along and replaced them, so there are still a big bunch of religions. They're all hooey. It all depends on where you come from. Now, my ancestors in Africa probably had different gods than we have here in America. I figure those old African gods weren't real and neither are any of the more modern American gods. It's all just mumbo jumbo. You'd have to be goofy to buy into any of that crap."

"I see."

"Yeah, you know, like those old Greek gods or the Roman gods, or the Viking gods. You know, Odin and Thor and all that. They were so important in their time and place, but they weren't real. I guess people make up gods to try and explain why stuff happens. They're just imaginary constructs, like Santa Clause or the Tooth Fairy. I guess they're harmless enough, but sometimes people get crazy about their religions."

I nodded in agreement.

"That has often been the case."

"Yeah, religion is a crutch. There's nothing wrong with a crutch, if you need one, but I don't need one." Diondro said, confidently.

We drove along in silence for a while.

"Are you a religious person, Mr. Tucker? I hope I

didn't offend you..."

I smiled.

"No not at all, Diondro. I'm not a religious person either. In fact, it seems to me, people who are religious tend to dislike people who belong to a different religion. Religion has been the cause of wars and strife for centuries."

"Yeah, that's right."

"Why do you suppose there are so many different religions?"

Diondro had his left leg drawn up and crossed over his right knee. He started tapping his ankle with his right hand.

"Well, like we said, people make up gods to try and explain why stuff happens, or to help them feel better about life."

"Why is that?"

"Life is hard and horrible things happen all the time, maybe volcanoes, hurricanes, earthquakes or other natural disasters. Those things scare people."

"Sure, things like floods and plagues and death." I said.

"Right."

"We all live just a short time and then we die. All people, everywhere, throughout all of time, have had to think about dying." I said.

"Yeah, that's why they make up stories about re-incarnation and stuff."

"Sure, life after death. It's the same reason there are mummies. The ancient Egyptians, and others, were preparing the bodies for the next life. It's also the reason for all those stories about ghosts, zombies, vampires and Frankenstein's monster. People are fascinated, wondering about what happens after we die."

He thought about what I said for a moment.

"Yeah, I guess so."

"Have you thought about what happens to us after we die?"

He took a moment to formulate his response. I saw he had now begun to shake his foot as an unconscious nervous habit.

"Well, nothing happens, I guess. Our bodies just decay and become part of the earth."

"What about the person who lived in the body?"

"What do you mean? The body is the person."

I waggled my head ambiguously.

"I tend to think of my body as just the vehicle that carries me around. The real 'me' lives inside the body, but the body is not 'me'." I told him.

"I know what you mean, but I don't believe that. People are just animals with bigger brains. We have all the same drives and hungers as the other animals."

I looked over at him.

"Really, Then you believe you are nothing more than your biological functions?"

"Uh, yeah, I guess."

"So then, you are no different really from a blade of grass or a banana slug?"

"Well, obviously I'm different, just like a fish is different from a butterfly." Diondro said.

I chuckled in response.

"Ok, but that difference is relative and completely unimportant. I catch and eat fish, and about five minutes ago, a butterfly splattered against my windshield. Are you saying the fish and the butterfly are just as important and completely the same as you are?"

He struggled with his thoughts for a moment.

"Not exactly, what I'm trying to say is humans are by nature animals, but we are more highly evolved animals. We are capable of more complex thought and communication, as well as a greater diversity of creative abilities."

"Oh, I see what you mean. No ape ever wrote a screenplay, designed a bicycle, or codified the formula for flight."

"Uh, yeah, I guess."

"I'll bet apes don't spend much time writing poetry, thinking about string theory, and probably haven't established many religions either. It appears apes really are little more than their basic biological functions."

"Well, I'm not sure about that. I think they have personalities and stuff."

"I wonder if a personality would be more than just a basic biological function?"

"Maybe, I don't know."

I left him to his thoughts for a moment, and then I asked another question.

"What about composing a symphony, designing surgical instruments, studying the complexities of science, comforting those who are hurting, and then of course, what about love?"

His response was quick, as though already re-hearsed.

"Oh, love really is just basic biology. We feel love, because we need to reproduce or for another reason that effects the survival of the species."

"So, all of the emotions are just functions of basic biology."

"Well, yeah, I guess."

"What about morality?"

"That's easy, too. Morality is just the generally accepted behavioral norms a society or group establishes to maintain the health and safety of the group." He stated confidently. "That's why people and cultures have such disparities about right and wrong."

I decided to challenge him on that point.

"Actually, they don't have many disparities."

"What do you mean?"

"I mean that all through time, and in virtually every culture there are behaviors which are deemed wrong. There are striking similarities, like generally speaking, murder is wrong, stealing is wrong, lying is wrong, and so on."

"Yeah, well, maybe, but that's because those things threaten the health and stability of the group."

"What about conscience? You know within yourself some things are right and some things are wrong."

Diondro thought about it for a second.

"Isn't it just instinct? If it threatens the survival of the species, then we just naturally feel it."

I smiled.

"Self-preservation is a powerful instinct too, perhaps the most powerful instinct. But when Mrs. Sawyer was being kidnapped, you didn't concern yourself about your own safety. You also didn't form a committee to study the morality of the incident. You didn't even ask others what they thought should be done about the situation. You saw something being done that was wrong, and you did what was right."

"Well, it seemed natural to do the right thing."

"Then why would a society or group change their minds about what is right and what is wrong?"

"I don't know. Do they?"

I changed lanes to pass an eighteen-wheeler. When I returned to the right hand lane, I looked over at Diondro.

"Of course, it happens all the time. People don't really have an unchanging moral standard. The rules change based on the people who make them. Take attitudes about homosexuality as an example. There are very few cultures that have always condoned it and think it's normal. Over the course of time, they often change their minds and decide it is acceptable, a change that usually signals the end of the culture. Again, generally speaking, murder is wrong, but it seems to be OK in some cultures, as long as you murder the right people. If you murder one person it is probably wrong, but if you murder ten thousand or three million people, then maybe you had a good reason. It's the sort of thinking that leads to genocide and infanticide, among other things. Other people groups see these murders and turn a blind eye, until it gets too out of hand. Marriage is another example. It exists in some form in pretty much every culture. Most figure it is between a man and a woman, but over the course of time, some figure there are no rules about marriage. They re-define it as a union between two or more loving individuals. Gender or the number of people in a 'marriage' is unimportant to them. You see, Diondro, when people make the rules, people invariably change the rules.

"Well, I guess that's because the consensus changes as more knowledge is attained."

"Oh, so you're saying basic instinct is unimportant. Conscience is unreliable, traditional morality is unfounded, and higher thinking or general consensus is the best determining factor. I think you just said morality is best determined by the majority in control?"

"Uh, I'm not sure that's what I meant."

I chuckled again.

"That's because you are marvelously smarter than any animal and there is much more to you, than just your basic biological functions. Diondro, let me tell you something... You are going to do very well in college."

CHAPTER 14

The drive back to Tyler was without incident. After the guard at the gate phoned him to get permission to let us through, we met Tony at his house in the gated community north of Tyler.

His sprawling, white, ranch style house with a big front porch was up on a hillside, situated in the middle of a five acre lot with trees surrounding it on three sides, and the top of a swing set could be seen rising above the privacy fence that surrounded the back yard. The house faced the road and had a view of the lake for which this gated community was named. Under the circumstances it seemed amusing to me, because it was called "Hide Away Lake."

In addition to the guarded gatehouse at the entrance, Tony had installed an electric gate at the end of his driveway. The gate was already open for us as we drove up to his house.

After I parked the car, Diondro and I emerged to find Tony was waiting for us, having just stepped out on his porch. We climbed the porch stairs to greet him.

"Tony, meet Diondro Taylor. Diondro, this is my friend Tony Escalante."

They shook hands.

"Pleased to meet you, sir, this is a beautiful location."

"Thank you." Tony said, looking around kind of wistfully.

I knew Tony was remembering when there had been more life here. He was remembering his wife and son who had died in a car wreck, a little more than a year before. The three bedroom house was too big for Tony alone, and every time he looked at the swing set out back...

"Tony is a Tyler cop, Diondro. Not just any cop either, he's the Detective Lieutenant, of the robbery/homicide division."

"Wow, that's impressive."

"Diondro, I want you to know I'm personally and professionally impressed by your courage in this thing. What you did for Mrs. Sawyer was amazing enough, but the way you are stepping up now... well, you're a special kind of man. Don't you worry either; we'll make sure you stay safe."

"Thank you, sir."

"Well, come on in and we'll get you settled."

Tony showed Diondro to his guest room and the guest bathroom.

Tony came back to the living room alone.

"So, tell me what happened in Arkansas." Tony said.

"Well you'll probably see something about it on TV, in about twenty minutes, on the five o'clock news. You might even see it on the national news."

"There was a reference on CNN to a shootout in Arkansas, just as you drove up, but they hadn't gotten to the story yet."

"I'll give you the overview and then we can watch the TV news."

"Fair enough, what happened?"

Just then, Diondro came back into the living room.

"Long story short, I was followed to Arkansas. I found Diondro and whoever was following me, found him too." I gave Tony a look. I could see he understood my veiled reference to the former Tyler cop, Kirby Wilson.

"Just as we were leaving, four armed men showed up, and all hell broke loose. Diondro's Great Uncle was killed, along with the gunmen, and some other folks were hurt. We escaped and we're here. I'll be interested to see what the news has to say, because we left before we knew everything that happened. The County Sheriff up there is a friend of mine, and he helped us get away."

"You make it sound like we just drove away from the shooting. Tell Detective Escalante what really happened," Diondro instructed me.

"Well, we kind of got stuck between the assassins and the men who were guarding a pot farm. We had to wade down a bayou and two of the gunmen jumped us there. I had to put both of them down."

Tony looked shocked.

I didn't want to talk about it anymore.

"Let's turn on the news." I suggested.

"Hang on a minute. Does Christine know you're alright?"

"Yeah, I talked to her on the way here."

"Good heavens, John! You might both have been killed."

I nodded.

"Yeah, it was a near thing."

"We need to talk..."

"I know, Tony. We'll go over all of it later. Right now, I'm tired. Can we just watch the news and go from there?"

"Yeah, I guess so. Are you sure you're OK?"

"Yes, I'm just a little the worse for wear. You understand."

"Yes, I sure do."

Tony turned on the TV which was still set to CNN. An image of Columbia County Sheriff, Wilson Livesque, filled the screen. He was cleaned up, and wearing his official Sheriff's department, flat brimmed hat, rather than the ball cap he usually wore. His usual cheery countenance was replaced with a very serious demeanor.

"... No, we are not able to answer that question at this time. This is an ongoing investigation."

"Can you tell us how many may have been killed?"

"There were five persons killed, one in the residence, one just outside the residence, and three more bodies were found in the bayou. At this time we have not identified all of the bodies."

"Is it true the homeowner, a man named Andrew Taylor, was killed inside his home?"

"We can confirm that the owner of the residence, a man by the name of Andrew Taylor was the man killed inside the residence."

"Sheriff Livesque, there has been some speculation that this appears to have been a drug related incident..."

"Again, we are conducting an active investigation at this time. As I said in the official statement; earlier today, at least four heavily armed men attacked this residence and killed the home owner. One of the Deputies from this department responded to the scene and engaged the shooters. They fired multiple rounds at the deputy. The deputy returned fire and shot and killed at least one of the men, the others fled into the woods behind me. We have recovered the bodies of three men from the bayou, who we believe were part of the group that attacked the residence and the deputy. There were five other people who received gunshot wounds in the violence and they are currently being treated in area hospitals. We are not releasing any other names at this time."

Did the deputy kill all three of the attackers?"

"That is unknown at this time.

"What is the name of the deputy who was involved in the shooting?"

"Again, we are not releasing any other names at this time."

"Was the deputy wounded?"

"No the deputy was not wounded in the incident."

"How many people were involved in the shooting?"

"Again, this is an ongoing investigation..."

"I understand that assault rifles with high capacity magazines were used. Do you know where or how the guns and ammunition were acquired?"

"As I said, this is an ongoing investigation..."

The reporter finally took the hint. "You can't get milk from an angry bull". She turned away from Buddy and faced the camera directly. The camera zoomed in for a close-up of the reporter.

"Thank you, Sheriff Livesque. So, that is all we have at this time. A 911 call was placed at nine forty seven this morning, stating that there was someone shooting at a residence here on County Road 3807 in Columbia County, Arkansas. This location is about fifteen miles south and west of Magnolia, Arkansas. CNN has confirmed that several people were shot, five of them fatally, including the owner of the residence..."

The image on the screen was an aerial view of the scene, clearly taken hours earlier and showing all the emergency vehicles parked at the end of the road, with their lights flashing and uniformed officers and firemen milling about the buildings.

Tony turned off the TV.

"Well, I'm sorry, Diondro. That must have been pretty horrible." Tony said.

"Yes sir, it was. It was kind of surreal at the time. I could hardly believe it was happening. If Mr. Tucker hadn't been there, I guess they would have killed me, for sure."

"Diondro, I'm sorry about your Great Uncle Andrew..." I started.

"... Pot farming? What were they thinking?" Diondro interrupted, shaking his head.

I realized he didn't want to talk about it.

"You need to call your mother. She may have seen the news or heard from someone in your family. Here, use my cell phone and call her, she needs to know you're alright."

"Yes sir, thank you."

I lay back against the couch cushions and closed my eyes.

"Mom, it's me. Yes, I'm fine. How are you? No, I'm back here in Tyler. I know, mom. No, really I'm fine. Don't cry, mom… I don't think I'm supposed to tell you…"

I shook my head.

"…but everything is fine. Don't worry. OK, I know, mom. I love you too. I'll call you again tomorrow. OK, good bye."

He handed my phone back to me.

"My cell phone is in my bag, but the battery is dead. Is it OK if I charge it up and use it?" He asked.

"You can charge it, but don't use it. Don't answer it if it rings. No texting either. This is only temporary, but it will be important you do not tell anyone where you are. That includes your friends and your family."

"That will be hard."

"Yep, but you can handle it. It is possible your phone could be used to determine your location. It's better to be safe than sorry. Only use that phone in a dire emergency. I'll get you in touch with your mother. Three weeks from now this will all be over and life should get back to something like normal."

"J.W., you look done in. Do you want to stay here with us tonight? I cook a mean frozen pizza."

"No thanks, Tony. I have things to do. I've been gone for three days and can you believe I have a dinner party to go to tonight? I'm leaving now to get ready for that."

I turned my attention back to Diondro. He seemed lost in thought or maybe he was just overwhelmed. It had been a busy and unimaginably stressful day for him.

"Good bye, Diondro, I'll probably see you tomor-row."

"Good night, Mr. Tucker, and... thank you. I should have said it before now."

"You're welcome, Diondro, it's all in a day's work."

"I'll walk out to your car with you," Tony said.

When we were outside standing by the rental car, Tony had some questions.

"Was that right? Four gunmen attacked you?"

I nodded.

"How could a street gang afford to hire four gunmen?"

"I doubt they had to pay much, maybe as little as five thousand dollars. The guys who came after us were killers, but they weren't real professionals. They would probably have done it for as little as a thousand bucks each. For the gang that hired them, that's probably only about one day of profit from drug sales, extortion and prostitution. The gang could easily afford it."

"This is bad, John, really bad. One of our own, a Tyler cop is mixed up in a murder for hire plot. This is about to get real ugly."

"Tony, I killed two men this morning. It's already ugly enough."

CHAPTER 15

Jim Fowler and his wife Maria had been friends of mine for a few years. Jim is one of the most prominent attorneys in Tyler. We are members of the same church. He and Maria are active supporters of the arts in East Texas. They helped sponsor a lecture series at the University of Texas at Tyler. I had handled a sensitive investigation for Jim a few years back, and ever since, Jim had always made sure I had a pair of season tickets for the lecture series. I usually only made one or two lectures each year, but I enjoyed those very much.

I had been pleased to get a dinner invitation.

"Hey, John, listen, we are having a little dinner party at the house, to honor one of the visiting lecturers. Maria wanted me to make sure you were invited. We're sending you an invitation with an RSVP in it, but I wanted to invite you personally. You can bring a date. Will you come?"

"Well, it depends. What are you going to be serving for dinner? You know what a picky eater I am."

Jim laughed.

"We thought maybe we could have beany weenies and soda pop."

"Well then, I'm in. When is this shin dig?"

Generally, I'm not a big fan of dinner parties, but I had accepted the invitation, so even though I was nearly exhausted, I found myself on my way to Jim and Maria's house. They seated me directly across the table from the visiting lecturer.

The conversation had turned political and the guest of honor, a middle aged man, named Calvin Worthington, was holding forth. I could see how he had become successful as an established columnist and author. I was also aware he had gained considerable notoriety with television appearances as a panelist on political talk shows. It was rumored he was about to get his own show on a major news network.

"This notion that our economy can be improved, by reducing and eliminating vital programs, and reining in government spending, is of course flawed in every conceivable way. The federal government is the single largest employer in the United States. We cannot afford to add to the unemployment numbers by curtailing people's jobs. We are the largest and most successful economy in the world. So, we will recover without having to touch any of our entitlement programs or other essential federal programs. The neocons will tell us we can no longer afford some of these programs. While they are wrong on that point, in a general sense, there is one area in which they are correct. Federal spending on the war machine must be checked. The military industrial complex is a shameful example of waste and corruption. We are sacrificing our young people on the altar of war, for the profit of big business. Big business is controlling our system and it must be stopped. The idea of imposing austerity on the citizens of this nation, while allowing banks, Wall Street, oil and gas companies, war mongers and other corporate capitalists, to make massive profits, is appalling."

A lovely lady whose name I had forgotten chimed in.

"Oh, I agree. Those super rich bastards only care about lining their own pockets with profits, stolen from the poor working class. Wall Street is destroying America."

Her husband who owned a local car dealership, nodded in agreement.

"Even though we as a nation have chosen a progressive course, corporate America has spent billions of dollars buying politicians, so they can get support for their own economic benefit. They produce their goods overseas, they pay little to no tax in America, and they control our government with their crony capitalism."

I was reminded again; this was why I didn't like dinner parties. There was usually someone who dominated the conversation and political discussions were particularly annoying. We live in a nation with a population of more than three hundred million people. We are ruled by less than seven hundred professional politicians, who ostensibly represent us. Virtually all of the politicians are wealthy. Most of the rest of us are not. It is only one of the many ways in which our system is broken.

"Well, if we don't get our spending under control we're going to face an un-payable debt. We can't continue to run the country on borrowed money. Sooner or later we will have that debt called. What will happen to our children and grandchildren if that happens?" Maria asked.

"My dear lady, that's nonsense! If we avoid the neocon approach to fiscal management, the federal deficit will be brought under control within the next sixteen years. Those greedy conservatives and the corporate fools, who control them, would steal the food from, and deny medical care for, our poorest and most vulnerable citizens. That kind of conservative thinking has been the cause of untold oppression of minorities, gay people and women." Calvin stated.

"Well then, we are going to have to raise taxes across the board. We have to increase income to offset debt. The money has to come from somewhere. The tax rate will have to be raised for every American, no matter his level of income. Everyone will have to pay their fair share," Jim said.

"No, if we do that, the rich will find a way to avoid it. The big corporations will get richer and the ordinary American will get poorer. As I said, we must not go down the old path of conservative thinking. We must once again raise taxes on the wealthiest Americans and on those greedy corporations. If we continue to redistribute their wealth, everyone benefits." Calvin replied.

He looked at me.

"You've been very quiet. What is your opinion, Mr. Tucker?"

I considered my answer. I decided to speak to the heart of the problem.

"I believe most people everywhere are stumbling around in twilight. They choose to live in shadow and twilight because they hate the light and they fear the darkness. Their thoughts, conversations and behavior are based on this hate and fear. Most of them have chosen leaders who are themselves blind. Trapped between the light and the darkness, they band together in the twilight, hoping they will not have to go in either direction. Everyone has an opinion and everyone is right in his own eyes. The road there in the twilight is broad and accommodates everyone. There is room for stumbling around. That wide road, in the twilight, eventually leads to destruction and death.

There is another road, but it is narrow and people shun it. The narrow road is hard to find and it's a difficult climb. It's completely out in the light, so it hurts the eyes of those who love the twilight. There have always been very few who choose this road, and fewer who succeed at walking in the light, but the narrow road leads to eternal life."

"Is that some kind of quote from the bible? What the hell is that supposed to mean?"

"It means, I believe those whom we have chosen to govern, often fail to realize they are unable to manage the complexities of these issues, without recognizing their own weakness and human limitations. When they think they are wise, they fool themselves. When they think they are powerful, they are but pawns in a bigger game. For these reasons, and others, I don't put my hope or trust in either the government or in any political leaders"

"Are you saying you don't vote? That's very foolish and un-American. Voting is the greatest privilege and responsibility of our Democratic Republic. We are a government 'of the people, by the people and for the people'."

"I do vote, Mr. Worthington. I agree, voting is a responsibility and a privilege."

"I don't understand you at all."

"No, you don't."

"I think what Mr. Tucker is trying to say is that he's a simple man who believes these issues are a bit too complex for him to understand. I'm right there with him," One of the ladies suggested.

There were a lot of knowing glances exchanged.

"No, that's not what I'm saying. My point is there is a God in heaven and He is sovereign over all things, including the affairs of men. He has a standard by which He judges both men and nations. He blesses a nation which honors Him. Those who do not honor Him are not blessed. I trust in the Lord. I know He has a plan and He will bring it to fruition."

Mr. Worthington threw his hands up.

"Well, there you have it. It's this kind of magical thinking, so common among you narrow minded, religious right wingers, which renders you stupid. Enlightened conversation is not something you people can attempt. Reality is beyond your limited grasp, because you believe in things that are not real. For you, it is all about voices in your head, fairy tales and 'pie in the sky, by and by'."

I caught his eye.

"I would prefer it if you would not tell me what I believe, Mr. Worthington. You are someone who claims to be tolerant of people who are different from you, yet it is apparent you are not tolerant of people who have a different value system from yours. Are you uncomfortable with basic truth?"

He looked away.

"No, it isn't that, no, not at all. It is quite the opposite in fact. Evidently, you were not listening to me. You would all do well to pay attention to what I tell you. I have a better understanding of the realities of life. I know what is real and that only what is real is true. What is not real is by definition, untrue. You people, who believe in a god, are delusional. You claim to love truth, while you believe in things that are not real, and therefor untrue. I don't hide bigotry and intolerance, under a cloak of religious self-righteousness. I have a distinct advantage over people like you. It's apparent I have a somewhat greater intellect, probably due to genetics, and my having had a more enlightened environment, in which to mature. You are not able to enter into an intelligent discussion, because you are not equipped. It's your own fault you are ignorant. You refuse to open your mind to reality. You just don't know any better. You're lost in childlike wonder, hypnotized by the shiny trinkets of religion. You really ought to be quiet, while the adults are talking."

Several people stiffened and frowned at that. I had to respond.

"I realize you have a right to your opinion and the right to express it. In my opinion, you are being rather judgmental, Mr. Worthington. I did not attempt to impose my views on you, rather you asked me for my opinion."

"Clearly, it was my mistake." He said, bowing graciously.

"Now hang on a second." Jim spoke up. "I'm not going to sit here and let a friend be insulted at my table. Calvin, when you insult John and basically call him stupid, and an ignorant, backwards, country bumpkin, just because he has a different point of view, I take it personally. Do you really think you are intellectually superior to us Texas folks, just because you live and work in New York City?"

"Indeed, yes I am. You gentlemen grew up in the Bible belt. You are a product of your environment. You are unable to grasp the nuances of sophisticated subject matter for the simple reason you have not had the requisite cultural opportunities afforded by exposure to a more metropolitan, diverse and progressive lifestyle. Not to mention my Ivy League education."

Jim wasn't having it.

"Mr. Worthington, you're a legend in your own mind. You state your opinions as if they were facts. Saying you're better or smarter than others does not actually make you an authority. Oh, and let's mention your education. I'm pretty sure you just suggested you're better than us, because you went to an Ivy League school. What's wrong with the University of Texas, Baylor, or Texas A & M? Just to name a few of our institutions of higher learning."

"Well, they are hardly to be compared with Harvard, Princeton or Yale, are they?"

"I expect we have better football players," I suggested, with a wink and a smile.

"Ah shucks, and whoooeee! I'll bet you are better at cow tipping as well," He sneered.

There was stunned silence for a moment.

"Why you pompous, egotistical, two bit dilettante, I oughtta throw you out on your ass!" Jim growled.

"Jim! That's enough," Maria said.

I started to laugh then, Jim glanced at me and

then he joined in, laughing.

In a moment, the whole room was laughing.

Laughter often breaks tension, but the truth about matters of deception and discernment, life and death decisions about good and evil, are not a laughing matter.

CHAPTER 16

Early the next morning, while driving on the south-west Loop, on my way to return the rental car, I gave Buddy a call.

"Hey, John, I guess this means you made it home OK?"

"Yes, thanks to you."

"What can I do for you this morning?"

"I was kind of hoping for an update. I don't think I'm getting the whole story from the media."

"Oh, ye of little faith."

I chuckled.

"Well then, let me tell you. The press is about to get the news, we found commercial marijuana production on the property. The Taylors and Carlisles will claim they had no knowledge of it, until recently. They'll say they encountered armed men on their property, and they suspected those men were guarding pot fields. Apparently Andrew Taylor had confronted the men and threatened to bring in the law. The men who attacked were Hispanic, and it appears at this time, the Hispanic men were responsible for the pot farm. So, we have possible illegal aliens, possible organized crime, trespassing, fully automatic assault weapons, commercial marijuana production, murder and mystery. As of today, we're going to have a whole alphabet soup of federal agencies involved."

"Have you accounted for all of the people in the fight?"

"As you know, the four men who attempted to ambush you are dead. On the other side of the bayou, we found three Carlisle men who were pretty badly wounded. I expect they had been the guards who shot it out with the attackers. They lost that fight, but they're in the hospital, and all three are expected to recover. I made sure they lawyered up. They won't say anything to law enforcement or the media about what really happened out there."

"So the news media is going to tell the tale of how the locals were the victims in this deal. Is that about right?"

"Oh, I can't speak for the press. We'll just have to wait for the news broadcasts. I'll be making a statement of course. As I said, it appears at this time the Hispanic men were conducting a secret pot farming operation and trespassing on the local folk's property, to do it. Apparently, when the locals found out and confronted them, the drug dealing Hispanics attempted extortion, and when the locals refused to buckle, the drug dealers decided to wipe them out. The locals fought back, and it was a mess."

"Well, Buddy, I'm sorry you're having these troubles in your county."

"Yeah, me too, I hope you won't come back and visit again, anytime soon."

I chuckled again.

"If I do, I'll try to make it more of a friendly visit."

"Seriously, John, you know we love you and we can't thank you enough, for what you did for Bud…"

"Don't thank me, Buddy."

"Right, I know. We thank God for Bud and we thank God for you too."

"You look good on the TV, Buddy."

"Thanks, I guess I'm getting a lot of free publicity

for my re-election campaign."

"You know what they say..."

"No press is bad press?"

"So I've heard."

When Christine picked me up at the rental car agency, she was pretty excited. She was driving my four door diesel, pickup truck. That was not the reason for her excitement.

"I saw the whole story on the news. How did you and Diondro get out of there without attracting any attention?"

"We left before most of the news people got there. No one up there feels any need to mention the Diondro connection. The Sheriff is a friend of mine, he has my back, and Diondro's family has his."

"Where is Diondro now?"

"Oh, I left him with a mutual friend. I expect at this moment he's sitting in your boyfriend's office, at the cop shop."

Christine scowled at me.

"If you're referring to our mutual friend, Tony Escalante, he is not my boyfriend."

"Now Christine, you and he are dating, aren't you?"

"Well..."

"And it seems to me neither of you are dating anyone else..."

I made a questioning gesture.

Christine rolled her eyes.

"And clearly you're a girl. Tony is a boy, and you're friends, who are also dating each other. So, ipso facto, he's your boyfriend."

"Go stick your head in the toilet."

"Awww, let's start over. Good morning, Christine! How are you today?"

Ten minutes later, I dropped her off at the office.

Tony called me as I was pulling to a stop at the Mexican Market where most of the day laborers hung out, waiting for someone to pick them up for a bit of short term work.

"J.W., the individual who was following you in Arkansas is working as a private detective."

"I'm aware of that, Tony."

"Yeah, but what you are not aware of is the fact he no longer works for the Tyler PD. He's working as a PI, period. That's his only job."

"How's that possible, did you fire him?"

"No, he had already been fired. He was fired last week, after an Internal Affairs investigation discovered he had been moonlighting on Tyler PD time. I-A had been investigating him for more than a year. There were some additional abnormalities related to him using his police badge to obtain information for his private business and dirty money making its way into his pockets. They tell me he had been providing muscle and running interference for some prostitutes, while in uniform. The Union didn't even try to defend him. They struck a deal with the department. If the department didn't bring charges against him, he would go away quietly. He turned in his badge and gun. The point is; Kirby Wilson was no longer a Tyler cop when he showed up in Arkansas."

"He had a badge and he flashed it when the local law stopped him for questioning."

"Maybe, but that's pretty thin gravy down here. He may have impersonated a police officer in Arkansas, but it would be their problem, not ours."

"What are you saying?"

Several Hispanic men had noticed me and were approaching the truck.

"We can't really connect him to the killers for hire. We only know he followed you to Arkansas and the killers eventually showed up there. J.W. can you prove he had any contact with them?"

I sighed.

"Yeah, you get my point." Tony said.

"Do you know where he is now?"

"No, I just got done talking with Internal Affairs. I figured I'd better let you know."

"OK, Tony thanks. Is the package with you?"

"Yes. All is well."

The good news was there was very little chance former Patrol Sergeant Kirby Wilson would be anywhere around Tony's office at the Tyler police station. The bad news was we couldn't pin anything on him that would take him out of the picture.

"Tony, I've got to go. I'll talk to you later."

I stepped out of my truck to greet the men gathering around.

There were five of them and they varied in age from about sixteen to about sixty. Each man was dressed for work in long sleeved shirts, ball caps and jeans. All of them had work gloves tucked in their pockets. Others were watching from a distance. It was after nine o'clock by now, which meant most of the good jobs had already been filled.

"Buenos días. ¿Alguno de ustedes habla a inglés?"

"Yes, I do, a little. So do I. We all do," was the general response.

"OK, I need men who are experienced concrete and general construction hands. Have any of you done construction work here, in East Texas?"

Two of them indicated they had done construction work in the area.

I addressed them.

"Dónde hiciste el trabajo?"

"We do some work near Lindale, Tyler, Longview, Kilgore, Whitehouse, but out in the country mostly," one of the men said, shrugging.

The other man nodded his agreement.

"OK, I'm paying one hundred dollars, per man, per day. Even though we're getting a late start, you'll still get one hundred dollars today. I'll also provide lunch today. I can only take you two men. Are you ready to go now?" I asked.

They both nodded. The other men began to wander off.

We got in my truck. The older of the two men appeared to be about forty. He sat in the passenger seat, up front beside me. The younger man appeared to be about thirty. He sat in the back seat, directly behind me.

I don't like to have strangers sitting directly behind me.

As we drove away from the Mexican Market, I phoned Gary.

"Where are you today?"

"We're building a big barn, a little ways outside of Troup, in Cherokee County."

"Congratulations again on getting the job as the crew chief."

"So, what can I do for you today?"

"I've picked up a couple of workmen. I'll bring them out to you, if you'll give me directions."

Gary gave me directions to the worksite.

Thirty minutes later, we pulled through an open farm gate and drove directly across the recently cut hay meadow toward the construction site. We passed hundreds of fresh square bales of Coastal Bermuda grass hay. It smelled like summer time.

The construction site was nothing more than a pad, cleared and leveled, at the edge of the hay meadow. As the day heated up, there would be little shade from the trees some thirty yards away.

Gary was supervising a four man crew. The men were building the forms for the barn's concrete foundation. They were working on a grid of re-bar. Lumber, roofing shingles, siding and other materials were stacked nearby.

The three of us got out of my pick up, as Gary approached us.

"Gary, this is Juan Vargas and Julio Garcia. They are ready to go to work."

Gary looked them over and nodded.

"OK, you men can start carrying supplies over to the others. Go over there and introduce yourselves."

When the men walked away, Gary spoke to me quietly.

"I've been re-thinking this thing, John. I don't think I have the authority to hire extra men."

"It might be a chance for you to show off a little. Show some initiative and get more work done, faster."

"Yeah, I don't think it's a good idea, my first day as a crew chief. Kevin Watkins is the Foreman and he'll be back by here sometime later today to check on me. He'll probably want to be here when the concrete truck gets here. He's a jackass, and I'd better not make him mad. If he shows up, I'll tell him some story about how you had hired these guys to work for you, but the job fell through, so you stopped by here to see if I needed anybody."

"Good plan, but I don't think it's going to be an issue. They're coming back here now."

Juan and Julio were hurrying toward us.

"¿Cuál es el problema?" I asked.

"We cannot work here, señor. We have had troubles with this company. We have worked with these other men before. We are all worried about the boss man. He won't like to see us here."

"Do you mean Kevin Watkins?"

They both nodded.

"Es un hombre malo. He will give us much troubles."

"I see... well, we can't have that. We'll figure out something else, don't worry. Get back in the truck. I'll be along in a minute."

I looked at Gary.

"Problem solved."

"Yeah, but I've never seen anything like that before. Those guys are scared."

"Yes, they are. It should be an interesting conversation on the drive back to Tyler."

Gary looked thoughtful.

"I'll try to get some info from these other guys, as the day goes on."

"Do that, but you be very careful and take care of yourself. It's going to be hot today."

CHAPTER 17

When I got back in the truck, I addressed the men.

"I'm sorry, this was the only work I had for you today..."

"... No es un problema, senor. We cannot work for this company." Juan interrupted.

I nodded in response.

"By the time I drive you back to Tyler, the morning will be nearly gone and there will be few opportunities to find other work. I tell you what... I promised you each one hundred dollars for today. If you will tell me everything you know about the company and why you won't work for them, I'll still pay you the one hundred dollars."

Juan turned and looked back at Julio. In the rear view mirror, I saw Julio shrug.

"Why do you want to know? If you are working for this company, you should already know." Juan enquired.

It was getting hot in the truck, so I started it up and got the air conditioning going.

"I don't work for this company. The crew chief on this job here is a friend of mine, and he told me if I could find a couple of extra men he would appreciate it. I just picked you up to help my friend. Why won't you work for this company?"

"Why are you willing to pay two hundred dollars to hear about it?" Juan demanded.

"I have already heard some bad things myself. I need to know if the stories are true. I can probably make some money if this company has bad practices. Do they?"

Juan and Julio were both thoughtful for a moment.

"You keep your money then. I think maybe it is not safe to talk about these things." Julio said.

"Why do you say that?"

"Esto es mal negocio, y no le conocemos," Juan observed.

"I agree Juan. It is bad business we are discussing. My name is John Tucker. I am in the business of helping people who have troubles. I know of a man who worked for this company and he was injured on the job. His friends and co-workers are afraid to tell what happened. They are afraid to tell about the bad things that happen to people who work for the bad company. I think you are both afraid, too."

Juan did not like hearing me say I thought he was afraid. His eyes blazed and he set his mouth in a firm line.

Julio was younger and had less self-discipline.

"We are not cowards, señor. If you knew what we know, you would not judge us so."

"So, tell me what you know, and I will be the judge of that."

"Why should we trust you?"

It was a fair question.

"Trust me because of justice. Debe hacerse justicia. When good men do not stand up for what is right, there is no justice. I intend to find out the truth about this company. When I do, I will make sure they answer to the law."

"Huh, the Norte Americano, white man's law? They will not listen to us. We are not welcome in the Estados Unidos. They will send us back to Mexico."

"You can tell me. I won't send you back to Mexico."

They were both silent for a moment.

"Por favor, Sr. Tucker, nos llevan de aquí." Julio entreated.

"Why? You are safe enough here in the truck."

"It is the bad man. If he comes here and finds us..."

"Do you mean Kevin Watkins?"

"Yes."

"This is the second time you've mentioned him. Is he dangerous?"

"Sí, él es... muy peligroso."

"OK, tell me more about him."

I put the truck in gear and started to drive away from the job site, waiving at Gary as we left. As we drove across the hay meadow, Julio opened up.

"This man is bad. He is cruel and he hurts people. He pushes and trips us as we work. He laughs about it. One day he pushed and taunted Eduardo so much, Eduardo pulled a knife on him. Eduardo is not a man to taunt. Eduardo is stupid, but very strong and fierce, and his knife was always very sharp."

"What is Eduardo's last name?"

"Ruiz, Eduardo Ruiz. He is from Mazatlan."

"What happened when Eduardo pulled the knife?"

"The bad man, he beat Eduardo, with this little whip thing he had clipped to his belt. It is small and short, no more than a foot long, but it gets long and thin. Senor Watkins knocked the knife out of Eduardo's hand, very quickly, and then he beat him with the stick. Then he cut Eduardo with his own knife."

"Did he kill Eduardo?"

"No, we did not see this. He hurt him. We saw him cut a mark into Eduardo's chest, but Eduardo did not die."

"Where is Eduardo now?"

"No one knows, señor. After the fight, Mr. Watkins drove Eduardo away. He said he was taking him home to get cleaned up, maybe see a doctor. Mr. Watkins came back to the job site, Eduardo did not. Not that day, or the next, or ever again. No one has seen him since that day."

"When did this happen? Cuándo sucedió esto?"

"Fue en Noviembre".

"Where?"

"Somewhere over east of here." He pointed over his shoulder.

"Do you think Mr. Watkins killed Eduardo?"

They both shrugged.

"Who can say? Maybe Eduardo, he just go somewhere else." Juan observed.

"Have you ever met the owner of the company?"

"No, only the bad man. He is the one who hires the men and he is the one who torments the men."

"Did you get a paycheck from the company?"

"No, always cash money."

"Why would anyone want to work for that company?"

They both shrugged again.

"We need money. There are many others who want the work. When the white man got hurt on the job, Mr. Watkins tell us to shut up and talk to no one about what happened. He say he know where we live, if we talk to anyone, he will find us and make us to pay, Julio and I decide we won't ever go near this bad man again."

"Were you there on the day the bricks fell on the white man?"

Juan and Julio looked at each other.

"Si', but we did not see it happen."

"The reason I ask is because we are going to make the company pay for what happened to that man, and we can make them pay for what they have done to you."

"Pay us what? What have they done to us? Nothing, we quit because we don't want to work there no more."

"Would you testify to what you know about the company and about how Mr. Watkins treats the men?"

They looked confused, so I repeated the question in Spanish.

"Se dan testimonio de lo que sabes sobre la empresa y sobre cómo el Sr. Watkins trata a los hombres?"

They looked at each other and then back at me.

"We are not Americanos. We will not talk in the gringo court. They would send us back to Mexico."

We drove along in silence for a little while.

"I will find a way we can get your testimony and not put you in danger. In the meantime, you must stay away from those people. You have earned your money today."

I gave each of them five, twenty dollar bills.

We drove the rest of the way back into Tyler, in silence.

After I dropped the men off at the Mexican Market, I phoned Gary and warned him about Watkins and his ASP.

"What is an ASP?" Gary asked.

"It's one of those telescoping batons some law enforcement types carry. Evidently Watkins is very good with one. You watch him closely. He may not show his meaner side to you on the first day, but he almost certainly will, at some point. Juan and Julio tell me he's very cruel, and he may even have murdered a man named Eduardo Ruiz."

"What has it got to do with me?"

"Eduardo Ruiz worked for your outfit. He got crosswise with Watkins on the job one day, and took the worst of it from Watkins. Ruiz got hurt and Watkins put him in his truck and drove away. Ruiz hasn't been seen since."

"Oh, that's just great! Do I get to collect hazardous duty pay?"

"If you feel like you need to pull out, I'll understand."

"Naw, remember, I'm a fireman. We run into burning buildings for a living."

"Yeah, well watch out for burning debris. You don't have any other firemen with you in this deal."

CHAPTER 18

The next call I made was to Tony.

"Tony, could you look into whether or not there have been any unidentified bodies found in the general area, between now and October of last year?"

"Well, J.W., you know on those rare occasions, whenever someone finds a body, it tends to be big news."

"Right, I know, but if no other information becomes available, the story just kind of goes away. I think I remember something from a few months ago, maybe over in Henderson County, but I'm not sure."

"OK. I'll look into it and call you back."

Ten minutes later, my phone rang. I saw the call was from Tony.

"You know, J.W. you continue to surprise me. Yes, there was a body found in January of this year, on an old abandoned oil well site, over in Rusk County, near the town of Henderson. That's why you thought it was in Henderson County. A guy riding an ATV found it."

"Oh, OK. Was the dead person a Hispanic male?"

I could hear Tony hesitate. I knew he was struggling to compose his answer.

"No one knew, at the time. The Rusk County Sheriff's department had to wait for the forensics people in Dallas to report back. Nothing was reported to the public. The remains were those of a male, of Hispanic origin. But of course, I expect you already knew that."

"Was he ever identified?"

"No. It says here the body was in advanced decomposition, and had been pretty well torn apart by animals. You know, first the vultures, then the coyotes or feral hogs. Mostly it was a skull and some bones scattered around. They had to work to gather all the remains."

"How did they identify the remains as being a Hispanic male?"

"Well, you know it's pretty easy to determine the gender and approximate age, from the bones. There was some other evidence at the scene and on the remains. Maybe DNA indicated it was a person of Hispanic origin."

"Was this person about thirty years of age?"

I could tell Tony was scrolling through the information displayed on his monitor.

"So it would seem, J.W."

"I guess we are going to have to have a conversation with the Rusk County Sheriff."

Tony groaned into the phone.

"What do you mean 'we', J.W.? I don't know anything about it. It has nothing to do with me."

"I think the body may have been the remains of a man who was murdered. He was a resident of Tyler. He may have been murdered in Tyler. If he was murdered, I believe he was murdered by a man who is also a resident of Tyler. Is that something that the Detective Lieutenant of the Robbery/Homicide Division for the police department of the city of Tyler, might be interested in?"

"Ohhh, man."

"I'll take that as a 'yes'."

"You said 'may be', maybe this and maybe that. For all I know there was no murder."

"There is sufficient information to conduct an investigation.

"Do you have further information you would like to share?"

"Was there ever a missing persons report filed, that might have fit this guy?"

"Not to my knowledge."

"Has anyone come forward to claim the body?"

I don't know, J.W. How about you answer some of my questions?"

"You only had one."

"Two"

"Two? No, I distinctly remember... oh yeah. You asked me why you should be involved, and you asked me if I had any further information to share. You're right, that was two questions. I already answered the first one. Well, Tony, call me when you get the appointment set up with the Rusk County Sheriff."

"Are you going to answer my questions?"

"That's it, stick to your guns. Now you're starting to sound like a homicide investigator."

In response, Tony growled into the phone.

"Take it easy, big guy. No need to use the rubber hose. I'll talk. Yes, I have further information, and I'll be happy to answer your questions."

"Come down to the station. I want you to make a statement."

"I was afraid you would say that."

"Right now, J.W., do it now."

Tony prefers to do everything by the book, and he's a stickler for procedure.

For me, rattling his cage is kind of like a hobby.

It makes me smile.

CHAPTER 19

I found Diondro sitting in Tony's office. They were in the middle of a conversation.

"... we'll be changed. We'll have bodies just like the body Jesus had after his resurrection," Tony was saying

"Hey," I said, by way of greeting.

"What's up?" Diondro asked, with a nod.

"The heavens," I responded.

Diondro considered my answer and chose to ignore it.

"On another subject - I hear you know something about a dead body."

"Some, maybe, it's too early to know enough. It isn't really a different subject, either. Tony was telling you about how our human bodies will be changed into glorified bodies, when Jesus returns."

"Yes, but it's pretty far-fetched, kind of impossible, really."

"Not really, a caterpillar changes into a butterfly."

"Yes, but the process requires a living caterpillar, a cocoon, and time for the metamorphosis."

"So, your problem isn't with the idea of the change, it's with the amount of time it takes?"

"No, the whole thing seems pretty ridiculous. It's like science fiction."

"Well, many things that used to be science fiction have become everyday facts. Take robots for example. Once they were science fiction. Today, mass produced robots do everything from assembling cars, to vacuuming our swimming pools, houses, and even mowing our yards. We learn new things every day. What we are used to today would have been considered magic not so long ago. Should we discuss cloning or bio-engineering?"

Diondro saw an opportunity to change the subject.

"I've been learning a lot about crime and our legal system, by just watching and listening to what goes on around here."

"I'll bet you have."

"John, I would like to learn a few things myself." Tony interrupted, pointing to the other chair in front of his desk.

I sat where I had been directed.

Tony pulled out a digital recorder, turned it on, and set it on the desk between us.

"I am Detective Lieutenant Anthony Escalante, of the Robbery/Homicide Division of the Tyler Police Department. The current time is eleven forty one, A.M., Friday, the sixteenth day of June. I am interviewing Mr. John Wesley Tucker, who wishes to make a statement about information he has, related to a possible homicide."

He looked at me.

"Mr. Tucker, you are not under arrest, so I don't need to read you your rights, but this is the first part of an official investigation into a possible homicide. Are you ready and willing to make a statement and to answer some questions?"

I smiled at Tony.

"Yes, Lieutenant Escalante."

He scowled at me.

"Mr. Tucker, will you please explain why you called me and asked me several questions about whether or not a certain unidentified body had been found in the general area?"

I smiled again.

"Yes, Lieutenant Escalante."

Tony gritted his teeth, his jaw muscles bunching.

"Please tell me why you made those inquiries and what information you may have about the remains."

I took a moment to gather my thoughts.

"I'm a licensed private investigator. One of my clients is a law firm, currently handling the legal affairs of a man who worked for a local construction company. Their client was injured on the job. They believe there was gross negligence on the job site, which was the cause of the serious injuries their client suffered. I have been tasked with finding witnesses to the incident and to gather any other information which might support their client's case."

Tony nodded, and encouraged me to continue, with a hand gesture.

"In the course of my investigation, I interviewed two men who had worked for the company in question. They told me a man they used to work with had been in an altercation with the man who is the foreman for the construction company. They told me the foreman beat their friend, and then took him away in his truck. They never saw their friend again," I concluded.

"Mr. Tucker, did these men tell you they thought their friend had been murdered?" Tony asked.

"No Lieutenant, they did not. They told me the foreman was cruel and vicious, but they didn't make any statement as to what they thought might have happened to the missing man."

"What is the missing man's name?"

"Eduardo Ruiz. He is or was a male of Hispanic origin, about thirty years of age."

Tony looked thoughtful for a moment, and then he stopped the recorder.

"J.W., that isn't much to go on. We don't have any kind of a missing persons report. It sounds like this guy could be an illegal immigrant, from south of the border somewhere."

"Yeah, Tony he is or was a Mexican national, from Mazatlan."

"J.W. did it even cross your mind he may have just gone back to Mexico."

"Sure, but the men I spoke with knew him and his family. They told me no one has ever seen him again. Around the time he disappeared, someone happened to find the decomposed and mutilated corpse of a Hispanic male. You know how I feel about coincidences."

Tony nodded, and started the recorder again.

"Is this why you contacted the department and inquired about missing persons or unidentified remains?"

"Yes, Lieutenant, I thought I remembered hearing on the news, something about someone finding a dead body, a few months ago."

"Is there any other information you have, that would help us identify the remains, or prove this Mr. Ruiz was murdered?"

"The missing man, Mr. Ruiz, went missing in November. Not one person saw him or spoke to him after he got into Mr. Watkins pickup truck. As I understand it, the unidentified remains were found just a few weeks later, near Henderson, in Rusk County. That's the same general area where those men were working, on the day Mr. Ruiz disappeared."

"Who is Mr. Watkins?"

"He's the foreman for the construction company and the man they told me had beaten Mr. Ruiz. I am told he also cut Mr. Ruiz with a knife, on that day, just moments before he drove him away from the job site."

"Is there anything you wish to add to your statement?"

"No, that's pretty much all I know, so far."

Tony nodded and turned off the recorder. He

leaned back in his desk chair.

"Now I have a question for you..." I started.

Tony held up his hand.

"I am not at liberty to discuss any of the details of an ongoing homicide investigation."

"What? I thought you said there was no indication there had been a homicide."

Tony looked over at Diondro.

"Diondro, would you go get me and Mr. Tucker a couple of cups of coffee?"

Diondro nodded.

"Sure, and I'll bet you would like me to take my time doing it."

Tony nodded back at him, with a rueful smile.

"No need to hurry."

When Diondro had left his office, Tony leaned forward on his desk.

"Well, J.W. Off the record, it so happens the coroner was able to determine a cause of death," he said, quietly.

"Oh boy, here we go. Fill in the blank. Death by...?"

"... Multiple stab wounds. There were nicks and cuts on several of the bone surfaces, consistent with a steel blade. These marks were not the marks left by the animals tearing the body apart. Some of the marks were on the bones in the arms and hands. Those would be consistent with defensive wounds. He was clearly stabbed to death, by someone who was enraged. And there was another rather odd mark..."

"... Let me guess. Was it found on the breast bone?"

"How did you know?"

My witnesses said Watkins carved a mark in Mr. Ruiz' chest, what was the mark?"

Tony sighed and looked down at his hands.

"It was a cross, J.W."

CHAPTER 20

That afternoon I went to the home of a man by the name of Frank Overton. Mr. Overton had contacted us with concerns his house might be bugged. He believed his telephone conversations and other communications in his home were being electronically monitored, by persons unknown. It was unusual because private citizens were seldom bugged, unless they were involved or suspected of being involved in some sort of criminal activity. Even then, it could be difficult for a police agency to get a warrant to do electronic surveillance, unless there was a suspected threat to national security or involvement in organized crime. My cursory check into Mr. Overton's business activities ruled out any sort of corporate espionage.

He was however, a Certified Public Accountant. It would not be unusual for a CPA, like Mr. Overton, to have conversations with clients in which sensitive private financial information might be discussed. In these days when identity theft is so common, nothing could be overlooked. Additionally, some accountants can have odd bedfellows.

I was pretty curious to see what was going on in the Overton home office.

I rang the doorbell, and was greeted by a man

of about forty years of age. He was tall, maybe six-two or so, and had what had once been an athletic build. The years had softened him and he was a bit on the heavy side now, with a balding head. What hair he had left was obviously dyed a deep chocolate brown and combed over the top of his head. He was wearing a white dress shirt open at the neck and dark grey slacks.

"Mr. Overton, I'm John Wesley Tucker, we spoke on the phone."

"Oh, right, right, yes. Do you have some form of identification?" he asked.

It was annoying, but probably to be expected of someone with cause for concern about their privacy and security.

"Yes, sir, will my driver's license do?"

"Is that all you've got?"

I produced one of my business cards as well. I have two types. One is my actual business card; the other just has a beautifully embossed name on it - Earl Hightower. It's an alias I've found useful on occasion.

He pulled a pair of reading glasses from his shirt pocket and proceeded to carefully study my credentials.

"Oh, OK. I guess you are who you say you are, come on in."

I entered a dark foyer that gave way to a darker living room. He had all of the window shades drawn and there were no lights on. The television was the only light source in the room, casting everything in a bluish hue. It was showing "Haunted humans" or some such "reality" drivel, about people searching for ghosts in old buildings.

I smelled a foul odor, but could not be sure of its source.

"What makes you think your home might be bugged?" I asked him.

He was lost in the television show.

"Mr Overton, I said, what makes you think your home might be bugged?" I spoke more loudly this time.

He looked at me and blinked several times.

"What makes you think it isn't?"

"I won't have any idea until I bring in my equipment."

"Well, go get it."

I went out to the truck and retrieved my RF, VLF, UHF and infrared scanners.

Mr. Overton took an interest in the scanners.

"Hey, that looks a lot like some of the equipment the ghost hunters use to capture energy from the spirits. Do you believe in spirits?"

"That would depend on what you mean when you say 'spirits'. There are many different ways the term is used."

"I mean ghosts and demons and unseen entities. They are all around us, you know? Only the gifted can communicate with them, though."

I considered how to respond.

"Are you a person who believes dead people become ghosts who stay around to haunt people and places they knew when they were alive?"

"Absolutely, it's why they have these TV shows."

"Well, if that's true, then there would have to be billions of ghosts. Can you imagine everyone who ever died, throughout all of human history, still here with us? They would be everywhere. I read in the Bible, it is appointed that people only die once, and after that they are judged. It says, to be absent from the body is to be present with the Lord. The Bible also says in several places and in different ways, it's evil to attempt to communicate with the dead."

"Phaw!" He spat. "You Bible thumpers are an ignorant lot. No one knows what becomes of our spirits once we die. They say sometimes a person's ghost stays around, because they have unresolved issues. I believe there are spirits all around us. I hear them sometimes, myself."

"Mr. Overton, I agree with you about unseen spirits. Have you ever heard of the Holy Spirit?"

"Phaw!" He spat again. "I'm not interested in organized religion. There is more that goes bump in the night, than you religious people can possibly imagine."

I decided to return to the subject of electronic monitoring.

Mr. Overton said he had no idea exactly which rooms might be bugged, so we started with his office.

This room also had a blue hue to it, magnified by the only light source, his computer monitors. There were three of them. One was showing the same television program as the one in the living room. There were no ground line telephones in the room.

"I only use my cell phone these days. I have a fax machine hooked up, as you can see, but it gets very little use, anymore. Almost any document is sent faster and more securely as a PDF file, attached in an e-mail."

There was a lot of electrical interference in the room, but I was able to determine there was nothing in the room that Mr. Overton had not put there himself.

After going through the rest of the house, I was certain there were no electronic listening devices or other devices, except those Mr. Overton had himself placed in the building. The temperature in the attic was at least thirty or forty degrees hotter than in the house. I sweated through my shirt in about two minutes. After a very thorough search, I was certain there were no electronic devices on the premises in any way out of the ordinary. I was surprised there was a television in nearly every room including the master bathroom. I also noticed a variety of totems, masks, and native artwork items in the house. These were from diverse parts of the world. Some I recognized as objects of worship in other, more ancient cultures.

The problem wasn't someone attempting to steal identities or other sensitive information from Mr. Overton.

The problem was much worse.

"Mr Overton, do you watch a lot of television?"

"Of course, it's never turned off. It's my source. I get all my news, weather and entertainment from it. There are great programs on the education channels which I find informative and thought provoking. I've learned a lot from TV."

"Yes, I can see you have. I'll bet you've learned a lot from the internet as well. How do you know whether what you have learned is the truth?"

"Truth, what is truth? I mean, you know, all truth is relative. What is true for you may not be true for me? Your truth is not my truth. What is true today may not be true tomorrow. It's all a matter of personal perception. Science has certainly proven that."

"Has it? Science hasn't actually proven anything. Proving things is neither the purpose nor the process of science. Science is merely the study of creation, through observation and experimentation. Occasionally, science arrives at conclusions, but they are often incomplete conclusions and frequently wrong conclusions. Science is all about studying evidence, gathering data and conducting experiments, not about arriving at conclusions."

He thought about my statement for a moment and then he changed the subject.

"If there are no bugs in the house, why do I feel as if I am constantly being watched? Do you think there might be hidden cameras?"

"There are no bugs or hidden cameras here, Mr. Overton. You are right about the spirits but they are not ghosts. If you're hearing the voices of unknown spirits, then you are in grave danger. It is important to test every spirit. I will pray God protects you, but you must be more careful about what you invite into your home, your heart, and your head."

"Nonsense, I don't believe in your God!"

This man was hearing voices and he believed in ghosts and other spirits, but he denied the existence of God. I knew this attitude was fairly common in our culture, except for the part about hearing voices.

"It seems you believe in many gods. It appears you have your own god. You said the television was your source. You might want to reconsider the altar, at which you worship."

"I don't need any advice from you. Clearly, you are some kind of a nut. Send me your bill."

I packed up my gear and looked over at Mr. Overton.

"Thank you, Mr. Overton. I'll be on my way…"

Frank Overton was lost in another daze. He appeared to be tuned in to his television program, but perhaps he was listening to other voices. Voices only he had been gifted to hear.

I let myself out.

It seemed like everyone was going crazy these days.

CHAPTER 21

When I got back to the office, I told Christine what had happened with Mr. Overton.

"So, there was nothing there? Christine asked.

"There was nothing there that he didn't bring into the house himself, certainly no electronic eavesdropping or video recording devices. Still, he was hearing voices and felt like he was being watched."

"Why do you think he was afraid of something that wasn't there?"

"He's a very strange man. I think he's opened himself to some pretty bad influences."

"What influences?"

"The Bible in the book of Ephesians refers to Satan as 'the prince of the power of the air'. It's an odd term. In ancient times, people thought 'the air' was where the spirit beings lived, the angels and demons. Some believed storms and other meteorological phenomenon were caused by these spirits. 'The air' was believed to be a different dimension from the one in which we live.

They could not imagine anything like what we have now, Christine. Can you imagine someone from the ancient world hearing a stereo or seeing a television image? It would seem like magic. Do you think it's just a coincidence we refer to television and radio broadcasts as being 'on the air'?"

"No, we also call some people 'on air' personalities, but are you suggesting radio and television are evil?"

"Not, exactly. Television and radio broadcasts are just things we've created by using natural phenomenon in new ways. A television is just an object, as are cameras, recording equipment, computers, satellites, and broadcasting equipment. The medium is not evil. However, as with anything else it can be used for evil, or by evil. With satellite uplinks and downloads, TV and radio are now universal and have the capability to reach billions of people in virtually real time. The medium is not evil, but the media may well be a tool."

"I guess it could be, but there are also very good programs and religious broadcasts, sharing the Gospel with people who otherwise might not have heard it." Christine said.

It's one of the things I appreciate about Christine. She always tries to see the good in everything, and she won't hesitate to challenge my thinking. I had to agree with her statement.

"Sure, and Billy Graham was the first evangelist to really make full use of the radio and television potential. God can use broadcast media, if He wants to. He created every aspect of the physics involved, but He does not need the medium, because He's omnipresent and omnipotent. Satan is neither omnipotent nor omnipresent. He can use the medium and he does need to use it, to spread his deceptions and lies throughout the world. There are people who believe pretty much everything they see on TV. They never question whether there might be an agenda into which they are buying. There are people who worship the TV and the people they see on TV or in the movies, as idols. They have been seduced into a modern form of idolatry."

Christine laughed.

"John, I know for a fact you watched 'American Idol'. Does that make you an idolater?"

"No, it doesn't, because I know the God of the universe. My worship and awe are for Him alone. I enjoy seeing people use the gifts God has given them, whether on a stage or in a sports arena. I enjoy fine art, music, good writing and good acting. There is a value to stories that reveal the truth in interesting ways. Watching television, listening to the radio or enjoying recorded media, is not a wrong or evil activity in itself, if we are aware of the message the messenger is carrying 'on the air'. Every broadcast carries a message. Sometimes the message is obvious and open, at other times its hidden and deceptive. It could be a bad thing if we fail to recognize the message and test the source. It could be a bad thing if it takes time away from more fruitful pursuits. It could be wrong or used for evil, if the people getting the message are drawn away into lies and deception."

Christine was thoughtful for a moment.

"Is that what you think is happening with Frank Overton." She asked.

"I'm afraid it's only one of the many things happening with that gentleman and his family."

"It's so sad. It sounds like he might be mentally ill."

"It is a possibility. There's a lot we don't know about brain chemistry and the things that cause changes in it. The term "mental illness" encompasses a huge range of attitudes and behaviors and the cause/effect relationship is not fully understood. In ancient times, this might have been called demonic oppression. Today we try to adjust brain chemistry through experimentation with prescription of psychiatric drugs. I wonder, do you think demonic oppression could create changes in brain chemistry which would cause mental illness? It might be hard to tell one from the other, sometimes. There have been studies of brain activity, observing the electrical impulses in the brain and the changes which occur under different types of visual and auditory stimulation. Think of all of the people who let their children have televisions in their rooms. They let the children watch pretty much whatever comes on. They let them listen to music and they don't know what the message is the kids are hearing. Their children play violent video games, some with demonic themes. Would you like to talk about what the average six year old can find on the internet? What changes to the brain might these things contribute to? We spend way too much time 'on the air'. It may not be good for anyone's mental health."

Christine pursed her lips and nodded her head in agreement.

"John, you make a good point, and we live in a world where media shapes the message."

"And, Satan is the Prince of this world and the Prince of the Power of the Air."

"That's a scary thought."

"Not when you remember his days are numbered. The fallen angel is not omnipotent, his power is limited. He can only do what God allows him to do, in the season he has left. God is just allowing him to act out his role for the purpose God has ordained. We have no reason to be afraid."

CHAPTER 22

Often, as I did my on-line research, I would listen to digital music I had saved as the playlist on my computer, my own personal groove. I'd been listening to some of my favorite music the next morning, but my ear buds were bothering me, so I pulled them out. Even as they were coming out of my ears, I heard the screaming.

It was coming from outside our office. I checked the video feed on the monitor. The cameras out in the hall showed a woman standing outside the elevator doors. She was screaming as she backed away from the open elevator

I jumped up from behind my desk and ran through the reception area, finding myself just a few steps behind Christine, who must have seen the same video feed I had seen. We burst out into the hall together and raced to the screaming woman.

That woman was no longer screaming. She had collapsed in a heap, leaning against the wall next to the elevator. She was sobbing now, and making the sign of the cross, in the air before her.

I left her to Christine as I stepped to where I could see into the elevator. The doors had just closed, but the elevator wasn't moving. I punched the button.

I was waiting when the doors opened.

The overhead lights in the elevator were flickering. A big man was standing with his back to me. He was standing in a pool of blood. Evidently the blood was his own, as there was no one else in the elevator. His shirt, which appeared to have been a white dress shirt, was completely saturated with it and had turned crimson. The shirt was slashed and shredded, and stuck to him like glue. In his right hand hung a club made entirely of twisted barbed wire, about two and a half feet in length. It had bits of flesh and fabric clinging on some of the barbs. Blood slowly dripped from the end of the twisted wire, each drop splashing into the congealing pool at his feet

He turned toward me, and fixed his eyes on me. Those eyes were cold and vacant, not unlike the eyes of a dead man. His face was spattered with dried blood. His mouth opened and he began to speak.

"We see you, Shepherd. You have opposed us for too long. We have grown weary of your interference. We think it is time for you to go away," he said.

There was mucous, slowly running down his upper lip, dripping from one of his nostrils.

"To whom am I speaking?"

"We are many. You are alone."

"No, I am not alone. I am never alone."

He growled a low, deep, guttural growl. Then he bared his teeth. Someone else might have mistaken it for a hideous grin.

"I come against you in the name..." I started.

He was amazingly fast.

He rushed me, just as the elevator doors began to close again.

He lashed out with the barbed wire and I felt cold blood spatter my face, as I lurched back away from the strike. I ducked under the next swing and slammed the heel of my hand up under his chin.

I heard his teeth clap together, as his head was knocked back. I had hit him hard, with the full weight of my body behind the blow. I had expected him to be nearly lifted from the floor, and knocked out cold, but he was barely effected and otherwise unmoved.

He stood ready to spring as I backed up against the opposite wall, in the now much too narrow hallway.

Blood ran down his chin from his lacerated tongue. He had bitten through it when I hit him.

I started to speak again, but he leapt straight at me, both hands now bringing the club down in a whistling, overhand arch.

I rolled to the side, narrowly missing having that club slam straight down on my head. It did burn its way down the outside of my thigh, shredding part of my sport coat and the outside of my pants leg.

He spun then and hit me in the head with an elbow, knocking me to the floor.

He towered over me for a second with the club raised above his head with both hands.

He was howling.

I shot him three times with my Browning, two in center mass, the last up through his head, spattering gore on the ceiling.

He fell directly on me, as if he had been a marionette and all the strings had been cut at once. I scrambled to get clear of his dead body.

My leg was bleeding much more than I would have imagined, more than Christine and I could completely control with our hands. Soon the police arrived, as did a fire truck and a couple of ambulances.

I knew the drill, so I had laid my Browning off to the side and identified myself to the first uniformed officers who appeared on the scene. An officer had taken the Browning, checked me for other weapons, and looked over my credentials. Christine and the cleaning lady from the attorney's office were taken away by a female uniformed officer. The poor cleaning lady was still crying and making the sign of the cross on herself, again and again.

An EMT put a pressure dressing on my leg and checked my vital signs. They hooked me up to an IV drip.

"Some of these lacerations are quite deep. At a minimum you're going to need some stitches, and a tetanus shot. We need to carry you into the E.R," The paramedic said.

I saw Tony just arriving on the scene. He was talking to the uniformed supervisor. The supervisor showed Tony my Browning, now ensconced in a plastic bag, which the uniforms had passed off to him.

"I'll need to talk to Lieutenant Escalante for a minute. Can you wait?"

"Sure, you're OK, for now. Just let us know when you're ready to go.

Tony bent down to examine the club of bloody twisted wire, where it lay next to the man's lifeless body, then he walked over to where I was sitting on the bench in the hall, outside the office of Doyle, Doyle and Starnes.

"Howdy, J.W., are you alright?

"I guess I need some stiches, but otherwise I'm OK. At least I'm way better than he is," I nodded towards the corpse.

They had not covered the body, awaiting the Crime Scene Analysis team to finish gathering evidence and for the coroner's permission to bag it, and remove it to the county morgue.

Tony nodded solemnly, in agreement.

"J.W., I'll need you to make a statement about the shooting. Can we do this interview now, or do you need to go to the hospital?"

I looked at the paramedic, who replied with a shrug.

"I can do it now."

Tony pulled out his ubiquitous digital recorder.

"I am Detective Lieutenant Anthony Escalante of the Robbery/Homicide Division of the Tyler Police Department. The current time is nine forty seven A.M. Saturday, June seventeenth. I am interviewing Mr. John Wesley Tucker, about his role in a fatal shooting, which occurred at this location at approximately ten minutes after nine o'clock, this morning."

He looked at me.

"Mr. Tucker, you are not under arrest, so I don't need to read you your rights, but this is the first part of an official investigation of the shooting that occurred here today. Are you ready and willing to make a statement?"

I nodded.

"Just tell me what happened," Tony prompted.

I told him the story, not leaving out any details.

"Did you know the man?"

I nodded again. I was getting very tired now. The adrenaline had worn off and the trauma was taking its toll.

I suddenly realized the recorder could only record my voice, not my body language.

"His name was Frank Overton. He had asked me to do some investigating for him. I only met him once. There was no trouble between us, but he was a troubled man."

"Now that's an understatement," The EMT interrupted.

"Why do you say that?" I asked.

"Well, look at him. His hands are flayed, cut to the bone. How could he do such a thing to himself, not to mention what he did..."

"Let's just finish your statement, Mr. Tucker,"

Tony snapped, glaring at the EMT.

"That's all I can tell you, Lieutenant Escalante. I shot him in self-defense, but I wish I could have stopped him some other way. I did try to do that."

Tony put away his recorder.

"I understand, J.W. I'm just glad you survived and Christine wasn't hurt."

The EMT asked if they could load me on the gurney.

"Yeah, OK. We're done here, J.W., unless there's anything you want to add to your statement?"

I shook my head.

"You sure you don't know what set him off?"

"I do know what 'set him off', Tony. It wasn't Frank Overton who attacked me..."

Tony held up his hand.

"Stop, right there, J.W., the body lying there is that of Frank Overton. We have witnesses and video of him coming into this building. We have the video from the security cameras here in this hallway. Christine and the cleaning woman have given us a statement. That dead man is Overton. It even says so, on his I.D, which was still in his pocket.

What you don't know is we have the bodies of his wife and child, which we found at his residence earlier this morning, after responding to a 911 call from his neighbors. We have the statements from his neighbors, attesting to what he did to his family. Now I understand what you're saying, but it won't help with the inquiry. You're pretty shaken up, as well you should be. Go on to the hospital and get patched up. We'll talk about this later."

Tony nodded to the ambulance attendants and they helped me onto a gurney and strapped me down. Then we got in the freight elevator for the ride down to the waiting ambulance. I knew the sinking feeling I had was a product of multiple, nearly simultaneous, descents.

CHAPTER 23

I didn't get out of the hospital for nearly six hours. Since my injuries were not life threatening, I was near the bottom of the list for treatment. Eventually they got me into an examining room and cut my shredded and blood saturated khaki pants off. When they got the mess all cleaned up, there were numerous deep cuts and bruises from my hip down to the top of my knee. After the doctor put seven internal stiches, thirty eight surface stitches and one anti tetanus shot into me, they were ready to let me go. They had bandaged my leg and I had been instructed not to get it wet for three or four days.

No showers for me, I would have to take bird baths… bring on the wet wipes.

Christine had followed the ambulance to the hospital and had kept me company through the whole ordeal. She took my prescription for antibiotics and my things, and left to get her car, while an orderly pushed me in a wheelchair to the front entrance. I limped outside, wearing a pair of borrowed, blue scrub pants, which really didn't match my dark brown, partially shredded sport coat or my blood spattered tan shirt.

I was met outside the front entrance, by a local TV news crew.

I saw Christine trying to bring her car to the curb, but the TV van had blocked her approach. The camera man and the reporter were between us.

"Mr Tucker, is it true you were attacked by a man named Frank Overton?"

The reporter was a pretty and vivacious, new girl, who I had not seen before.

I paused to consider my answer.

"You have a history of violence, Mr. Tucker. What did you do to provoke Mr. Overton?"

I stiffened at that.

"Why didn't you call the police?"

I tried to ease past her to get to Christine, but she stepped in front of me, blocking my way and thrust her microphone in my face.

I brushed it away, and hobbled toward Christine's car.

"We called 911." I mumbled.

"Did you have to shoot and kill him, Mr. Tucker? Why did you have that gun?" the reporter yelled.

That nearly stopped me.

I wanted to tell her I almost always had "that gun". I wanted to tell her that if I had not had "that gun", there would have been more dead people, before Frank Overton was eventually stopped. I wanted to tell her I would certainly have been the next person he killed, but probably not the last. I wanted to explain the situation to her, but more than anything, I just wanted to go home and lie down.

Christine had gotten out of her car and opened the passenger door. She looked ready to attack as the reporter followed me to the car and continued to badger me with questions.

As we pulled away from the curb, Christine gave a loud sigh, and apologized.

"John, I'm so sorry. I went out the side door to get to the parking garage, and I didn't know they were waiting to ambush you at the front entrance."

I shook my head.

"Not your fault. I just couldn't deal with it right now."

"I guess it's just part of the cost of being a local celebrity."

"No, that's not it. She was pushing for an angle. She had an agenda. It wasn't enough her patience had rewarded her with an exclusive interview opportunity. If she had approached me differently, I might have made a statement."

"It sounds like she has a lot to learn."

"We'll see. It all comes down to what the news director was looking for. The reporter may have messed up, or she may have done exactly what the news director wanted."

"You sound kind of cynical, John. Do you mistrust the media?"

I gave her a look, and she snorted out a most un-lady like laugh.

"Who all called me earlier, while they were sewing me up?"

"Gary called. He told me to tell you, he hasn't been able to get any of the men who have been working with him, to talk about anything. He asked them about someone named Eduardo, and they all clammed up."

"Yeah, it figures."

"Tony called to check on you."

"Odd, he didn't call me on my phone."

"Well uhhh, no, he called me on my phone."

"I suppose he probably figured I couldn't talk on my phone."

Christine frowned slightly.

"Well... not really."

"OK. What did you and he talk about?"

She glared at me this time.

"I told you, he called to check on how you were doing."

I wagged my finger at her.

"Yes, and it was the only time you left the room. You were gone for like fifteen minutes. It wouldn't take ten seconds to say, 'Oh, John is just fine, the doctor is using him for quilting practice'. Then, you could have handed me the phone. So, what was it you were discussing with Tony?"

Christine blushed.

"That's really none of your business."

I chuckled.

"No, it surely isn't… Or is it?"

Christine rolled her eyes.

"Ok, we were wondering if you could uh… baby sit, tomorrow night."

"Ahhhh, Tony wants me to hang out with Diondro, while you and he go out on a date."

I winked.

"OH! You are insufferable. I told Tony he should be the one to ask you."

"Probably, but I'll be happy to do it. It's about time I have a talk with Diondro. Besides, I don't think I'll feel much like dancing anyway. Y'all plan to go on and have a good time."

"Don't think we won't, because we will" She said, bobbing her head and holding up her hand.

"Testify sister!"

"Um hmmmm."

We both laughed.

Later, as the local anesthetic began to wear off, my leg felt like it was on fire.

CHAPTER 24

We decided since Tony was going to take Christine out, I would meet Tony and Diondro at Christine's apartment. Diondro and I would stay there and wait for Tony to come back with Christine. That way, if anyone was watching my apartment, they would never see Diondro there. If anyone tried to follow me, Christine's apartment was in a gated complex requiring a card or an access code to get in. It provided some sense of minimal security. Anyone following me wouldn't be able to follow me into the apartment complex, without me spotting them.

I had been keeping a sharp lookout for anyone tailing me since I came back from Arkansas. Tailing a person without being spotted is not easy, whether on foot or in a vehicle. If you have multiple people or vehicles taking turns, keeping the subject in sight is easier to do without the person being able to detect the surveillance. I was pretty sure no such involved planning or resources were being employed against me. One person alone, attempting to tail another person, is pretty easy to spot, especially if the person being followed is looking for someone tailing them.

Manned aircraft are an excellent way to maintain

surveillance on a subject, but it is very expensive and problematic. Unmanned aircraft fitted with a camera are often the best way to go for tailing someone. They are hard to hear or see from the ground. They are fairly inexpensive to operate and the person controlling the aircraft can be miles away, or even on a different continent. That's why the military uses them for surveillance both at home and abroad. In war zones and conflict areas, some drones are armed and lethal. Any number of our nation's enemies has been killed by our unseen drone aircraft. Fortunately, our government would never use them against our own citizens in our own country, right?

I knew a variety of these aircraft, in various sizes and configurations are available to the general public. These drones were being used more and more in commercial applications, and were even being used by the paparazzi, voyeurs and other criminals. The FAA was struggling to regulate their use. I'd purchased a couple of different styles myself. The only ones I could afford were not nearly as sophisticated as the military versions. Mine were smaller and confined to a pretty short range, and I had to be within about a mile of the aircraft and more or less in line of sight to control them, but they had excellent cameras. That's where I'd invested the most money, in those extremely high tech cameras and gimbles. I was very pleased with the quality of the images sent back to my monitor. I hadn't had occasion to use one on the job yet, but I knew the opportunity would present itself.

I doubted anyone who might be trying to use me to find Diondro, would be so sophisticated, but it pays to be alert.

I arrived at Christine's apartment at about 6:30 the next evening, and was delighted to see Tum Tum again.

"Tum Tum" whose name is actually Mr. Tumescence, is Christine's rather obese cat.

Christine thinks the name is funny.

Go figure.

A couple of hours after Tony and Christine left on their date, Diondro, Mr. Tumescence and I were left sitting in the apartment, watching some vapid comedy on the Boob Tube

"Diondro, have you ever noticed how the laugh track comes in after nearly every comment a character makes?"

"What? Oh, uhh yeah, I guess."

I picked up the remote control and pointed it at the television.

On the screen, the fat man made a comment, and the laugh track kicked in. Another character said something, and I hit the mute button, for a second. The next character said something, and just as the laugh track started, I muted it again.

"See what I mean? You don't get to decide whether the dialogue is funny or not. They insert the laughter, wherever they think it should go. If you take the laugh track out, very few of these programs are actually funny, at all. It takes clever writers and skilled performers to be consistently funny. Hollywood is the home of mediocrity, in a flashy package. They provide neatly packaged junk entertainment, available 24/7."

We stared at the antics on the screen for a little while, until Diondro picked up the remote and did his own test.

"Rats! You've ruined it for me. I used to like this show. Now it just seems shallow and silly."

Diondro turned the television off.

I laughed.

"Sorry. I guess it was kind of mean. I wanted to talk to you for a minute."

"What's up?"

"How are you handling the isolation?"

"It's OK, I guess. There's nothing to do. Most days, I just sit in Tony's office at the police station, and read."

"What are you reading?

"Oh, I don't know. Fiction mostly, I guess."

"What kind of fiction?"

"I like science fiction and fantasy books."

"Ahhh, Asimov, Tolkien, Robert Jordan, and the like?"

"Yeah, like that."

"Have you ever read any C.S. Lewis?"

"Was he the guy who wrote the Chronicles of Narnia series?"

"Yes, and some other really excellent books, The Screw Tape Letters, and the Out of the Silent Planet trilogy, and several others."

"I saw one of the Narnia movies and it was OK, I guess, but it was kind of kid's stuff."

"I recommend actually reading the books."

"Yeah, I know what you mean. The books are almost always better than the movies."

"Tony has a pretty good collection of books."

"Yeah, it sure helps. He doesn't do much reading himself. He mostly just reads the Bible."

"Well, Truth is always better than fiction."

"I guess there is probably some truth in the Bible, but it's mostly just made up stories to illustrate a point, or poetry and prose for the sake of maintaining the God myth."

"Where did you hear that?

"I think I read it somewhere, but everybody knows that."

"So, you haven't actually read the Bible yourself?"

"No, it's really hard to read and even harder to understand."

"Not for a smart guy like you."

"Naw, I don't think I'd get much out of it."

"You would be surprised. Where do you think

great writers like those we mentioned have gotten their inspiration?"

"I thought you said you weren't religious."

"What does religion have to do with this conversation? I thought we were discussing literature."

Diondro shrugged.

"What's bothering you?"

"I've been thinking about what you and Tony said about life after death."

"Why? Does thinking about death upset you?"

"I haven't had much experience with death. I had never seen a dead body, until that day, in the bayou,"

"Not even at a funeral?"

"Yeah, from a distance, when I was a kid. But this was different. I saw those men die."

"Seeing men die, is upsetting, Diondro. It tears me up, too. I've seen far too many die."

"It doesn't seem to bother you. You just killed another man, and he nearly killed you. You've killed three men in less than three weeks. So much death, one minute they were alive, and then..."

I let him think about it for a minute.

"Diondro, it bothers me more than you know. I hate death, any way it comes. Everyone dies, eventually. Sometimes, it happens suddenly, maybe even violently, and sometimes it happens slowly. I didn't set out to kill anyone. Those men in the bayou brought it on themselves. Some people live long happy lives; others are miserable for their entire lives, however long or short. Children die, old people die, rich or poor, everyone has to face death at some point. You might think of death as a natural part of life. How or when we die is not what matters. How we live is the thing that matters. We remember and celebrate the lives of people, not their deaths. Some people live and love and make a difference in this world and in the lives of other people, making their lives better and being remembered fondly. Others live in hate and stumble around lost and confused, leaving broken things and wounded people in their wake. How we live is the only part of life that matters. Death is just a single, small part of life, the last part, for far too many people."

"It's not fair though. Some people suffer horribly, even little children. They didn't choose to suffer. How is that living a 'good' life?"

"Diondro, the life we live in our physical bodies is just a moment in time. One small lifetime in a physical body, is just the blink of an eye, compared to eternity. Some people are walking around in a healthy and strong physical body, but they are spiritually dead on the inside. When the physical body dies, those people will still be spiritually dead, just like when they were in the physical body. The thing is they will go on that way forever. They will be physically dead and spiritually dead. I mean for eternity. Think about hundreds of thousands of years, and then multiply that by millions of millions of years. Today, some people are suffering in their physical bodies, but on the inside they are spiritually alive and well, knowing great joy. They will continue that joyous life forever, but they will have glorified, new, healthy bodies."

"How do you know who is spiritually alive?"

"The Bible says everyone is spiritually dead and separated from the knowledge of God, until they are re-born as His children."

"See, that's what I'm talking about, Religious mumbo-jumbo. That's why I don't read the Bible."

"Would you say you are spiritually alive?"

"What kind of question is that? Of course I am, as much as the next person."

"Are you?"

"Hell yes."

"Then why are you so upset?"

"Because you lied to me," he snapped.

"How did I lie?"

"You said you were not religious, but you talk like

a preacher."

"I'm not religious. I'm not a fan of the various religions man has made for himself."

"Then why do you keep talking like a preacher?"

"I am a servant of God."

"See? Right there! There you go. God this and God that. It's the way all you religious people talk."

"How people talk is immaterial, Diondro. I don't play in the NFL, but I can talk football as well as anybody. The difference is important. It's the difference between reality and imagination. There are plenty of people who talk religion. People who are religious are like sports fans. They may be experts, able to recite all the rules, regulations and statistics. They call in to the sports talk radio programs, raving about this or that. They can talk the talk and they love to watch the show. They have their favorite teams or players. They may even wear their favorite player's number or jersey. They choose up sides, but they are not actually in the game. Sometimes they think they are players, maybe they even play the game as a hobby, but they're only on the outside, looking in. Do you understand the difference?"

"So, you're saying only people who go to the right church are spiritually alive."

"No, I'm not saying anything like that. Most people who go to church, a synagogue or temple, are just watching the show. Many of them are very religious, but they've just picked a team and they're ardent fans. Some are convinced their religion is the best, or the only true way to get to God. 'Go team, Go!' They are fanatical fans who hate any other religion because it is not the 'right' religion. Others have adopted religion as a hobby, and have become experts on the doctrine and dogma. All these things are religious, but they are only on the outside, looking in. Man makes up religions as a systematic way to search for God."

"I don't get it. What difference does it make?"

"God is Holy. That's the difference."

"Whatever!"

"Man has invented all sorts of religions as a way to find God, or make other people follow their system. But God has made the way Himself. It's not important to belong to the 'right' religion. It's not important to practice a religion or system in the 'right' way. Only one thing is important. Do you know what one thing is important?"

"OK, I'll bite. What 'one thing' is important?"

"It's important to know the way that God has provided."

"Oh, fine. We have just completed the circle. You said yourself religions are the way man finds God."

"Well, sort of, but not exactly. What I'm trying to say, is men do not know how to find God. That's the reason there are so many different religions. People are trying to find some god, somewhere, somehow. Being religious might be a way, but it's not the way. God alone has decided how we will know Him. God is Holy, and we can't even begin to grasp the wonder of the way He does things.

Jesus said "I am the way, the truth, and the life. No man come's to the Father, but by me." We are saved by grace through faith. That is a gift from God. It isn't what we humans do; it's what He did, for us."

"Aren't all religions good, helping point you toward God?"

"Again religions are man-made. Some people, who are truly searching, will find God through religion. Still, if they are earnestly seeking Him, they may find Him almost anywhere. Most people make the mistake of substituting a religion, or any combination of religions, for actually knowing God. They think being religious, or practicing the rituals and customs of a religion, is the same as having a relationship as a child of the Holy God. They think wearing the jersey is the same as being on the team. The Bible says anyone who wants to know God must first believe that He is, and that He always rewards those who diligently seek Him. Once you know Him, you can decide if there is a religion you might want to participate in."

"Why? According to you, it doesn't matter where you start, or what religion it is, if you are looking for God, you will find him."

"Do you believe there is a God? Are you searching?"

"I don't know. I'm just saying maybe I could believe there is some kind of God."

"Good. The devils believe, and tremble in fear."

"You're kind of creeping me out, right now. Let's change the subject."

I laughed.

"Sure, this is not easy stuff to understand."

"Yeah, and I don't even want to understand it. I'm not really interested in myths and mythologies. One thing I do know though…"

"What is it?"

"… You are one peculiar dude."

I laughed.

"Peculiar? Maybe, but I still say, I'm not religious."

CHAPTER 25

We talked about what Diondro might be interested in as a career choice. I wasn't surprised he was
thinking about criminal justice or practicing law.
It led to a discussion of college classes and degree
programs.

"You are obviously very smart, and I think you
can accomplish pretty much anything you set your
mind to do, Diondro."

"Thank you, Mr. Tucker."

"Something is lacking however, and it is the most
important thing of all."

"What is that?"

"Where will you spend eternity, when this life
is over?"

Diondro threw his hands in the air.

"Oh man. Here we go again…"

"I just want you to do a little research. Do some
reading and some serious thinking. You can do it
easily enough, right? Until the trial starts, you have
some time on your hands; with nothing more important to do."

"Yeah sure, I guess."

I want you to read the New Testament in the Bible. Start with the Gospels, Matthew, Mark, Luke
and John. Then, continue on from there."

"Really, I mean... really?"

"Yes."

Diondro made a face.

"I don't understand all the 'thou shalt' and 'sayeth thee' stuff, man."

"Tony has some modern language versions you might like. Focus on Jesus and the things he said. Think about what it means, if what he said is true."

"Why? What did he say?"

"It would be better for you to find out for yourself."

Christine and Tony came back at about eleven o'clock. We could hear them, out on the landing, laughing and making small talk. Then there was silence for so long a time it became awkward for Diondro and me, as we waited inside. At first, the cat, Mr. Tumescence, acted indifferent, but as time stretched by, he altered his attitude.

We exchanged glances at each other, among the three of us. Diondro's eyes got real big, as he made a funny face. I started to whistle a happy little tune, and Mr. Tumescence stared at the front door, as if he were attempting to open it with his mind.

Diondro and I were both stifling our laughter, when Tony and Christine eventually came into the living area. I thought I even saw the cat looking amused.

"What is so funny?" Christine demanded.

Tony was just shaking his head and looking embarrassed.

"Oh, uhhh... Mr. Tucker was just showing me this trick with the remote control. Did you know you can mute the laugh track, on a comedy show?" Diondro asked.

"No, why is that funny?" Christine asked.

"Well, when you do, it gets real quiet for a long, loong, looong time." I said, looking at Tony.

Tony grinned and looked down at the floor.

"Oh! Good grief, y'all are a bunch of children!" Christine snapped.

The next morning, as I was driving to the office, I spotted my homeless friend Dustin. We have an odd relationship.

Dustin was wounded in the war, and most people would say he's not quite "right" in the head. Dustin would agree. He appreciates his limitations.

I appreciate his gifts.

Dustin was pushing his shopping cart down the sidewalk, along the edge of the park named after a lady named, "Rose".

I found a place to park and walked down the sidewalk to meet Dustin. Even though my leg was healing quickly, I couldn't help limping a little.

"Hey, Angel, you that good angel," Dustin called out his usual greeting to me.

"Good morning, Dustin. How are you today?"

"I be truckin' along just fine. Better'n you, I expect. I aint seen you in many a day, Angel man."

As usual, Dustin was gazing around, as though he were not really talking to me.

"I've been pretty busy lately, but I wanted to see how you're doing."

"I be doin' what I's supposed to do. Just like you."

I thought about that. I often wonder if I'm doing all I'm supposed to do.

Dustin was studying me. He said, "Ummm hmmm. I see you worried. You got a pack of wolves be snappin' at you."

I nodded in agreement.

"The last few weeks have been pretty rough."

"Don't forget."

I puzzled at this comment for a moment.

"Don't forget what?"

"Whooeee. You done forgot already."

Talking to Dustin can be… challenging.

"What did I forget, Dustin?"

"Angel man, you gots to take a hold of them horns."

"Patience is a virtue", I reminded myself.

I waited a moment before I asked the question.

"What horns?"

"You grab onto them horns of the Alter, in the city of refuge."

I had to search through his statement, looking for a clue as to what he might mean. He seemed to be referring to the days thousands of years ago, when the children of Israel lived under the law which required that if a man killed another man, then the killer had to flee to a city of refuge, until a court of elders could be appointed to conduct a trial. He would enter the city and place his hands on the "horns" at the four corners of the alter. He would be safe in a city of refuge, but if he left the city limits, the avenger of blood could kill him on sight.

"You got blood on your hands, Angel man."

I looked down at the ground.

"Yes, I do."

Dustin nodded, and then he caught my eye.

"Are you the avenger of blood?"

"No, of course not, I'm just a Shepherd."

"… with blood on your hands?"

I looked away, and nodded.

"But the sacrifice is already done, the price is paid, you a citizen of a better city now, a city without no city limits."

I grinned.

"I guess I had kind of forgotten, for a moment there."

"No, no, no, good Angel. Don't you never ever forget."

"I hear you. I won't forget."

"You gots to watch out for them wolves, too. They won't never let you be. You fight the fight, today, tomorrow and the next day. Don't you tire and don't you quit."

I nodded in agreement.

"Not till He returns or calls me home."

"That's all then. You can go now. I done told you what He told me to tell you."

I chuckled a little, at his abrupt dismissal.

"Yes sir, Dustin. I believe you have."

CHAPTER 26

"You're not going to believe what I found out," Gary said.

I was driving toward the office, feeling a little better, after my talk with Dustin.

I was enjoying the fact I only had to push a button to be able to talk on the telephone. It hadn't been too many years ago, I would have had to stop and use a payphone to talk on the phone. The first cellular telephone I had ever owned had been a big, heavy, bag phone. Now my cellular phone was synced with my truck. I didn't have any wires involved, and it was completely hands free.

"What is it?" I asked.

"Watkins is a skin head."

"Really, you think he's a white supremacist?"

"I know he is. At least he claims he is. He's proud of it."

"How did you get him to tell you?"

"I didn't even have to try. We were on the jobsite getting the roof joists in place, when he showed up. You should have seen the way his arrival motivated the men. Anyway, he and I were standing over in the shade, watching the men working, and he said he thought 'wetbacks' were better workers than 'niggers'."

I took a slow, deep breath, as Gary went on.

"I played along, you know. 'Sure', I said, 'I expect life is so much better here, than it is south of the border, they just naturally want to earn as much as they can, to send home to their families'."

"No," Watkins had said, "I mean they are better suited to do this kind of work, than most of the other 'mud people', especially them 'niggers'. You know what I mean?"

"So, I just pretended to agree with him." Gary continued.

"You and me think alike." Watkins had said. "Now, you take them wetbacks. They'll work from daylight to dark thirty, and never complain. You smack um around a little and they just work harder. Niggers won't, and they won't stand for any kind of goading, neither."

"I pointed out that all American citizens are protected by the law," Gary said, "It's not legal to assault anyone, and now days, non-whites of every variety, are well represented and have a seat at the table of our political power base."

"Hell, yes. Don't I know it?" Watkins had said, "It's part of the problem, but some of us are fighting for God and country. We mean to see the mud people are put back where they belong... under our boot leather."

I interrupted Gary with a question.

"He said that? Watkins called non-whites 'mud people', and talked about subjugating them?"

"Oh, it gets worse," Gary replied. "He went into a long, drawn out spiel, about how God never intended for white people to become a minority in America. He said traitorous politicians had allowed the 'mud people' to rise up and get involved in politics, when they should have been put in their place. He said he was a member of a group that intended to restore America to her better days. His group has plans to punish the traitors and they will not tolerate any of the 'mud people' being uppity." Gary added.

"Did you ask him what group he belonged to?" I enquired.

"Yep. He said he's an officer in the Righteous Army of God."

When I got to the office, I called Tony.

"Hey J.W. what's up?"

"Have you ever heard of an organization called the Righteous Army of God?"

"The RAGs? Sure, they are one of those neo Nazi, white supremacist, hate groups. You know, wanna-be militia types. They have secret meetings and march around with arm bands and weapons. They shout slogans and racial slurs at people of color. They hate anyone who is not a white, 'Christian'. They're real punks, and there's often a connection with loud punk rock music."

"Do they use a swastika as a symbol?"

"Sometimes, but the symbol they have on their flag is... Oh no, I don't like where this is going."

"Is it a cross?"

I heard Tony sigh, before he answered.

"Yes, it is. They have a blood red flag, with a black cross on it. It's a cross with a big "R" at the top, a big "A" on the left side with a little "o" in the middle, and a big G on the right. Did you see it somewhere?"

"No. I just thought you might want to know, Watkins is a member of the group."

"I was afraid you were going to say something like that."

"Is it enough for you to get an arrest warrant?"

I heard the squeak of Tony's chair as he leaned back in it.

"No, all we have is a dead body, with evidence of having been murdered, and a report of a missing man, last seen in the company of Watkins. We don't have any way to positively identify the body, and we can't put Watkins at the scene of the homicide. In fact, we don't even know where the crime occurred. We have the remains, found at a particular location, but no way of knowing if that was where the crime occurred. We don't have any actual witness to a homicide. Being a member of a hate group is not a crime."

"I have never understood how people, who are so filled with hate, can call themselves Christians."

"I know. What it really means to them is that they are not Jewish, Muslim, Buddhist, Hindu, or whatever else. I guess they figure that if they aren't one of those, and they live in America, then they can just call themselves 'Christian'. When in fact, what they really are is ignorant, white, trash." Tony said.

"It must make Jesus sad."

"It makes me angry"

"Have you talked to the Rusk County Sheriff, yet, Tony?"

"I have. I told him what we have so far, and he wants to meet. Is this afternoon, at about two o'clock, good for you?"

"I'll make it work. How about I take you and Diondro to lunch, and we drive over there together, after that?"

"Yeah, I'll take you up on the offer. Come by here about noon."

I spotted my tail shortly after I walked out of my office building. It was almost too easy. So easy in fact, at first I thought it wasn't even real. Maybe, I was just being paranoid.

I noticed the car as I was getting into my truck, in the big parking lot that surrounds the building where my office is, on the south loop. The car was parked one row away and there was a black man with a shaved head, sitting behind the wheel. The car was a dark grey, Toyota sedan. I recognized the plates. I don't believe in coincidence, but I tried to shrug it off. I started the truck and drove toward the nearest exit, which empties out onto Copeland Rd. I changed my mind, when the car started to follow me through the parking lot.

When I reached the driveway exit, I stopped my truck and got out. I had blocked this exit onto Copeland Rd.

The black guy behind the wheel of the Toyota watched me approach his car, with a smirk around the corners of his mouth, which was not reflected in his eyes. His eyes watched me intently as I approached.

He rolled down his window, so I leaned toward him and spoke as I watched his hands on the steering wheel.

"Well, as I live and breathe, if it isn't Kirby Wilson. What a coincidence meeting you here, Mr. Wilson," I said, by way of greeting.

"What's up, Mr. Tucker?"

"I don't know. Were you following me, again?"

"I was just coming in to see you in your office, when you came out. So, I figured I'd just follow you to wherever you're going, and we could talk there."

I nodded and looked around the parking lot. Other cars were beginning to come up behind his.

"OK, so here I am, what would you like to discuss?"

"It's too hot to stand around in the parking lot, blocking traffic. Let's talk somewhere else."

"Sure, let's do that, somewhere else and some other time. You can make an appointment with my associate. Right now, I'm meeting a friend for lunch."

"Yeah, who's that?"

"I think you know him, Lieutenant Escalante, of the Tyler P.D.?"

"Yeah, we've met."

"Maybe you would like to join us for lunch, my treat."

"No thanks. My business is with you."

"Ok. Like I said, you can make an appointment with my associate."

"Whatever." He said.

I looked him in the eye.

"Whenever, wherever." I replied.

As I got back in my truck, I was wondering why Kirby Wilson had gone to the trouble of deliberately catching my attention.

CHAPTER 27

"I don't like it." Tony started. "What if Wilson followed you here?"

Tony had sent Diondro away, ostensibly to get more coffee, so we could have a moment to talk.

I shrugged.

"I was watching for him, and after I got headed toward downtown, I never saw him again. If Wilson did manage to follow me here, he would see I was coming to the cop shop to have lunch with you. Just like I told him I was going to do."

"It would seem likely he's trying to find Diondro again."

"Could be, but we don't know for sure."

"I don't like it," Tony repeated.

"Well, the trial is only a week away. I'm confident we can avoid putting Diondro into any kind of danger, until then. Those street thugs aren't really trying very hard. Putting Kirby Wilson back on my tail, at this late date, would be kind of a weak and uncommitted measure," I pointed out.

"It probably took a little while for them to figure out what exactly happened to the crew they sent to get you the first time, and more time to arrange for another crew."

"Not enough time. These gang banger types are

not particularly smart. They're not well connected to professional killers, and they won't want to waste any more money on amateurs. They're probably planning to just come after Diondro themselves. The usual way they handle something like this is with a drive by. Just a bunch of guys in a car firing all their guns out the window as they drive by, hoping to hit their intended target, but you can't fire a lot of bullets at anyone, until you know where they are. At this point, they have no idea where Diondro is."

Tony considered my statement for a moment.

"I think we'd better do something to protect Diondro's mother," He said.

"Good night! Why didn't I think of that?"

"Think of what?" Diondro asked, as he walked back into the room.

"Diondro, does your mother work?"

"No sir."

"Is she usually at home during the day?"

"Yes sir. Why do you ask?"

"I'm going to ask Christine if she would have your mother stay with her, until after the trial."

"Oh, I don't know if she would do something like..."

"I think she'll be happy to do it, Diondro. Christine is really good about this sort of thing, and she has an extra bedroom."

"No, I mean my moms. She wouldn't be comfortable staying with a strange white... uhh, what I mean is, she wouldn't want to impose."

"Sure, I understand, but we think she would be safer if she stayed with Christine."

"Are you saying you think they would go after my moms?"

I shrugged.

"They might try to use your mother to get at you," Tony said.

Diondro looked shaken.

"Diondro, use Tony's desk phone there. Call your

mother and ask her to join us for lunch. We have to go right through Chapel Hill on the way to Rusk County. We'll pick her up, and she can come with us to Henderson."

Diondro looked at Tony.

Tony smiled back at him.

"Sure, it's an excellent idea. I look forward to meeting your mother."

Diondro tried to call his mother, but the phone went unanswered.

"Huh! I wonder where she is. My moms is usually home at this time of day. I'll call her back in a few minutes," Diondro said.

Tony and I made eye contact.

"We need to get on the road. You can use my cell phone to call her on the way there," Tony said.

We piled into Tony's unmarked Crown Victoria and worked our way through the lunch time crowds, on the streets of Tyler.

When we reached the junction of Loop 323 and the Henderson Highway, Diondro tried to call his mother again. He tried, but there was no still answer.

"Is there an answering machine?" I asked.

"No sir, she has caller ID and if she misses a call, she figures anybody who knows her will just call back later."

The house where Diondro's mother lived was a modest frame house, on about a quarter acre lot, maybe a half mile south of the highway. There were shade trees in the yard and flower beds, at the front of the house.

Her car was in the carport as we pulled up to the curb.

We all got out of the Crown Victoria and walked up the walk, toward the house.

The front door was ajar.

Diondro started to rush forward, but Tony and I stopped him, as we pulled our guns.

"You stand over by the car until we tell you it's safe. If there is any trouble, call it in. Help will be on the way." Tony instructed him.

Diondro didn't like it, but he knew better than to try going past us.

Tony and I took up positions, one on each side of the front door. We could feel the cooler air from inside the house, being quickly heated and humidified, as it spilled out through the partially open door.

"Mrs. Taylor? Are you at home? Hello, is anybody there?" Tony called into the house.

There was no response.

"Mrs. Taylor, this is the police. We are coming in. Can you hear me?"

We looked at each other, and Tony pointed his finger at himself and then upwards into the house. I pointed back at myself, and then downwards into the house, indicating Tony would lead, going high and I would follow, going low. He nodded in response.

Tony reached out and pushed the door open, all the way. We paused for a second and then ducked into the house. Tony swerved a bit to the right, slamming the door against an end table, and I stepped to the left.

The living room was small, but tidy and tastefully furnished.

There was no one in the room.

My phone rang. I had forgotten to turn off the ringer.

Tony scowled at me, keeping his gun pointed in the general direction of the hallway and the kitchen doorway.

I glanced at the caller ID, as I cut off the call. It was an unidentified, local number.

Just then, we heard Diondro shout something, outside.

As we rushed from the house with our guns in hand, we saw Diondro approaching a heavy black woman, as she was getting out of the back seat of a Lincoln Town Car, which had pulled into the carport, and was parked behind Mrs. Taylor's car.

When the big woman saw us, her eyes got huge, and she had something to say.

"Get down, Diondro!" she screamed.

Tony and I were putting our guns away, but we had not been fast enough.

The woman was digging through her purse, and as we approached, she produced a can of mace.

"No Momma, wait," Diondro said, as he tried to pull her arm down.

He was no match for the sheer strength of the woman, who thought she was protecting her child. Of course she did out-weigh him, by about two to one.

Tony and I were back-peddling, as fast as we could.

The woman, whom we now assumed was Mrs. Taylor, wore a fierce countenance, a blonde wig, a pink straw hat with flowers on it, and a dress with a floral print.

She started toward us, basically dragging Diondro with her.

"What you doin' in my house?" she enquired, menacingly.

The driver of the Lincoln jumped out, looking worried and confused.

He was a middle aged, black man, dressed in a suit and tie.

"Now, Sister Taylor, calm down. Let's just ask these gentlemen to explain themselves..." He started.

"Momma, take it easy." Diondro added.

"Oh, no I won't! Nobody comes into my house and threatens my son. I'll tell you one thing."

"Mrs. Taylor, I'm Detective Escalante. You know me. We've talked on the telephone," Tony stated.

Mrs. Taylor looked at Diondro, who nodded his affirmative. She seemed to realize for the first time, Diondro was clinging to her wrist.

"Oh, my baby!" She cried, wrapping Diondro in

her embrace.

For a moment he was lost to sight.

When Diondro emerged from her embrace, he looked none the worse, for his near death by suffocation.

Mrs. Taylor turned back on us.

"I axed you, what you doin' in my house?"

"Mrs. Taylor, we were worried. When we got to the front door, we found it open. Your car is in the carport, but there was no sign of you," Tony replied.

I was keeping my distance.

Another lady appeared, stepping out from the passenger seat of the Lincoln. She was of a similar age to Mrs. Taylor and similarly dressed. Her wig was grayish brown, with silver highlights and she had no hat.

"Is everything alright, Sister Taylor?" She enquired.

"I expect it is, Reverend Jefferson. I believe these are the police, who been takin' care of my boy."

"Yes ma'am, that's correct. I'm Lieutenant Escalante with the City of Tyler Police Department, and this is my friend John Wesley Tucker," Tony said by way of introduction.

"Well, praise the Lord. I'm Reverend Jefferson of the Glory to God Church of Heavenly Holiness. This is my husband, Brother Ed."

"Momma, where were you, and why was the front door open?"

"I was at the church house, gettin' my baptism on. I must've forgotten to lock up, when I left."

Diondro's mouth dropped open.

"Momma, you've never been religious."

"Could we go inside, Mrs. Taylor? There is something we need to talk to you about and it's getting pretty hot out here," Tony suggested.

"Umm hmmm. Now that's what I'm talking about. You can come into my house, when I invite you."

"Momma!" Diondro interjected.

"Hush yo' self. I'm fixin to invite um."

CHAPTER 28

We were all crowded into Mrs. Taylor's living room. Because the front door had been open for so long and there were so many warm bodies, it was uncomfortably warm and humid in the room, but it was still better than standing outside.

The Reverend Mrs. Jefferson was seated on the couch beside her husband Ed. Mrs. Taylor was seated in one of the two easy chairs and Tony was seated in the other. Diondro and I stood.

I was standing where I could see out through the lace curtains, watching for approaching cars.

Mrs. Taylor was fanning herself with her hat.

I caught Tony's eye, and tapped my watch, to remind him of the need to be moving on down the road.

"Mrs. Taylor, I wish you would reconsider our offer. We think it would be best if you came on with us. The trial is just a few days away, and I'm concerned you will not be safe here." Tony tried again.

The Reverend Mrs. Jefferson, spoke up next.

"That won't be necessary, Bless God. The church will keep her safe, Amen. She is a member of my flock now, and I won't let nobody mess with her, Hallelujah!

"I know that's right. Now don't you worry, Sister

Taylor, you in the family of God now. I'll get some men together and we'll watch out for you, right round the clock." Ed Jefferson added.

"You need to understand something. These are common street thugs. You won't be able to reason with them. They may just drive up and shoot anybody in sight." Tony indicated.

"Umm hmmm, and we have a couple of local police in our congregation, Praise the Lord. I'll call on them to step up, into the service of the Lord, Bless God."

It was my turn to speak up.

"Actually, it's an excellent idea, Mrs. Taylor. These folks here want to help you. They may not have the skills we have, but they love you and they want to keep you safe. I think they can do it, for just the few days until the trial. After the trial, I believe the threat will have ended."

Tony looked surprised at my comment.

"How about you, Diondro, do you want to stay here with your mom, or would you rather come with us?"

"You stay with us, son, we'll look after you too, in Jesus' name, Hallelujah!" Reverend Jefferson suggested.

Mrs. Taylor looked at Diondro, hopefully.

I could see Diondro struggling with the choice. He wanted to be sure his mother stayed safe, but he was also clearly put off by the Reverend Mrs. Jefferson.

Tony saved the day.

"I'll tell you what, Diondro. Why don't you stay here with your mom, while J.W. and I go take our meeting with Sheriff Andrews? It will give you some time to figure out what you want to do. We'll stop by on our way back to Tyler. By then you'll have a better understanding of what you want."

"Yes sir, thank you."

"Amen, Bless the Lord!" Reverend Jefferson pronounced.

She was giving me a long, appraising look.

I smiled back at her.

"That was weird." Tony stated, as we drove away.
"Not exactly what we're used to is it?"
"Not by a long shot."
"It's better."
"Better than what?"
"Tony that's the way it's supposed to be."
"What are you talking about?"
"People taking care of each other. Mrs. Taylor has become a member of a church family. Those folks didn't hesitate, even though it involves possible danger and personal sacrifice, maybe even legal complications. She's a member of their church and they are there for her."
"Yeah, I guess I can see that. But the preacher lady is weird, J.W."
"I'm former military, and you've been a cop, for a long time. The people we usually deal with every day tend to pepper their speech with vulgarities and foul language. Unfortunately it's what we as a society are used to. It has become virtually a cultural norm. That lady chooses to salt her speech with language which doesn't use the name of the Lord in vain, and we call her 'weird'."
"I see your point, but still..."
"... Yeah, completely different from what we're used to."
"Amen, brother. Hallelujah."
I laughed at his attempt.
"I guess I'm just uncomfortable around people who don't talk and act the way I think is normal." Tony admitted.
I nodded.
"It reminds me of the way people tend to think about God. We want God to be more like us. We're made in His image, so in some ways we are kind of like Him, in the same way a photo is kind of like us,

but it is not even close to actually being us. We're sort of like Him, made in His image, but He is not like us. He is holy, and utterly beyond our limited comprehension of what the term means. He's completely different from what we're used to. People tend to struggle with the concept. We want God to fit into our preconceived notions of what we think He should be like. We want him to be all loving and forgiving. We want to forget He is also just and righteous. That part scares us. We want him to give us what we want. He wants us to give Him what He deserves, but we definitely don't want Him to give us what we deserve."

Tony nodded in agreement.

"Right, we want mercy and forgiveness, not justice. We get hung up on the idea life should be fair. We want to be the ones who decide what fair is, and make God do things our way."

"We are no more capable of understanding the mind of God, than Christine's cat is able to understand how this car's engine works." I suggested.

"Sure, but Christine's cat is content, without thinking about how the car's engine works."

"That's only one of several ways in which we are different from the animals."

We drove along in silence for a while, thinking our own thoughts.

CHAPTER 29

"… We also have what was left of the clothing we found at the scene. The forensics people in Dallas sent all of it back to us. Maybe someone will be able to identify the clothing. It's in terrible shape, all slashed and faded by exposure, but still recognizable." Rusk County Sheriff, Tom Dempsey, concluded.

"Did you find a ball cap?" I asked

"We did, yes. The hair in it matched that of the victim. How did you know?"

"It was just a guess. The ball cap is kind of standard with men who work outside. They are easy to come by and easy to replace."

"We have the work boots and his slashed gloves as well. What will they tell you?"

I shrugged.

"… After being out in the weather for weeks, probably nothing. The ball cap does tell me something though."

"You haven't even seen it," Tony pointed out.

"If you killed someone and then had to haul the body off to dump it somewhere, would you bother to carry the ball cap along?"

"It's hard to say, too many variables."

"Sheriff Dempsey has indicated they found everything the man had on him when he was killed, except one thing."

"What's that?" Sheriff Dempsey asked.

"His knife, I believe Eduardo Ruiz was probably killed with his own knife. You didn't find it at the scene, even though you found everything else the corpse had on him, even the cash and change in his pants pocket, but not the knife."

"The murder weapon, sure, it could be. It's one of the reasons we aren't sure where the killing took place. We found no weapon. The remains were scattered. Time and the weather had washed away any blood or other indicators."

"You found everything but the knife and the killer." I said.

"It's our turn now, Tom. Let me tell you what we know, so far." Tony said.

He laid out everything I'd told him. Tony even told Sheriff Dempsey about Watkins membership in the Righteous Army of God, hate group

"Well, you boys have some pretty compelling information. I suggest we conduct a joint investigation. It's entirely possible, perhaps even probable; the victim was killed here in Rusk County. Evidently the victim lived in Tyler, and you have a possible suspect who lives in the city of Tyler, in Smith County. We don't have any confirmation the victim really was Eduardo Ruiz. So, we can't definitively tie your guy to the victim, but we have some pretty useful things to work with," Sheriff Dempsey said.

Tony nodded.

"Agreed, we'll work on gathering evidence and information on our suspect from our end. Has the body been disposed of?"

"It was buried. No one came forward to claim it, so it was buried by the county, in Potter's Field. The forensics people in Dallas have preserved some evidence and they took a lot of very detailed photos, especially of the blade marks on the bones."

"They might not be good enough to stand up in court. If we find a weapon which might be the murder weapon, we may need to have the body exhumed."

"Not a problem."

"OK. We'll stay in touch."

"Tony, can I speak to you privately for a moment?" Sheriff Dempsey asked.

Tony looked at me.

I took it as my cue to stand up.

"I'll meet you out in the hall, Tony. Sheriff Dempsey, it was a pleasure to meet you," I said, as we shook hands.

"No offense, son. It's just a law enforcement matter."

"None taken, I understand. I hope we'll have occasion to talk again some time."

"I'll look forward to it, and I appreciate your help with this investigation."

I usually have to finagle information out of Tony. He is a stickler for P.P.P., or proper police procedure. He doesn't like to deviate from the tried and true training, of which he's a product.

That was not the case this time. When he walked out of the sheriff's office, I could see he had something on his mind. The minute Tony got the car started; he began telling me what he and Sheriff Dempsey had discussed.

"You won't believe this; Sheriff Dempsey told me the FBI has its eye on the RAGs. Apparently they have reason to believe the RAGs are getting more militant and may pose a threat to some local government officials, and others. This is very much under the radar, because the feds don't know who to trust. Sheriff Dempsey says the FBI didn't even contact him until they had investigated him thoroughly. This is an incredibly bad situation. Apparently there are members of the RAGs in positions of authority in several parts of East Texas and the feds believe law enforcement in this area is seriously compromised."

"Why would he trust you with this information?" Tony looked startled.

"You got to that very quickly. It's a very good question, and I've been asking myself the same thing."

"You probably should've asked him."

"It crossed my mind. I was so fascinated by what he was telling me, I let it go."

"It might be a test."

"It might be, but what kind of a test?"

"I suspect the relationship between the Tyler PD and the FBI is not very cordial. I'm pretty sure there is no love lost between the two."

"Of course, even though the Federal building is only a few blocks from my office, I hardly ever see any of those people. We have a love hate relationship. Whenever the feds get involved in one of our cases, they pretty much just take over and freeze us out. Federal charges trump local charges, most of the time. We hate that. On the other hand, they have data bases and other resources which are pretty vital to us. We love that."

"I'll bet if the FBI investigated Sheriff Dempsey before they trusted him with any intel on the RAGs investigation, then they're probably doing the same thing with Smith County and the Tyler PD."

"Yeah, it makes sense." Tony agreed.

"Maybe the feds are looking at you."

"Oh come on, they should know I can't be a white supremacist."

"It doesn't mean they trust you." I said.

"Well, that's annoying. Obviously I can be trusted."

"Of course you can be trusted. It's not as if you would tell anybody about this..."

Tony rolled his eyes and then he gave me a dirty look. I laughed.

"Hey, don't worry. Your secret is safe with me."

CHAPTER 30

As we made the turn onto the street where Diondro's mother lived, we found a Chapel Hill police cruiser parked facing us, about a half block from the house. The officer inside the car flashed his lights as we approached. Farther up the street, we could see there were pickup trucks parked in front of Mrs. Taylor's house, and there were two men with shotguns sitting in chairs in the shade provided by the carport.

Tony flashed his lights and rolled down his window, as he stopped his unmarked Crown Victoria beside the Chapel Hill P.D. cruiser.

"Good afternoon, sir. May I ask who you gentlemen are and what business you have in this neighborhood?" The officer asked.

I had to smile. Not long ago, it was a common practice for white police officers in white neighborhoods, to stop cars with black drivers and ask the same question. This was the exact reverse scenario.

I was pretty sure the Chapel Hill cop was aware of the irony, and he found it just as amusing as I did.

"I'm Lieutenant Escalante with Tyler P.D. and this is my associate, Mr. Tucker. We are friends of the Taylors, and they're expecting us."

"Yes sir. Go right ahead."

Tony drove up to the house and parked behind

one of the trucks. The men with the shotguns had shifted over in front of the house.

Diondro came out the front door and waved us in, indicating to the armed men we were not a threat. He held the door for us as we went inside.

Inside, we found Mrs. Taylor and the Reverend Mrs. Jefferson in the kitchen, enjoying each other's company, over coffee and some homemade cookies.

"Mamma, Mr. Tucker and Tony are back," Diondro announced.

"Well, well, that's just fine. Would you gentlemen enjoy a cup of coffee and some fresh cookies?"

Tony started to shake his head, but I cut him off.

"Yes ma'am, we surely would."

"Get you a cup. They's hangin' over there, under the cupboard."

I grabbed a coffee mug off a hook and headed for the coffee pot. My blue mug said Chapel Hill Bank & Trust in gold letters. I saw Tony had grabbed a green mug with East Texas Feed & Seed, in white letters.

"Diondro say you went to see the Sheriff, over to Henderson."

"Yes, ma'am," Tony said.

"Praise the Lord for law and order. The Lord instructs us to do justice, to love mercy and to walk humbly... Amen?" asked the Reverend Mrs. Jefferson.

"Yes, ma'am."

"Sit yo'selves down," instructed Mrs. Taylor.

Tony and I joined the women at the 1950's vintage dining table, topped with harvest gold colored Formica.

"It's nice to see the police car down the street. How long do you think they will be able to provide that service?" I asked Mrs. Taylor.

The Reverend Mrs. Jefferson replied for her. "Bless God. There are two police in our congregation, and the Chief of Police is my nephew. We'll have a police sitting right there, until this trial is over. Hallelujah!"

I tried to hide my smile.

"Those men out side, with the shotguns..." Tony started.

"Glory to God! Those brothers are members of my flock, and some men who live here in this neighborhood have volunteered as well, so someone will always be there, till this trial is over, umm hum. Praise the Lord!"

"Reverend Jefferson, there's an ordinance against..."

"This is private property. Are you a Chapel Hill police?" the Reverend Mrs. Jefferson asked, holding her hand up and pointing at the ceiling.

"No ma'am." Tony answered.

"Well then, you might want to mind your own business. Thank you, Jesus!"

Tony was now struggling to hide his own smile.

I decided to change the subject.

"So, Diondro, will you be staying here with your mom, or coming with us?"

"The trial is just a few days away. You said you and Tony think it will be a slam dunk, right?"

Tony and I both nodded.

"Do you still think they'll leave us alone, once that punk goes to prison?"

I looked at Tony, hoping to have him answer the question.

"The only reason y'all are in any danger now, is because the guy you jumped is the current gang boss. He hates you and he gives the orders. Once he gets his sentence of twenty to life, there are guys just standing in line to replace him. Whoever is the heir to his throne has no beef with you; in fact you will have helped them ascend to power."

Diondro looked to me.

"I agree. If there is any indication that's not the case, we'll help them change their minds."

Diondro thought about it for a moment.

"Ok. I want to stay here with my moms."

"Hallelujah! Glory to God! That's the right answer. You a fine young man, Diondro," said the Reverend Mrs. Jefferson.

"Oh, my baby, I'm so happy. I've missed you so much. Thank you, Jesus!" Mrs. Taylor said.

Diondro managed to look happy and consternated, all at the same time.

"Mr. Tucker, may I speak to you and the Lieutenant outside, for a moment?" asked the Reverend Mrs. Jefferson.

"Yes ma'am. We are just on our way out."

"Before you go, I just want to say thank you. Thank you both, for taking care of my boy," Mrs. Taylor said.

"It was my pleasure, ma'am," Tony replied.

"I'm glad we could help. Diondro, you feel free to call me, if you need anything. We'll get your TJC admittance things squared away, as soon as the trial is over," I added.

"Yes sir, thanks again." Diondro said, shaking my hand.

He walked over and shook Tony's hand as well.

"Thank you for all you've done, sir. I won't ever forget the things I've learned hanging out with you."

"Don't be a stranger. You come around the cop shop any time you like, Diondro." Tony said.

Outside, the Reverend Mrs. Jefferson got right to the point.

"Diondro says you're both Christian men. That true?"

Tony and I exchanged a look.

"Yes, ma'am," Tony answered.

"Praise the Lord. You know God sent you into this boy's life?"

"Yes ma'am, I suppose so." Tony said.

Reverend Jefferson fixed me with a look.

"I believe I would like to have a word with you alone, for a moment."

"J.W., I'll wait for you in the car," Tony said.

We watched him walk away. He seemed to be in a terrible hurry. It must have been because he wanted to get in the car and get the air conditioning going.

She turned to me.

"Is you an angel?"

"I beg your pardon…"

"There is something about you… more than meets the eye."

"Of course not, I'm as human as you are. I've just been around a lot longer."

"You a Shepherd, aren't you?"

"Isn't that the function of a church pastor? You know, someone like yourself. A shepherd has a flock. You have a flock. I do not."

"There are shepherds who lead the flock, and there are shepherds who guard against the predators."

"Don't most shepherds do both?"

"Umm hmmm, and there are Shepherds who seek the lost sheep."

I nodded.

"So there are."

"Umm hmmm, so there are. Thank the Lord!"

I winked at her, and went to join Tony in the car.

As I walked away from her, I was hurrying a little myself.

CHAPTER 31

Christine came into my office and closed the door behind her. She was wearing a coral colored, knee length sleeveless dress, with contrasting turquoise jewelry. The jewelry looked to be some old Navajo pawn pieces. The necklace was a heavy, handmade chain, with big Kingman cabochons. She had matching earrings and a bracelet. The effect was stunning and made her look like a red headed fashion model. I wondered where she had found shoes that matched her dress.

"John, there is someone here to see you," she said.

Her coming in to speak to me was odd, because just by glancing at my monitor, I could see the man waiting out in the reception area. She could have just called me on the intercom.

"Ok. What's up?"

"He says he's with the FBI."

"Well then, show the man in."

"John, you aren't in any trouble are you?"

"Oh, so that's it. No, I'm not in any trouble, not that I know of. Go ahead and send him in."

Christine walked to the door and held it open.

"Mr. Tucker will see you now," she said, with a big warm smile.

She could be dazzling when she wanted to.

The man who entered my office was about 5'10" and about 200 pounds. He was well dressed, in a pin striped charcoal suit, had longish hair, stylishly greying at the temples, and he wore expensive Oxford loafers. His face was only slightly off balanced by a nose which had clearly been broken, at least once. The overall affect was that of an attorney who liked to cage fight, and he was clearly dazzled by Christine. He could hardly take his eyes off her.

I stood to greet him.

He shifted his attention to me, as Christine stepped out of the room, closing the door behind her.

"Mr. Tucker, I'm FBI Special Agent Douglas Booker. I'm the Special Agent in charge of the Tyler office.

"Agent Booker, I'm pleased to meet you. I remember you from the child abduction case last year, although we never met," I said, as we shook hands. "Please have a seat. Can I offer you a cup of coffee?"

"Thank you, no."

We sat and regarded each other for a moment, across the top of my desk.

I was wondering if his heavy brow was a by-product of using anabolic steroids.

"I imagine you're wondering why I'm here..." Agent Booker started.

I waited.

"First, let me send greetings from a friend of yours. Jack McCarthy, asked me to say 'howdy' for him."

I nodded.

"How is Jack?"

"He's doing well. He's now a Regional Director with DHS."

"That's nice."

"I must say, I'm surprised by your appearance. What I mean is; I was expecting an older man."

"Why?"

Well, Jack said you and he had worked together as agents in DHS, for several years, up until maybe five or six years ago?"

I nodded.

"Yeah, sounds about right."

"Huh, you and he are both about the same age, but neither of you looks to be over thirty," he observed.

I didn't like the direction this conversation was going. I changed the subject.

"I guess you would know a good bit about me, if you've been talking to Jack."

"Yeah, he shared your file, although your file says you are quite a bit older than you look. No offense intended, but if you've had some work done, it's extraordinary. You look like your photos from your days in the Navy."

I wondered what file he was referring to. My DHS employee file was one thing. Was there another file about which I had no knowledge? Did DHS know my history? This was bothersome. I needed to steer him away from this line of thought.

"Clean living. Surely you didn't come here just to see what I look like."

"Uhh, no, just an observation. As I said, no offense intended."

"What can I do for you, Agent Booker?"

He studied me for a moment, and then he appeared to make a decision."

"You attracted quite a lot of attention last year, when you and Lieutenant Escalante found those missing kids."

I waited.

"Your name popped up several times in the news and you have become something of a local celebrity. You will remember the child abduction was a federal case, because of the little boy who was transported across state lines."

"I remember."

"Then a couple of funny things happened."

I stared at him.

"Well, not funny, exactly. More along the lines of 'odd' I would say."

I continued to stare.

"Your name came up in a conversation some of us were having, about a local hate group."

I shrugged and made a "move along" motion with my hand.

"What is your connection to the Righteous Army of God?"

I felt a wave of relief roll over me. This wasn't about me. My secret remained secure.

I considered my response.

"If you're referring to the white supremacist hate organization, I have no connection."

"It was reported to me you have informed the local LEOs you suspect a member of the RAGs, in an apparent homicide."

"I do."

"How did you arrive at this suspicion?"

"In my investigation into a matter on behalf of one of my clients, I stumbled onto it, quite by accident."

"What do you know about the RAGs?"

"I know more than I want to and somewhat less than I will, before this is finished."

"Uh huh… Jack told me you played your cards close to the vest."

I shrugged again.

"You had a top secret clearance, when you worked for the Department of Homeland Security."

I stared at him, some more. Where was he going with this?

"Look, we may have gotten off on the wrong foot."

"I still don't know why you are sitting in my office."

Special Agent Booker nodded.

"Fair enough, let's start over. Mr. Tucker, as you know, domestic terrorism falls within the scope of my agency's duties to protect and defend the citizens of the United States. The FBI is actively engaged in an investigation of the Righteous Army of God. The RAGs is a larger organization than most people realize. There are active chapters in at least half of our states. The Federal prison system is full of them, as are many of the State prisons. In addition, the RAGs have ties with other hate groups and they are a significant part of the white supremacist movement in this country. We have reason to believe they are planning some sort of major event. Perhaps even on the scale of Oklahoma City."

I considered the information for a moment.

"Is that the connection between your agency, the FBI, and the Department of Homeland Security?"

It is, yes, one of the connections. It was through that channel I came to have information about you."

I wondered what "information" he was referring to.

"Again, why are you here, in my office?"

"I was just getting to that. You have apparently developed some sort of information source, or connection with a person of interest in our investigation of the RAGs."

"... And you want me to back off?"

"No, not at all, on the contrary, we want you to develop the relationship, if you can. We need all the information we can gather. We have a source ourselves, but an additional source could be very helpful."

I rocked back in my chair and gathered my thoughts.

"Agent Booker..."

"Call me Doug," he interrupted.

"Alright, Doug, I have a very tenuous contact with a member of that group. One of my people is in a position to interact with him, but it could all end tomorrow. I intend to see justice is done in the murder of a Mexican national. If it turns out your, so called 'person of interest,' is the killer, I'll do everything I can to see he gets put behind bars."

"Now hold on, this is a much more important matter than the supposed murder of some illegal alien."

"I thought you government types are supposed to call them 'undocumented immigrants' or just immigrants."

"Whatever, the point is - domestic terrorism is a far more serious threat to the people of the United States."

"It depends on your perspective; I understand, but..."

"... Let's just take this one step at a time and see where it leads us," he interrupted.

I took a deep breath.

"OK, sure. We can work together. We both want to see justice prevail. Like I told you though, this could all fall apart tomorrow, maybe even today."

"I'm not looking for promises, just a little cooperation."

I nodded.

"I'll keep you in the loop, as my operative reports his progress, but I do need a promise from you, as well."

"... And that is?"

"My operative is on the edge of a very dangerous situation. He's risking his job, his personal safety, maybe even his life. I want you to promise me if this gets too dicey, you will help me get him out."

"We'll be happy to assist him in any way we can. Do you have a lot of confidence in this guy? I want to meet him, of course."

"He's a fireman by training and occupation. He only works for me part time. He's using vacation and sick days to stay on this case. At some point very soon, he won't be able to do that anymore."

"What's his name?"

Agent Booker was starting to annoy me.

"Show me your credentials."

By the look on Agent Booker's face, I could see I had just returned the favor.

"I thought we were past this." He said

"I don't know you and I don't trust you. You can be sure I'm going to check you out."

"Fair enough," Doug said, as he handed me his badge case."

I quickly photographed the info on his photo ID

card and his badge number with the camera in my smart phone...

"You're pretty thorough aren't you?" Doug asked.

"My clients expect me to be thorough, and I've found it's better to be safe than sorry."

I handed back his creds.

"You'll find you can trust me," he said.

"Time will tell, Doug."

"No worries."

"Just one more thing, Doug..."

He raised his eyebrows.

"I asked you to promise me you would help my operative, if I asked you to. I was speaking to you. You answered 'we'll be happy to assist him in any way we can.' I'm not interested in ten layers of bureaucracy. I had more than enough of that, when I worked for Uncle Sam. I'm dealing with you. I'll hold you responsible, not the entire government, not the FBI, not the local Field Office; just you, personally. Do you understand what I'm saying?"

Doug pursed his lips.

"You're kind of a hard ass, aren't you?"

"I just want to make sure we understand each other. If you can't commit to it, tell me now."

"Trust is a two way street. I don't know you either."

"Well then, have a nice day, Special Agent Booker."

He stood up, and started to turn away.

"Now hang on a minute. Ok, I get it. You want me to promise you my help. I can't make some sort of blanket promise, to do whatever you want me to do. You understand I work for the Federal Government, right?"

I spread my hands.

"Still, yes, I promise to personally help your guy in any and every way I can. OK, is that what you want from me?"

"That, my friend, could be the start of a beautiful relationship."

CHAPTER 32

I was thinking about the implications of my meeting with FBI Special Agent Booker, when Christine buzzed me on the intercom.

"John, you're three o'clock is here," She said.

I checked the monitor and saw Mrs. Clark. She was at least as attractive as she had sounded on the telephone.

"Thank you. Please send her in, Christine."

I stood up behind my desk as the lady entered the room.

From the moment Evelyn Clark came into my office, I could see she was working hard to maintain her composure.

"Good afternoon, Mrs. Clark, I'm John Tucker. Please have a seat." I motioned toward one of the high backed upholstered chairs in front of my desk.

I sat down as well.

We studied each other for a moment, before I broke the silence.

"How may we help you today, Mrs. Clark?"

She drew a somewhat ragged breath.

"I would like you to follow my husband."

"I see. May I ask why?"

"... Because he's having an affair, of course."

"Are you sure?"

Her eyes jumped around the room, not really looking at anything, especially me.

"Oh, I don't know. If I knew for sure, I wouldn't need you to follow him."

"I see. So then, you suspect your husband is having an affair, is that correct?"

She nodded several times.

"Do you have any idea with whom he might be having an affair?"

"... With whom? Of course not! If I knew who it was, I wouldn't need you."

I conceded the point.

"Why do you think your husband is having an affair?"

"All the usual reasons I suppose. He's a man. He likes women. He's bored with me."

"Are you bored with him?"

"What? No, this isn't about me, it's about him, or us, I suppose."

I waited her out.

"So, what will it cost me to have him followed?"

"My rate is $500.00 per day, plus expenses. I figure a day is eight hours. I bill for each accumulation of eight hours. I have other clients, and some part of every day is spent on the needs of each of my clients, so typically, I would not be billing any single client every day, for the work we do on a case. Surveillance can often stretch out over several hours, on any given day. It may take several days to obtain any useful information. It is one of the most expensive services we provide."

"I can afford it."

"Yes ma'am. May I ask, does your husband monitor or manage your accounts?"

She paled, as she thought about the implications of my question.

I nodded.

"Do you carry a gun, Mr. Tucker?" she asked.

"Yes, ma'am, I do. Why do you ask?"

"I want you to kill him."

I regarded her for a moment, and then she broke down in tears.

I pushed the button on the intercom.

"Christine, would you please come in here?"

Christine walked in and gave me a 'what's up?' look.

"Mrs. Clark has just asked me to kill her husband." I said, as casually as possible.

"Oh my! Whatever for?" Christine asked.

Mrs. Clark was sobbing now.

Christine knelt down beside her, and wrapped and arm around her.

I pushed the box of tissues over to where Christine could reach them.

"It seems there are problems in the marriage, and Mrs. Clark suspects her husband is having an affair."

"I'm so sorry to hear that. Do you really want John to kill him?" She asked Mrs. Clark.

Mrs. Clark shook her head. Her mascara was running down her face.

"I, I just want to know... Oh, I don't know what I want."

"Of course you don't. This is horrible for you. Have you talked to your husband about this?"

Mrs. Clark shook her head again.

"I can't, I just don't know how, or what to say..."

"You could ask him straight out, if he is having an affair." I suggested.

"He would just lie, wouldn't he?"

"Mrs. Clark, have you ever considered marriage counseling?" Christine asked her.

The lady just shook her head in response.

"Do you think your husband might be open to going to see a counselor with you?"

"I, I don't know." Mrs. Clark sobbed.

I caught Christine's eye and nodded at her.

"Honey, let's you and I go to the ladies' room and

have a private chat. We'll get you cleaned up and put some cool water on your face. How does that sound?" Christine asked her.

Mrs. Clark nodded in agreement and Christine helped her to her feet.

"John, if you will excuse us for a few minutes, we'll be back shortly," Christine said, as she turned toward the door and guided Mrs. Clark in that direction.

"Certainly," I said.

I gave Christine a wink.

She made a face, in response.

When Mrs. Clark was again seated in my office, she was much calmer, and appeared to be thinking more clearly.

"Mr. Tucker, please excuse me for asking you to…"

"Not at all," I said, interrupting her. "I understand you are quite distraught. Sometimes it helps just having a friend to talk with. Mrs. Clark, here is a card with the contact information for a friend of mine. She does marriage and family counseling. Please make an appointment with her. I think you will find her a much more beneficial person to help you with this issue than I can be. She can encourage you and help you figure out what it will take to save your marriage. Perhaps your marriage can't be saved, but if it can be, do you want to?"

"Yes, yes I do. I came here thinking it was too late and there was no hope. I don't know, but I want to try."

"That's good then. I'm glad you came in today."

"I am as well. You and Christine have been very kind."

"If there is anything either of us can do for you, even if it is just listening, please come see us again." I stood up to show her to the door.

"It's funny, I came here frightened and confused, but y'all have helped me feel better."

I opened the door, and Christine greeted her with

a smile.

When she had gone, Christine came in and sat down in one of the two high back arm chairs upholstered in a green fabric, with a hunt scene theme, which sat in front of my massive hand carved oak desk.

I was reminded again, Christine had been the one sent to turn my drab, one man agency into what it was now. She had chosen this space and all of the furnishings.

"That was the strangest appointment we've had in a while," Christine observed.

"Not particularly profitable either."

"There is more than one kind of profit, John. I feel really good about being able to just comfort and befriend her."

"Me too, but as they say, it don't pay the bills."

"A contract to kill her husband might have paid a few bills. Taking her on as a client and doing the surveillance on her husband would have put some cash in the coffers."

"Not the reason for the appointment."

Christine was thoughtful for a moment.

"Mrs. Clark thought it was."

"Mrs. Clark didn't make the appointment. She just made the phone call." I said.

Christine smiled.

"I think you're right. It was a divine appointment, wasn't it?"

I smiled back.

"They are the best kind."

CHAPTER 33

It was the first opportunity to get together and shoot since I had gotten back from Arkansas. Christine, Tony and I met at the indoor shooting range where we routinely meet and spent some time and ammunition practicing.

Afterwards, as Tony, Christine and I emerged from the building; on our way out to dinner, we spotted a big black man leaning against the tailgate of my pickup, with his arms crossed.

"Is this trouble, J.W.?" Tony growled beside me.

I shook my head.

"I don't think so…"

We spread out as we approached my truck. We wanted to make it more difficult for the man to hit moving targets, if he decided to start shooting. We also wanted to look for other possible threats; realizing one man might be just a diversion.

Ironically, most people going into, or coming out of a shooting range are carrying guns that aren't loaded.

The man leaning against my truck didn't move, except for his head which turned from one to the other of us as we approached. He was grinning.

"Whoooeee, y'all sure are careful," he said.

"What can we do for you, Mr. Wilson?" I asked.

Kirby Wilson slowly uncrossed his arms and casually held his hands up.

"I'm not looking for any trouble. I just want to clear the air."

"Yeah, I recognize you." Tony said.

"Christine, this is Kirby Wilson, lately of the Tyler Police Department, now in private practice."

Christine flared her nostrils and set her mouth in a thin line.

"A pleasure to meet you ma'am, I hope I didn't scare you folks none," Wilson smirked.

"What do you want, Mr. Wilson?" I asked him.

"I told you I wanted to talk."

"I told you to make an appointment."

He nodded and grinned again.

"I did make an appointment, this is it."

How did you know where to find us?" Tony asked.

"Oh please. Like this is some sort of secret. Everybody knows the three of you come here to shoot, on a regular basis. It don't take much of a detective to figure it out."

"Again, and for the last time, what do you want?" I asked.

"Well, I don't want y'all to think badly of me. Sure, I had a little falling out with the department. I know you probably disapprove of my work and my client list, but why can't we all just get along?"

"You tailed me to Arkansas and nearly got me and my client killed."

"Oh come on now, that was just business. I never lifted a finger against you or the boy."

"No, you just marked the target, so somebody else could do the killing." Tony observed.

Kirby Wilson shrugged.

"Nothing personal, just business."

"I trust the business we had between us is no longer an issue?" I said.

"Yeah, I got no further interest. I wanted to tell you I think y'all have done a fine job of keeping the boy safe. I know all three of you were involved. It's my understanding the threat to him is pretty much just... going away, if you catch my drift."

"Good, then I assume you won't be following me around, any time soon."

"Oh, I don't need to follow you, to find you, not any of you. I can find any of you anywhere, at any time, as you can see." He was grinning like the Cheshire cat.

"I suggest you stay far away from me, my friends and my clients."

"Oh, now that sounded like a threat. Lieutenant, did you hear that? This man is threatening me."

Tony just continued to scan the area, ignoring Wilson completely.

Wilson shrugged.

"Fine, I just wanted to let you know I hold nothing personal against any of you, and I have no intention of bothering you in the future."

"Good answer."

"But, business is business. You mind your business and I'll mind my own."

"...As long as your business doesn't interfere with my business."

He shrugged.

"Time will tell."

"I'm telling you now, stay away from all of us." I said.

He nodded.

"Nice talk," he grinned again.

Then, Kirby Wilson straightened up and started to walk away. He turned his head and called back over his shoulder.

"Like I said, business is business."

CHAPTER 34

"Business is business. This is just a business decision, baby. There's no money in it and we don't want to pursue it any further." Melody Doyle said.

She was standing at the side of my desk. She leaned forward and put her hands on my arms.

"Melody, this has become more than just an investigation into negligence on a job site. It looks like one of the workers was actually murdered."

I was trying not to look down the front of her blouse. Trying, but failing.

She caught me looking and smiled seductively.

"See anything you like?"

I pushed my chair back and stood up.

"Let me walk you back to your office. We can discuss this further as we walk."

"I'd much rather dance, baby. Come on and dance with me," she purred.

"Ms. Doyle, I'm serious. We can't just drop this case."

"It's done, we're done. The construction company isn't worth the time and the resources we've already committed trying to bring a suit against them. We would probably win in court, but we wouldn't ever collect. The money just isn't there, you as much as said so yourself. You're the one who told us all about how the business is organized."

She had put her hands on my shoulders.

"Oh, John, you're so strong."

The door opened and in walked Christine. From the way she moved and the look on her face, for a moment, I thought she was going to punch Melody right in the face!

"May I interrupt, whatever this is, to conduct some business?" she asked, between tightly clenched teeth.

I saw Melody turn bright red. I figured she was embarrassed.

I figured wrong.

"What, your mommy never taught you to knock on a closed door?" Melody snarled.

"What, your mommy never taught you not to throw yourself at a man?" Christine retorted.

It was like watching a snake eat a mouse. I didn't want to see it, but I just couldn't look away.

"Why don't you mind your own business?"

"This is my business! May I remind you whose office you're standing in?"

"Oh, I see how it is. You want him for yourself. Well, John and I have a thing going, and you aren't woman enough to get between us."

I couldn't believe what I was seeing or hearing.

"If you don't walk right out of here, I'll drag you out by your bleach bottle hair." Christine spat.

"OK, stop it! Now that's enough," I interrupted.

There was something wrong with me. My voice didn't sound right. It was much too husky. I didn't want them to stop. I wanted to watch them fight and tear each other's clothes off...

Fortunately, Melody turned and stormed out.

Christine slammed the door behind her.

"Have you lost your mind?" She demanded, as she whirled around to face me.

"Uhhh, I uhhh... I umm..." I stammered.

"Oh good grief, men!" she barked.

I held up my hands.

"Hey, I didn't invite her here. She just walked in, and…"

"Well, it's a good thing I just walked in, isn't it?"

I chuckled.

"As a matter of fact, it is. Thank you."

"I walk away from my desk for five minutes, and this is what happens."

"Look, I don't know what brought all this on. Oh yeah; Doyle, Doyle and Starnes are pulling the plug on the gross negligence case we were working for them.

"Good!"

"No, not good, this isn't something we can just drop. They won't be paying us, but the investigation has to go on."

"The good part is that woman won't have any occasion to wend her way into your… office."

I nodded and took a deep breath.

"Or do you want her to?"

I went back to my desk.

"I have to admit, it sure was tempting."

"Which was the whole point, don't you think?"

"I wasn't thinking very well then, but I am now."

"We'll see…"

"… Bleach bottle hair?" I asked.

Christine giggled.

"I'm just saying."

CHAPTER 35

I managed to contact Gary by phone.

"Are y'all still building that barn?"

"No, the construction is finished. The painters are the only ones over there."

"Can you meet me there in about an hour?"

"Sure, in fact I need to run by there and make sure the painters are on the job. The job we're on now is only about ten minutes away from there."

"Good, I have news and some things we need to discuss."

An hour later, Gary and I were sitting in my truck, with the engine running and the air conditioner keeping us comfortable.

"I've seen him with a knife. I don't have any way to know if it's the same knife your dead guy had."

"Give me as detailed a description of the knife as you can."

"OK, it's a folding, lock blade knife. It's one of those cheap ones from India, China or wherever. The blade is about five inches long, so the knife is about five and a half inches long, when it's closed. The handle is clear plastic, so you can see the picture in it. The picture is a painting, or whatever, of a hawk or an eagle killing a rattlesnake."

"Wow, that's a pretty complete description."

Gary shrugged.

"I've seen the knife two or three times."

"You know the symbol of the golden eagle and the rattlesnake is a traditional Mexican motif?"

"Yeah, I saw it on a Mexican flag or something, somewhere."

"Kind of odd a white supremacist would be carrying a Mexican knife, don't you think?"

"Like I said, it's a cheap knife. You can get knives like that at flea markets and gas stations, pretty much anywhere."

"OK, on another subject... This is complicated and I don't know how to tell you all of it, exactly."

"Just lay it all out, man."

I gathered my thoughts.

"One, Kevin Watkins is now a suspect in a murder investigation. Two, Kevin Watkins is a member of a hate group that may be planning to do something horrific."

"And three, is that Watkins was the guy who was overseeing the job when our client got hurt, right?" Gary asked.

I opened my mouth to answer, but closed it for a second.

"What those things have in common is you, Gary. You're the only person I know who can get close to Watkins."

"Yeah, it's pretty cool, isn't it?"

"There are some serious problems with that."

"Well, there's something I've been wanting to tell you..."

"OK."

"I put in for my retirement from the fire department."

I was stunned and I had too many questions.

"What the, when, why?" Was how it came out of my mouth.

"Yeah, I like this work. I'm getting paid by you, to

play detective, and I'm getting paid by the company to work with my hands. It's all good."

"About that, here's the thing... The client has dropped the case."

"Oh, you've got to be kidding, right?"

"No."

"Ouch, it sucks to be you!"

"Gary, I can't keep paying you, if no one is paying me."

"Yeah, I see that."

"This is bigger than the money. You're in a position to do something important, and you're the only one who can do it. I hope you'll choose to continue, but I'll understand if you can't, for whatever reason."

"Wow, I'll need to think about this."

"Sure and here is something to add to the things you're thinking about. If Kevin Watkins gets any idea you're looking at him as a possible murder suspect, or as a member of the Righteous Army of God... you could be in danger."

"Yeah, he's a pretty nasty guy. I wouldn't want to have him as an enemy."

"Gary, he isn't your friend now. He is your enemy, but he just doesn't know it. Do you understand what I'm saying?"

Gary nodded quietly.

"How soon do you need my answer?"

"No hurry, take your time and think it through. I can't tell you what you should do. And, Gary... I'm sorry I got you into this."

"Hey, it's been good, up until now."

"Well whatever you decide, I'm with you all the way."

I felt terrible as I drove away from the construction site. I would never have advised Gary to retire from the fire department. He'd joined when he was 19 years old, and had put in twenty years. All that training and experience was just being thrown away.

If he had stayed on with the department, he might have been able to advance farther up the command chain. I knew he enjoyed construction and he had worked at remodeling as his part time job, before he started working for me, but I hadn't expected him to quit the department. I hadn't made any promises about him being able to work full time for me, but this sudden end to his income from our client, had to be a shock.

Now, I was asking him to put himself in danger, without even being paid to do it.

I decided to call Agent Booker and fill him in on the details. I also needed to call Tony and tell him about the knife.

"That's good, very good, a huge step in the right direction! The knife is essential, if it is the murder weapon." Tony said.

"Are you going to arrest Watkins?" I asked.

"No, we don't have sufficient probable cause. Even if we caught him with the knife on him, and if it turned out to be the murder weapon, he could claim he found it somewhere. We can't tie him to the killing, yet. We have far too many 'ifs', if this and if that. There is something you can do though. I want you to show the pictures of the clothes and the cap that were found with the remains, to whoever last saw the victim."

"Sure, Tony. I can do that, but even if they do identify the effects, I can't make them swear to it in a court of law."

"I've spoken to the DA and brought him up to speed on this thing. He understands the only witnesses are afraid of Immigration and Customs Enforcement. He's spoken to ICE and they have agreed to look the other way, if we can get those people to testify."

"It may make all the difference, Tony."

I called SAIC, Doug Booker on his direct line.

"Doug, its John Tucker. Do you have a moment to talk about the RAGs thing?"

"I have a moment, but that's about all."

"There's been a monkey wrench thrown in the gears. My client has pulled out, which means I can't continue paying my man to investigate Watkins, or the RAGs."

"I can see how that could be a complication. Why'd they decide to drop the case?"

"They figured the return isn't worth the investment."

Doug was silent for a moment. I think he was considering his response.

"Listen, John, I'm in charge of this investigation. If the only issue is money, we can probably make your man a paid informant. I'll send the request upstairs immediately."

"Actually, it isn't the only issue. I don't like to see him in danger."

"I understand how you feel, John, but your man is important. We need him to get as close to Watkins as he can." Doug said.

"I don't think Watkins is going to be running around loose for very much longer."

"Why do you say that?"

"There's a preponderance of evidence building against him for the murder of Eduardo Ruiz. At this point, it's all circumstantial, but I think an arrest warrant is going to be issued very soon."

"That is a complication. Still, we may be able to use it to our advantage."

"I just called to let you know what's happening."

"OK, thanks, John. When can I meet this guy who's working with Watkins?"

"I'll see what I can arrange."

CHAPTER 36

"All right, Agent Booker, I'm in," Gary said.

Gary had agreed to meet at the barn, one more time. Doug and I drove out there together in my truck. As soon as Gary met Special Agent, Doug Booker, I could see he would do just about anything to be a part of the "team".

"Gary, you want to back out of this, now is the time..."

"I can handle it, John. If I can help the FBI in an official investigation, then that's what I want to do. I get to collect my entire pension from the department, I make a decent wage working for the construction company, and I get to be an undercover informant for the FBI. Man, it just doesn't get any better than that."

"Do you think there's any way you might be able to get into the RAGs?" Doug asked him.

"Sure, they'll accept anybody who hates colored people."

"What about the more dedicated inner circle of the RAGS?

"Probably... I've been playing along with the whole racist thing. I was raised by a racist, so I know the way they talk. I just pretend I'm my stepfather. He was a member of the KKK. Watkins thinks I'm as prejudiced as he is. I haven't asked Watkins anything about the RAGs, but I'm pretty sure I could."

"You need to be very careful about how you do it, Gary. Most of those guys are quite a bit younger than you are. An older guy asking about how to get into the RAGs might look suspicious to him." I suggested.

"He can work it to his advantage. Listen Gary, Watkins is about your age, right?" Doug asked.

"Yeah, he's no more than five years younger than me. Why?"

"You can tell him you would like to be a part of an organization of real men who are serious about making some changes in America, but you don't want to be a part of a bunch of post-adolescent punk rockers, like the RAGs."

"It might put him on edge," I pointed out.

Gary nodded.

"It might, but I think it would throw him off guard. He might even respect my attitude."

I conceded the point.

"You know him better than we do."

"Actually, I like that approach. I can act like I'm sick and tired of things getting worse and worse for white people in America. I'll tell him I think it's time for the grown men to stand up and fight back."

Doug was nodding his agreement.

"We believe the radical element is made up of men who are about your age and older, Gary." He said.

"Well, there you go. Us grown men will show those young posers, how the cow ate the cabbage."

Doug was grinning.

"Say, I think you could be pretty convincing."

"You're damn right!"

"Easy does it, 'De Niro'. If you over act, you'll show your hand."

"No, John. You're mixed metaphor aside, I think Gary's got a pretty good handle on this thing." Doug observed.

Gary winked at me.

After I dropped Doug off at the Federal Building, I swung over by the Mexican Market, to see if I could spot Juan and Julio. There was no sign of them, this late in the day.

As I was headed for the office, my phone rang. I pushed the button on my truck's steering wheel and said, "Hello."

"J.W., you're not gonna believe what just happened." Tony said, by way of greeting.

"OK, fire away."

"I just got a visit from the Chief of Police and the SAIC of the FBI, for the entire Southwest Region. They brought another guy along with them, a suit with the Department of Homeland Security..."

"Oh no..."

"Oh yes."

"What's the situation?"

"They informed me they were aware I was conducting an investigation into the murder of a certain illegal alien, and in the interests of national security, the FBI would be taking over as the lead agency in the investigation."

"Just like that, they just took over and tossed you out?"

"Not exactly, J.W."

"What is it then?"

"They want me to go ahead and arrest Watkins."

"What? I don't understand. Why?"

"They plan to flip him."

My mind whirled through the various scenarios likely to ensue. There was something else niggling at the edges of my conscious thought. Something about the way Tony was speaking, or the way he sounded.

"Tony, do you have me on speakerphone?"

Tony paused for a second.

"Yes, I do, J.W."

"Why? Tony, are they there with you, right now?"

A different voice responded.

"Mr. Tucker, I'm Special Agent, Mark Mansfield of the FBI. We would appreciate it if you would come down here to the federal building, right now."

I hit the turn signal, in preparation for turning back toward downtown Tyler.

When I walked into Tony's office, there were only three people in the room with him.

"Mr. Tucker, I'm Special Agent, Mark Mansfield, I'm the SAIC for the Southwest region. I believe you know these other gentlemen."

I looked at Tony, Special Agent Doug Booker, who appeared chagrined at the whole situation, and then the fourth man in the room.

"Hello, John. Long time no see."

"Hello, Jack. How are things in the DHS?" I said, reaching out to shake his hand.

I looked over at Doug.

"Did you know about this?"

Doug started to shake his head, but he was interrupted by SAIC, Mansfield.

"I'm afraid Agent Booker was not in the loop on this. He just got here himself. It's my understanding he was meeting with you and someone who works for you. Is that correct?"

"Yes, one of my associates is working for the same construction company Watkins works for."

"As Lieutenant Escalante has informed you, this is now a Federal matter. The Bureau is now in charge of this investigation. Any assets you have in the field are now our assets. I'll need to be brought up to speed on everyone involved, and be briefed on the details of the progress you've made thus far, any questions?"

I was so tired of these same old lines. I'd used them myself, when I worked for DHS.

"Yes, I do have questions. Who the hell do you think you are?" I asked.

Special Agent Mansfield stiffened slightly.

"Easy, John, there's no point in getting angry," Jack McCarthy interjected. "You'll have to excuse Special Agent, Mansfield, if he seems a bit rude..." He shot Mansfield a look. "... He's just trying to get his footing here."

"He'll be lucky if he doesn't get my foot up his..." I started.

"John!" Tony snapped.

Doug looked like he was going to be sick.

"Ok, let's all just take a moment to calm down and discuss the issues here." Mansfield suggested.

"Sure, here are the pertinent issues. I'm a private citizen. The people who work for me are private citizens. I don't answer to you and neither do they. Do you have any understanding of this concept, Mr. Mansfield?"

I have to give him credit. Mansfield didn't even blink.

"Certainly, I understand, Mr. Tucker. I was also given to understand, you had been instrumental in the investigation of Mr. Watkins as a possible murder suspect. I was told you have an employee, who is in a position to further our investigation into the intentions of the radical element of the Righteous Army of God. Further, I was told you would be a very useful and cooperative ally in this investigation. Clearly, I was misinformed on that point." He shot a look at Jack.

Jack stepped away from where he had been leaning against the wall. He put his hands in his pants pockets and approached us slowly. He acted cool and maybe a little bit hip. I had seen him do this before.

"Ahhh gee, fellas. We need to remember we're all on the same side here.

Agent Mansfield, Try to understand, John is not particularly fond of the Federal government. He did his bit for God and country. I know, because I was there for part of it. As you can see, he has certain passive/aggressive tendencies.

John, you know how it is with government types. Sure, Mark is a little pushy; he's just used to having people jump, when he snaps his fingers. Boys, we have a common enemy and the threat is eminent. We don't have time to fight with each other. Now shake hands and try to play nice."

That's the thing about Jack; he's an expert at finding common ground. It didn't surprise me he had worked his way up in the ranks at the DHS.

"I'm sorry if I offended you, Mr. Tucker," Agent Mansfield said, extending his hand.

"... Likewise." I replied, reluctantly shaking his hand.

I turned on Jack.

"Exactly how eminent is this threat, Jack? What do you know that we haven't been told, and why are you here?"

CHAPTER 37

"Domestic terrorism is at the top of our list these days." Jack said. "We've all been aware for some time that some American Muslims have become radicalized into full blown jihadists. When that happens, they start looking for ways to commit acts of terrorism, right here at home. We also have enemies within our country who are equally dangerous, but motivated by a different ideology.

The Righteous Army of God was not considered a real threat, because most of the membership was just a bunch of young racist punks. Sure, there were occasional incidents of violence against people of color, but nothing organized or threatening to the general public. We took our eye off of them for a while, and it was a mistake."

He paused and looked around the room.

"There have always been a few in the movement who were more committed to the cause of white supremacy. We now know some of them are violently committed to the cause. The leaders are older men and most of them are here in East Texas. They have organized an elite sub group of the RAGs into an extremist wing, determined to conduct acts of terrorism, at venues and events where many people will be killed or injured. They are also planning to target any individuals in law enforcement who have obstructed or prosecuted any of them. We came by this information from informants in the prison system. We have reason to believe some members of this militant wing are prominent and possibly even powerful members of the local community. Some of them may even be in law enforcement."

"Why do you believe the threat is eminent?" Tony asked.

"Our sources have indicated that now is the time. We are told they're planning some sort of an attack, likely to occur in this area, very soon. Because this is a domestic criminal conspiracy, without any ties to any person or group outside the United States, it falls within the charge of the FBI. That's why they have the point on this." Jack concluded.

"That said; we want to move on this guy Watkins. We mean to convince him we have enough evidence to get him put away for murder, maybe even facing a death sentence. We'll offer him a deal. If he becomes a confidential informant for us, we'll make the murder charges go away." SAIC Mansfield interjected.

I didn't like it. Watkins couldn't be allowed to go back on the streets. He was almost certainly a cold blooded killer. It would mean putting Gary's life at risk.

I understood the notion that one man's life was a small consideration when saving many lives was the goal. From the perspective of the federal government, one dead Mexican was no longer important in the whole big scheme of things. I understood that too, but I still didn't like it.

Tony and I made eye contact for a moment. He gave me the slightest nod, and then he spoke up.

"I know you've cleared this with the Chief and the DA, Agent Mansfield. Still, I would remind you, the murder investigation is a local matter and not within the jurisdiction of the bureau. We don't have to let you take over our murder investigation, or let our suspect go free as a bird." He pointed out.

"That's technically correct, Lieutenant, but I would remind you - matters of national security trump all other considerations." Jack replied.

"In matters of national security, you can throw all the rules out the window. Is that it, Jack?" I asked.

"In a word, yes, John," he replied with a shrug. "Just to simplify everyone's thinking on this."

"Let me ask you a question. Do you think we could wait a few days before you make the arrest?" I asked.

Jack was rubbing his chin. He looked over at SAIC Mansfield, and shrugged again.

"Possibly, why do you ask?"

"My man is in a position to try to get into the inner circle within the radical wing of the RAGs. He'll need some time to do it. If you snatch up Watkins, he'll lose his connection and there goes the opportunity."

"Yes, I see. It would be to our advantage for him to get into the RAGs. If it doesn't work out, we'll make the arrest immediately. If it does work, we'll make the arrest at a more opportune time, when our man won't need Watkins anymore." Mansfield mused.

"The thing is; if Watkins starts working for you, he could rat out my man to the RAGs. Getting an FBI informant killed would help cement Watkins' position in the group. I won't put my friend in that position."

"We can prevent Watkins from trying something like that."

Also, he won't be able to testify against Watkins, if he's part of an ongoing counter terrorism operation." I looked to Tony for a response.

Mansfield waved that off.

"It won't matter. Watkins won't be standing trial, once we flip him." SAIC, Mansfield said.

"I think you mean if you flip him. There's no guarantee he'll take the deal." I observed.

"In my experience, if properly presented, they always take the deal." SAIC, Mansfield replied.

"Maybe, but can you really trust them not to crawfish on you, the first chance they get?"

"Excuse me..."

"What John means is, he's wondering if they don't sometimes back out of the deal." Tony interpreted.

Jack and Mansfield made brief eye contact.

"When we flip someone, we only trust them as far as we can see them, and they don't try to back out. Not if they want to stay alive." Jack said.

That night, I called Gary and told him the whole story.

"Oh man! This is some pretty serious shit. I didn't think the RAGs were really all that big of a deal."

"Gary, this has gotten completely out of hand. I think you should consider your options. You don't have to do it."

"No way, man, I'm gonna stick with it. No offenses to you, John, but you're not my boss in this thing. I'm being asked to go undercover in a Federal anti-terrorism operation. How can I turn that down?"

"It could get you killed."

"I understand the risks, OK? Can you imagine being able to say you were part of something this important?"

"Yes, I can. I can also tell you when you're swimming in a cesspool, there is no way to stay clean. There's no way to predict the things you will have to do, or the ways you will suffer. I can tell you seeing your friends die is not fun. I can tell you there are things in life that are even more important than this is. There are other people who can shoulder this responsibility."

"Wow, I never thought I would hear you say something like that."

I took a deep breath.

"Gary, once you go in, you can't just quit. You can't back out. Those people will hunt you down. If you do this, you'll have to go all the way. You won't be able to bail out, because you won't have a parachute. You'll have to stay in it till it gets all wrapped up. There is no guarantee the feds can pull this off. You can't count on them to protect you, either. Do you understand what I'm saying?"

"Sure, I understand what you're saying. 'Praise the Lord and pass the ammunition'. Do you understand what I'm saying?"

I took a moment to reflect.

"Yes, I do. I've said it myself, and lived to regret it."

CHAPTER 38

"Si' that is the... ummm, cómo se dice... cap, he always wore it. I cannot say for sure about the pantalones. The camisa? You say, Tee shirt? Si' he wore it that day. " Juan told me, as he and Julio examined the pictures.

Julio was vigorously nodding his head in agreement.

"Does this mean Eduardo Ruiz is muerto?" Juan asked, as he made the sign of the cross.

I nodded solemnly, in response.

"I'm sorry."

"It was the hombre malo, no?"

"Eso puede ser verdad. No se'."

Both men hung their heads.

"It must be so. We saw Mr. Watkins drive away with Eduardo. No one has seen him since. These are his clothes. Where were they found?"

"Not far from where you were working on that day."

"Ese monstruo merece morir." Juan said, as he handed back the pictures.

"Will you say these things in court?"

They looked at each other.

"I will say it." Julio replied. "Even if they send me back to Mexico, I will say it."

"Sí, lo diré también." Juan agreed.

"I've been promised they will not send you back

to Mexico. You will be treated as if you were any other American. ¿Entiendes lo que estoy diciendo?"

"Sí, eso es muy bueno escuchar." Juan replied, as Julio smiled and nodded in agreement.

"Do you remember the knife Eduardo had with him on the day he had the fight with Watkins?"

"Sure, it was the same one he always carried."

"Can you describe it? Dime lo que parecía."

"It was a knife about this long, one that could be closed up." Juan held his fingers about five inches apart. "Tuvo el escudo mexicano en él."

"The symbol of Mexico, was in the handle? Está usted seguro de?"

"Very certain, Señor Tucker. Do you know the story of how it became our national symbol?"

"Not really."

"Do you know about my ancestors, the Aztec people?"

I shrugged. "I know a little."

Julio wanted to tell me some of the story.

"For two hundred years, the Aztec people were searching for a sign from the gods to show them the place to build a city. When the Aztec king saw an eagle, perched on a nopal, with a snake in its beak, he knew it was the sign they had been seeking. The gods had spoken. The gods led the Aztec people to Tenochtitlan. Today that place is the capital of Mexico, Ciudad Mexico."

"Wasn't Quetzalcoatl, the feathered serpent, one of the gods of the Aztecs?"

"Oh, si, señor and of the Mayas and the Toltecs, he was worshipped for thousands of years. He is still revered in many parts of Mexico, even now.

"Do you believe there are many gods?" I asked them.

"Me, I am a Catholic, pero quién puede decir?" he shrugged.

"Quién puede decir? Who can say?" Julio agreed.

"I know. I can say. There is one God and only one true God. There are many things that are called gods, but there is only one God."

"It is the teaching of the Church, Senor, pero quién puede decir?" Juan repeated.

"It is not important." Julio observed.

"It's the single most important thing anyone can ever know. It is the first thing. Es la cosa más importante"

"As you say, Señor," Juan said, philosophically.

Julio appeared uncomfortable with the discussion. I let it go.

"Mr. Watkins will probably be arrested very soon, but he will not be in court for a very long time," I observed.

"How long?"

"Quién puede decir?" I asked, with a shrug of my own. "Sólo Dios sabe."

"That's it then. If they'll testify they recognize the knife and the clothing, the DA will authorize us to arrest Kevin Watkins, on a charge of murder in the first degree. We can probably add kidnapping and assault to the charges. We have witnesses who saw the fight, they saw the knife, they recognize the clothes the victim was wearing, and they saw Watkins drive away with the victim, who was never seen alive again. If the knife turns out to be the murder weapon, Watkins' goose is cooked."

"Since there were no witnesses to the actual killing, Watkins can try to claim it was self-defense, not murder."

"How he tries to defend himself is not our concern. We can prove he had motive, means, and opportunity. The victim was stabbed multiple times and had obvious defensive wounds. There is no evidence Watkins was ever even in a fight, other than the one where he gave Ruiz a beating."

"There's no proof the remains are actually all that's left of Eduardo Ruiz."

"Stop trying to present the defense, J.W. There's more than enough evidence to prove the remains are those of Ruiz, at least beyond a reasonable doubt. Watkins did it and we know it."

I waited a moment.

"The question is, when do you arrest him?"

"That, my friend, is the sixty four thousand dollar question. The feds will make the big decision. Has Gary contacted you about his attempt to make the RAGs connection?"

"No, I haven't heard from him for a couple of days."

"It's too soon to worry."

"Yeah, I know."

"I heard Diondro was a very good witness, in his testimony at the trial of Hector Lopez."

"Huh, Hector Lopez, I thought his name was 'El Vibora', the viper."

Tony laughed.

"Yeah, that's his street name, but Lopez won't be back on the streets for at least twenty five years. He isn't eligible for parole until then and there is no possibility of time off for good behavior, as if he were capable of good behavior."

"There is hope for him Tony. Many people have become Christians during their incarceration. For some, it's the first time and place that they have ever heard the gospel. They come out of prison as better people than they were when they went in."

"Yeah, and for others, they come out worse people than they were when they went in.

"You are such a pessimist. Have you seen Diondro, since the trial?"

"Yeah, he stopped by here yesterday afternoon."

"Did he tell you we got him registered and he'll be starting at TJC in the fall semester?"

"He sure did, and that he's really looking forward to it."

CHAPTER 39

I found Jack in the makeshift office that had been temporarily provided for him, in the Federal building. I think it had been a storage room. Jack was seated behind a desk that was too small to be efficient. I was standing on the cracked and scuffed linoleum, in front of his desk, like a bad boy reporting to the principles' office. The difference was that I was the one who intended to call him on the carpet.

"Jack, I don't understand why you're here. You've done a pretty good job of trying to make us focus on the FBI, but you are here, in Tyler. Exactly why are you here?"

"I told you, the DHS is concerned about the situation here."

"This thing with the RAGs? That dog won't hunt."

He regarded me quietly for a moment.

"Private life hasn't dulled your wits much has it?"

"Not that much. A local matter like this, with the FBI on top of it, no way DHS sends a Regional Director to handle it. You've got whole sub departments and a host of field agents to do that."

Jack shrugged.

"So what's up? You might as well tell me the truth."

"Truth, what is truth?"

"You've been in government service too long."

"Sometimes I think so."

"So…" I made a rolling gesture with my hands.

"What if I told you I know that you were involved in a shootout at a pot farm in Arkansas, a few weeks ago?"

"I'd say you were mistaken."

"Truth, what is truth?"

"What happened in Arkansas is not relevant to my question."

"Don't you want to know how we found out?"

I shook my head.

"It doesn't matter. You're just trying to distract me from the subject at hand."

"There you go again."

"I worked with you too long, for you to get away with your old tricks."

"… Clearly."

I waited him out.

"OK, this thing with the RAGs is big, bigger than you realize. If they pull off some sort of terrorist act, it will have huge implications in our society."

"Duh, and …?"

He almost squirmed under my scrutiny.

"Alright, there is more. As big as the RAGs thing is, this is even bigger. We believe that concurrent with the threat from the RAGs, but not related in any way, is an additional threat from some local jihadists."

"Local jihadists?"

"Does that surprise you? Did you think radicalized Islamists were only to be found in the big cities?"

"Well, no not exactly, but not really here in East Texas…"

"That's what I'm trying to get across to you, John. Pretty much every state has some of them. There are hundreds of them, scattered all over the country. Maybe only a couple of them here or there, mostly in large metropolitan areas, but in some more rural areas, there are individuals and loosely organized cells. These cells are small groups of radicalized Muslims preparing to unleash a series of attacks against the general population. In the name of Islam, they'll target shopping malls, theaters, restaurants, sporting events, pretty much anywhere where people congregate."

"Churches, are you saying they're planning to attack churches?"

"No, at least we don't think so. They aren't out to get religious people specifically. If they attacked churches, it would open up a whole new world of ugly. No, they hate America, so they will attack those places that represent ordinary, everyday American life."

"Are you thinking maybe suicide bombers, like in the Middle East or Europe?"

"No, John. These cells will sometimes use improvised explosive devices, but they won't be suicidal. They plan to hit and run. They'll set off some bombs in a theater, and the next day, they'll whip through a shopping mall, shooting everyone in sight. A week later, they'll hit a baseball complex, then a crowded restaurant somewhere."

"It's madness."

"It's genius. They don't need to try and pull off some huge and highly complex event like they did on 9/11. Doing this, they can completely terrorize the population of the United States from coast to coast, and shut down our economy, with multiple attacks, at seemingly random places and times. They know they are less likely to be filmed by security cameras in more rural areas. They can hide out in the countryside without the neighbors being suspicious."

"Are you saying you think this could happen here in Tyler?"

"I'm saying this is the place we believe it will all start. Tyler and this area, within one hundred miles of here, will be ground zero for a whole new kind of terrorism in America"

My mind reeled.

"How could you possibly know this?"

"Between the NSA, CIA, DHS, FBI and a host of other agencies, both here and abroad, we've pieced it together. We've monitored certain people as they traveled overseas, we've intercepted communications, we've researched activities and interests, we've had tips from informants and other interested parties, we've followed money trails, and we have certain other resources I can't even tell you about."

"All that data and analysis has led you here, to Tyler?"

"Yes, John, it has."

I grabbed a folding chair from over in a corner, and sat down.

"So you're here to what... try to prevent it from happening."

He nodded.

"Yes, as part of a multi-agency anti-terrorism task force. DHS has the point on this, John. I've been given this assignment."

I was stunned.

"I'm sorry I asked."

"If you and I didn't go way back, if I didn't know you had once held a top secret clearance, I wouldn't have told you. Now that I have told you... I have to kill you."

The old joke wasn't funny today.

"What does any of this have to do with me?"

"Probably nothing, at least nothing I'm aware of, but I've known you a long time, John. You're like a lightning rod. When the worst storms hit, you're usually right in the middle of it. I wasn't particularly surprised to find you here, and already on the trail of domestic terrorists. Of course, this could all just be a coincidence."

"I don't believe in coincidence." I reminded him.

He shrugged.

"Does FBI Special Agent Doug Booker know about this?"

"Not in any detail. The Director and I think Doug should stay focused on eliminating the threat posed by the RAGs."

"I thought Mansfield was in charge of the RAGs investigation."

"He's been re-assigned. Mansfield has turned the ball over to Doug. He is now the man in charge."

This was more information than I had been prepared for. It was not easy to process.

"Do you really believe these local jihadists are capable of doing something like you've described?

He nodded.

"They are fully capable and they intend to do it soon. We believe they need a little more training, but they have the will and determination, right now."

"This is horrible. I don't want to believe it could happen here."

"It is what it is."

"Please, God, not this" I prayed.

CHAPTER 40

"I can't do it, John." Gary said. "I told Watkins I would be seriously interested in joining a group that was committed to seeing changes made in America. I told him I wasn't interested in the RAGs, because it seemed to me it is mostly just a bunch of immature belly-achers and posers. Young wannabe Nazis, covered in tattoos. I told him, that sort of thing, just didn't interest me.

He said he knew what I meant and agreed the image of the group was pretty pathetic. He told me there's actually a group within the group, real men who share my point of view. He told me these men are dedicated to action, not just demonstration, but violent action.

I told him I could join a group like that."

"How did he respond?"

"A couple of days later he told me they had checked me out. They have some pretty good sources. They knew my step father had been in the KKK. They knew I had been in the fire department. There are some pretty racist people in the department, just like any other group of people in the south, so I guess it wasn't a problem. They knew I worked part time as a private detective. They even knew I worked for you, specifically."

"Is that a problem?"

"No, he seemed to think it was interesting. You are sort of famous around here. He asked what I did for you. I told him I just did surveillance of people suspected of cheating on their spouses."

"So what's the problem?"

"He said there's an initiation or a bona fide that's required from anyone who wants to join up."

I closed my eyes for a moment. I knew what was coming.

"What is it?"

"Watkins said I would have to kill one of the 'mud people'. ... So, that's the end of it. I'm out of this thing, John."

"Did you tell him that?"

"No, I said I figured I could do it. He went on to tell me, I would have to prove I had done it."

"How? There might be some way we could fake it."

"I don't see how. I asked him if he had done it himself, and he kind of puffed up, real proud like, and told me he had killed a 'wet back', and showed the body to some of the members of the group."

"That, my friend, was a murder confession."

"I know, but there's more. He pulled out the pocket knife he carries and showed it to me. He told me it was the same knife he had used to 'stick that Mexican pig'. He was real proud of the fact he had killed the man with his own knife."

I took a deep breath.

"I need to talk this over with Doug and Tony. Don't do or say anything else about this, until Doug or I get back to you."

"There isn't anything I can do. I just want out."

"I understand, Gary, but they're not going to let you just walk away. You know too much."

"You've got to help me, man."

"Calm down. They don't expect you to just go out and kill someone today. I'll get with Doug, and we'll figure out what to do. You'll hear from one of us, shortly. In the meantime, just go on about your job, as usual. Act like you don't have a care in the world, and believe God will make a way."

"That's easy for you to say..."

I called Doug and arranged to have him meet me at Tony's office.

"It shouldn't be a problem. All he needs is a dead body," Doug observed.

"No. We'll go ahead and arrest Watkins on the homicide charge. Gary can testify against him and you federal boys can arrange to get Gary into the witness protection program." Tony said it, like there was no other option.

"I'm afraid that's not going to happen. He knew what he was doing when he went into this thing, and he's just going to have to see it through to the end." Doug replied.

"He's scared to death. How do you propose to pass him off as a stone cold killer?" I asked.

"Forget it, there's no way I'm going to sit back and let a private citizen be jerked around like this." Tony stated.

Doug looked at me.

"Will you explain to the Lieutenant here, that he doesn't get to dictate anything to us? This is a matter of national security and I'm running this show, not him."

Tony stood up from behind his desk and pointed his finger at Doug.

"You listen to me, hot shot. If you have something to say to me, you look me in the eye and say it. You treat me like I'm a child, and you're the one who'll get spanked."

"Take it easy, Tony. It isn't anything personal. The feds just love to pull that 'matter of national security' line, like you or I would pull a gun." I advised.

"I don't care about their agenda, and neither should you. Gary is a friend. You can't let these guys use him, like a worm on a hook." Tony glared at me.

I looked Tony in the eye.

"I know, buddy. I advised Gary not to do this. I told him straight up that once he started into this mess, he couldn't back out. All we can do is support him and help in any and every way we can. But Doug is right, the feds are running this. If you try to 'kick against the pricks'... It won't do any good, and it will only hurt you."

Tony slammed his hand down on his desk.

Doug spoke up.

"Look, Tony, I understand how you feel. I've already promised John, and now I'm promising you - I will personally do anything I can to protect Gary in this thing. OK?".

Tony sat down again.

"Well how exactly do you propose to do that?" he asked.

"This isn't the first time we've encountered this kind of thing. Our undercover operatives get put into all sorts of compromising situations. This one is actually pretty simple. Gary isn't being asked to commit a murder in front of witnesses. We've seen that plenty of times. In this case, all he has to do is present a dead body and claim he killed the person."

"How is he supposed to pull it off?"

"We'll locate a suitable dead body, even if we have to have one flown in, and then we'll arrange for Gary to show it to whoever needs to see it."

"You make it sound so simple."

"... Piece of cake." Doug replied.

I knew it had to be much more difficult and complex than Doug had indicated. Gary needed the dead body of a person of color. The body had to be fresh and killed in a manner that would appear to be Gary's handiwork. It couldn't be a death that would cause attention from family or friends. The person's death or disappearance couldn't be widely reported, because someone would figure out Gary couldn't have had anything to do with it. The FBI had to find the right body and arrange for Gary to take delivery of it. This would probably involve violating several laws related to the handling of the remains. We had to create a story of how and why Gary had killed the victim, and it had to be good enough to be believable. We had to figure out some way to plant a fake story in the local news that would appear to support Gary's story.

It only took three more days, for it all to come together.

CHAPTER 41

"They're flying the body in from New Orleans. The guy was killed about two hours ago, in a shootout with the local P.D. down there. It was a drug bust, gone bad. The guy was not a stranger to the NOPD and he has no known relatives. The story will barely get a mention in the local press down there, and no description of the victim will be given.

He's a black male, about 28 years old. He died of a single gunshot wound to the head. The FBI was on the scene, because they were preparing to intercept a cargo coming into the Port of New Orleans, when the shooting took place right in front of the local agents."

Doug reported.

"We'll set the chopper down in a remote area, where Gary can prepare a shallow grave. Then, he'll call Watkins and tell him he has something to show him." He continued.

I had all sorts of reservations.

"What will his story be? Who was the guy supposed to be, and how did Gary supposedly kill him?" I asked.

"We'll have Gary say he saw the guy hitchhiking, near Kilgore. He picked him up and took him to the grave site and shot him in the head."

"No, it won't work, Doug. There won't be any evidence of the killing at the scene. He'll have to say he killed him somewhere else and is burying him far from that location." I pointed out.

"It doesn't matter where he says he did it. It's dark and will be even darker where we'll dump the body. We'll plant a story in the local paper and on the TV news, about a missing young black man. We'll say he was last seen somewhere close to wherever Gary is supposed to have killed him." Doug said.

"This has far too many things that can go wrong with it. We need to buy some time. Gary needs some time to prepare and wrap his head around this. A helicopter flying into the same place where the body will be buried might attract too much attention. Gary can meet the chopper wherever they want to land it, offload the body, and haul it to wherever he wants to put the shallow grave. He can call Watkins from the scene, and arrange to show him the body, first thing in the morning. That will give us some time to get set up." I said.

"Set up for what?" Doug asked.

"We need to get some of your agents into position where they can provide onsite backup for Gary. Don't' you want to have pictures of Watkins at the scene?" I asked. "That would be hard to do in the dark, without him noticing."

"Yeah, and he might even bring somebody else with him to view the body." Doug observed.

"He might, at that."

Doug picked up his telephone.

An hour later, we were gearing up to go out to the place Gary had indicated he would dig the grave.

"Game cameras, you've got to be kidding?" Doug asked.

"No, we've used them before. They can be quite effective. The problem is getting them placed and hidden from human eyes."

"That wouldn't be easy to do in the dark. No, Gary has picked a place that's low and kind of torn up, from logging. According to GPS and the satellite imagery, it should be easy to get on higher ground above the grave site. We'll be able to use state of the art lenses and get great images from two or three hundred yards away."

He was right. His team's cameras probably would produce better pictures and the photographers might be able to move around unobserved to get better angles.

Doug was watching me think it through.

"Don't worry, John; my guys have done this a lot. They've taken pictures at everything from sporting events to mob funerals. Nobody will see them."

As the sun came up, Doug and I were positioned about a quarter of a mile above the grave site, on the edge of the woods, beside the fifty or so acres of land that had recently been clear cut. Below us, scattered here and there, were piles of brush, limbs and whole discarded trees, ready to be burned. Gary had chosen the spot, because no one would notice a freshly dug grave on land which had so recently been torn up by heavy equipment.

We could see Gary's truck where it was parked on the far side of the lot, at the edge of the logging road. Gary had spent the last couple of hours trying to sleep in his truck, after he finished covering the body with a tarp and a thin coat of dirt.

What we couldn't see, were the other agents and snipers hidden in and around the acreage, ready to leap to Gary's defense, if or when Doug gave the signal on his radio.

My eyes were grainy from lack of sleep. We had

arrived at the location a little after two o'clock in the morning. It had taken the better part of two hours to position the photographers and snipers. I knew there were half a dozen men hidden in and around the fifty acres of clear cut, but I couldn't spot a single one of them, anywhere.

I continued to slowly scan the entire woodlot with my high powered binoculars, still seeing nothing.

Gary had called Watkins at just after midnight and arranged to have him meet him at six thirty. He had given him detailed directions on how to find the woodlot.

At six twenty, Doug put his hand to his ear for a second.

"We have two vehicles approaching on the logging road, a truck and an SUV." He said

Doug keyed his mic and gave the final instructions.

Even at this hour in the morning, it was about eighty degrees. The air was damp with the morning dew and I figured the humidity was at about eighty percent. Maybe that was why I was sweating. The thick dust and sand were sticking to my clothes. The air was heavy with the smell of cut timber and crushed vegetation.

I saw the occasional flash of a vehicle through the trees, before I heard the vehicles approaching, then they came out of the forest and stopped behind Gary's truck, briefly obscuring our view, as the dust quickly settled.

Two men got out of the pick-up. I recognized Watkins from the photos provided by the FBI. Two more men got out of the SUV.

I had no idea who any of the three strangers were, but they looked rough and ready for anything.

Gary stepped out of his truck and greeted Watkins. From our position uphill from where Gary and the men were, we couldn't hear what they were saying, but the binoculars brought every detail into sharp focus.

We had considered putting a wire on Gary to monitor and record the conversation, but abandoned the idea, in favor of Gary's safety. It was a good thing we hadn't put a wire on him; because two of the men grabbed him and a third man searched him thoroughly. He found the .40 caliber handgun the FBI had provided Gary, and tucked it behind his back.

Watkins had watched the search without any obvious concern.

The two men holding Gary shoved him against the tailgate of his truck, and then all four men fanned out in front of him, two of the men produced hand guns, holding them down at their sides.

I looked at Doug.

He shook his head slightly.

I put the binoculars back on the group below us. They were having a conversation.

I watched Gary closely. I could see he was scared. He appeared to be telling the story we had briefly rehearsed. It all came down to this. Could he convince them?

A moment later, one of the men made a gesture toward the woodlot.

Gary led the four of them over to where he had dug the grave, at the edge of one of the big piles of forest debris.

From where we were, the pile of debris nearly blocked our view. All we could see were the heads of the men as they watched Gary bend over and pull the tarp away from the body.

Another conversation ensued.

The other men disappeared from view for a moment as they examined the body more closely.

When they stood back up, the man who had Gary's handgun, pulled it out and dropped the clip, pocketing it. He ejected the shell in the chamber and bent over to pick it up. He handed that bullet to Gary, then he thumbed the slide closed and dry fired the gun. He put the clip back in and handed the pistol back to Gary.

Gary looked up the hill, directly at where we were hidden. He took off his cap and smoothed his hair down, jerking the cap back on. It was the all clear sign.

I breathed a sigh of relief.

All five men engaged in another brief conversation. It looked as though Watkins was introducing Gary to the other men. They were shaking hands all around.

Shortly, Watkins and the others walked back to their vehicles and climbed inside.

As they drove away, Gary was busy burying the body.

CHAPTER 42

"I've never been so afraid in my life. At first, I thought they were on to me and they were just going to kill me. I swear, my knees were actually knocking."

Gary was talking fast, the adrenaline rushing through his blood stream.

"They started by asking me if I was a cop, then they wanted to know why I wanted to join their group. I didn't know what was going to happen. I didn't know what I was saying. I tried to remember the story, but I felt like I was just babbling. It's a wonder I didn't wet myself."

"What do you think caused them to change their minds?" SAIC Doug Booker asked.

"It was the body. When they saw that man's body; it was what really convinced them. They saw me, the body and the gun. They put two and two together and it was enough! One of them complimented me on the shot placement! Another guy said he thought I had picked a good place to dispose of the body."

Doug slapped Gary on the back.

"This was the desired outcome, Gary. So, I expect we have some excellent photos, but it will speed things along if you can remember their names." Doug prompted.

"Right, right, let's see... The guy on the right of

Watkins was named Tommy Turner, the guy next to him on his left was Bill Brown, and the other, older guy was named... Scott something, it started with an... Gosh, I can't remember his name."

Gary was actually trembling, just enough that I could see the tremor in his hands. This was evidence of the adrenaline leaving his blood stream.

"It's OK; chances are it will come back to you. The important thing is you did great, really great. We were watching you the whole time. I never doubted you for a moment."

"Now what happens?" Gary asked, dully.

I could see he was starting to feel the let-down after the exhilaration of the adrenaline rush.

"You go on about your business, Gary. If all goes well, at some point, they'll contact you about the next step." Doug replied.

"Oh, does that mean I'm done here?"

"Yes, you can head on out. We'll finish up here."

Gary looked around.

"What's left to do?"

"We'll all need to be picked up, for one thing. We don't have any transportation here."

"I could give y'all a ride out to the county road, if you want to pile into the back of my truck." Gary offered.

"No, that's fine. You go on. They may be watching for you to come out of this place."

"Right, OK then, I'm outta here." Gary said.

Doug shook his hand.

"Again, Gary, thanks, you did a great job. You let one of us know the moment they contact you."

I gave Gary the thumbs up sign, as he headed for his truck.

As Gary drove away, other agents began to show themselves, slowly working out the kinks from the cramped conditions they had been in for the last few hours.

A backpack with several bottles of water in it appeared. We all sucked the water down greedily.

Doug called for the extraction team.

"OK, gentlemen; flip a coin to figure out who gets to dig up the body." Doug instructed.

"What if they come back to see it again?" I asked.

"Well, they'll be SOL, because by one o'clock this afternoon, that body will be on ice in the morgue in New Orleans. This guy will only have gone missing for less than eighteen hours. No one is expected to claim the remains, but if someone does; he'll be right where he's supposed to be."

"Our tax dollars at work." I observed.

"Uncle Sam is the helpful hardware man."

"Yeah, but if the body spends much more time in this heat, he won't be anything like hardware. I expect that fact alone will keep them from coming back to see it again. Not to mention, nobody likes digging in this heat."

Doug wiped sweat away from under the camo boonie cap he was wearing.

"It isn't even eight o'clock in the morning yet, and I'll bet its well over eighty degrees. I hate Texas in the summer time." He stated.

"Where are you from, Doug?"

"Eureka, California."

"You ain't seen nothing yet, amigo. Wait till August." I said, as I watched two FBI agents digging up the body.

I imagined this was not the glamorous life they had signed on for when they decided to join the FBI.

Shortly later, three, big, black SUVs came down the logging road in a cloud of dust, I was glad I would get to ride in the command vehicle with Doug, instead of the one with the hot, black vinyl 'bag o' body', in the cargo space.

We loaded up and headed for Tyler.

Doug looked over at me.

"I've got to tell you. I didn't really have much faith

Gary could pull it off."

"It all came down to faith. I trust in God. So does Gary."

"Yeah, I heard you were some kind of a religious fundamentalist. However it worked out, I'm glad it did. We've got great pictures of the men and the license plates. We'll upload them with the names and have positive ID and addresses within the hour."

"What will you do with the information?"

"I'll advise my superiors at Quantico and they'll send it on to the US Attorney General, requesting permission to collect evidence via wire-tap and ultimately to issue arrest warrants."

"You're certain the RAGs are getting ready to launch a strike that's likely to result in a number of people being hurt or killed. Is that correct?"

Doug nodded, grimly.

"Is Gary the best source of evidence you have?"

Doug rubbed his jaw with one hand.

"Probably so, we have informants in prison, members of the Righteous Army of God who have told us there is a conspiracy and some of the possible plans, but no names and nothing we can arrest any- one for. We have another guy inside the 'RAGs', but he's on the fringes with the punks. Gary has gotten inside the dangerous circle and that's what we need."

I thought about what might happen next. I re- membered something Doug had said.

"Earlier, when you referred to me as a religious fundamentalist, did I detect some scorn in that?" I asked him.

"I'm just sick and tired of you religious people talking about your god. If there is a god, he, she, or it, is a vicious and brutal bully. I don't like thugs of any kind, but the concept of a heavenly being, one who picks and chooses who lives and who dies, disgusts me."

"That's because you don't have any idea what God is really like."

"… Which god, the one that inflicts horrific diseases on the world, destroys whole communities with catastrophic storms and earthquakes, the one who will drop a church roof on his groveling worshipers, just for grins, or the one who sends his faithful out to murder innocent people in his name?"

"Again, you have a distorted understanding of who God is."

"All I know is that you weirdoes, who claim to serve some god, are a dangerous bunch of mentally deficient fanatics. As far as I'm concerned, there is no difference between you, the RAGs, or the proponents of Islam. The world won't be a better place until all you religious people are rotting in the ground."

I hadn't expected a vitriolic response like that.

"Why are you so bitter?"

"Why are you so delusional?"

I didn't reply.

We rode the rest of the way in silence.

CHAPTER 43

That afternoon, Doug was very grim as he briefed Tony, Jack and me on the IDs of the men who had arrived on the scene at the burial site. He had already alerted his agents.

"The name Gary couldn't remember is, Scott Hollister," he said.

"... The same Scott Hollister who ran for the state Senate?" Tony asked.

Doug nodded.

"He has millions. He inherited a fortune from his father's frozen foods business, and then he made another fortune in investment banking. He has that new industrial development right by the interstate in Longview. Everything he touches turns to gold."

"He owns a huge mansion right off highway 80, just east of Longview. His face is on billboards, but I didn't recognize him this morning." I said.

Doug shrugged, and added, "Tommy Turner is a ranking officer in the Smith County Sheriff's office."

"What? I know him." Tony said, clearly stunned.

"The other guy, Brown, owns a trucking company in Rusk County. He's the only one with a criminal record. Two DWIs and one assault charge." Doug added.

We all considered the new information.

"You're telling us, all three of those guys are

members of the radical wing of the RAGs? They have nothing in common." Tony said.

"Don't forget to add Watkins to the mix." I said.

Doug nodded.

"Racism and Christianity is what they have in common, and maybe they enjoyed punk rock when they were younger." Doug replied.

"Sin is what they have in common. They're expressing hate and rage, directing it against the government and people of color, but their problem is more… essential. The sin of hatred has nothing to do with Christianity. It stems from some personal hurt, or inability to recognize their individual fears, limitations and failures. They form a bond of racism. A psychologist might say racism was a form of projection" I said.

"Whatever! You say potatoes…" Doug started.

"No, John is right. Racial hatred is just an expression of a deeper more personal issue. Maybe even ignorance. It doesn't really matter though. The point is we have to stop them." Jack spoke up.

We all nodded in agreement.

"We have enough evidence against Watkins to arrest him on the murder charge, right now." Tony pointed out.

"I think we need to wait on that." I said.

"I thought you were the guy who wanted to see justice done for the dead Mexican."

Doug said, clearly showing irritation.

"Justice, yes I do. I don't want to see Gary implicated in the arrest of Watkins though. Watkins is just one spoke in a bigger wheel."

Doug frowned.

"When I sweat Watkins, I can leave out any reference to information we got from Gary."

"I'm not sure you can, or that he won't figure it out. Besides, there are other people taking a pretty close look at Gary."

"That's a chance we'll just have to take. We need

to flip Watkins right now." Doug said.

"We didn't know a ranking officer in the Sheriff's Department was a part of this. What happens when we arrest Watkins? We can't put him in the Smith County jail." Tony was thinking out loud.

"We arrest him, bring him here to the federal building, and put the screws to him. Once I flip him, he won't be going to jail." Doug stated.

I looked at Jack. He nodded back, imperceptibly.

"I think we'd better hold off on arresting him. You have Gary inside the same group Watkins is in. Gary doesn't need to be flipped. If you snatch up Watkins, it will send up all kinds of red flags, which might jeopardize Gary's position. We need Gary on the inside. He's more valuable to us. Later, we can arrest Watkins, anytime we want to." Jack suggested.

"My orders are to arrest Watkins and flip him. End of story." Doug said.

"Those were your orders before Gary passed his initiation this morning." I observed.

"I would remind you, as you are so fond of pointing out, you're a civilian. I'm in charge of this investigation. So shut up." Doug snapped.

I saw both Jack and Tony stiffen at that last part Jack cleared his throat.

"John, would you mind stepping out. Those of us who have official capacities in this investigation need to have a few words in private" He met my eyes.

"Sure, I apologize if I've over stepped my…"

"Thanks, we'll keep you in the loop." Jack interrupted. He pointed toward the door.

I nodded, got up from my seat and left the three of them in the Federal building.

Tony called on my cell phone as I was driving to my office.

"The feds aren't going to arrest Watkins right now." He said.

"That's a relief."

"Yes, it is. Let me tell you what happened. After you left, Doug relaxed quite a bit and started talking about planning the arrest. Jack stopped him and asked him to call the Director of the FBI. The Director, John! It really confused Doug. Jack asked Doug if he would make the call, or would he prefer that Jack did it. Doug asked him why he should call the Director of the FBI. Jack just held up his cell phone and hit a speed dial button. He put the phone on speaker mode and set it on Doug's desk. When the ringing stopped, Director Driscoll answered!"

"Oh my…"

"I know, right? Anyway, Director Driscoll said, "Is that you, Jack?" to which Jack replied it was and he was sitting in Special Agent Doug Booker's office here in Tyler, Texas, with me in attendance. "How do you do, Lieutenant Escalante," the Director said…"

"I don't need to hear all that, Tony."

"Oh, right. The upshot of it was, Director Driscoll told Doug he should follow the advice of Agent McCarthy, whom he held in high esteem! I thought Doug was going to puke."

"Yeah, Jack has always had a certain flare for the dramatic."

"J.W., who is he exactly, that he has the Director of the FBI on speed dial?"

"If I told you, I'd have to kill you."

Tony chuckled.

"Then I don't really want to know. I guess he's some kind of high level spook."

"He's very high level, Tony."

"I get the impression life as we've known it, is never going to be the same."

"No, I'm afraid it won't be the same, and it won't be better, either. I suspect we are going to see changes that will cause great sorrow."

"Well then, 'the just shall live by faith', right?"

"Till He returns or calls us home."

CHAPTER 44

The next day, I was watching one of the morning network news channels. I like to channel surf for stories that don't include Hollywood scandals, weight loss or foolish political behavior. I was drawn to an announcement that the Vatican and Pope Gregory III were calling for the re-building of the temple in Jerusalem. The United Nations and Secretary General, Hosan Mushareff, were in complete support. They were all in agreement the temple could be re-built without encroaching on the sacred Al-Aqsa mosque commonly known as the Dome of the Rock.

"If the Holy of Holies is built to the same proportions as the Tabernacle in the wilderness, there will be plenty of room for the building and the inner court yard. The outer courtyard would be the entire world." The Pope was saying.

I was startled to learn how much of the Arab world seemed to be open to the idea.

My phone rang and caller ID indicated it was Gary.

"Hey Gary, what's up?"

"Morning, John. I just wanted to touch base."

"How's it going? Have you learned anything useful?"

"No nothing new, so far, John. I'm going to be overseeing a small building demolition job down in Bullard, starting today. I won't see Watkins at all. He's overseeing a bigger project outside of Chandler. They're building some apartments and he'll be tied up with that for the rest of the month. You might want to pass that along."

"OK. Is there anything I can do for you?"

"No. I just wanted to check in."

I could tell he was feeling isolated.

"It sounds like you'll be getting a break from some of the drama for at least a little while." I observed.

"Yeah, I suppose so."

"Don't feel like you're out there all alone. You can call me any time, day or night. If you just want to talk about football, we can do that."

"Since you mentioned it, did you see the game Monday night?"

I chuckled.

"Yeah, I did. Do you remember when it was unusual for a game to have a combined score of more than forty points?"

"I know, right? Now it's common to see sixty or seventy combined points in a game..."

We talked about football for a few minutes and ended the call.

The next morning, a little before ten o'clock, I was sitting at my desk when my cell phone rang.

"John, this is Doug Booker. Can you come down here to my office?"

"Sure Doug, when do you want me there?"

"Come now, John. There's been an incident."

"Is Gary alright?"

"We don't know. Please come down here right now."

I couldn't get to the Federal building. There were police barricades for two square blocks around both that building and the courthouse, on the square. I had to park about a quarter of a mile away and walk back to a barricade. I introduced myself to a uniformed officer and told him that I had been summoned by the SAIC of the FBI office. The officer got on his radio and a supervisor showed up. I explained the situation to the supervisor, who got on his radio. He examined my ID. Eventually the supervisor got permission to let me through. He had been instructed to escort me.

"What's going on?" I asked him, as we walked toward the Federal building.

"I'm not at liberty to say much. I can tell you what's already being reported on the news though. Both the Sheriff and the DA of Gregg County have been shot, outside the courthouse, in Longview. The DA is dead. The Sheriff is in critical condition at Good Shepherd."

As we approached the Federal building, the heat was stifling. I figured that the mercury was probably somewhere north of a hundred degrees. I had already sweated through my shirt. I also knew that, a cold front was forecast to blow in and drop the thermometer by thirty or forty degrees in a matter of hours. I could see storm clouds building to the northwest, a "blue norther" on the horizon.

I could also see police snipers on the surrounding rooftops.

At the entrance, we were met by an FBI agent wearing a black jacket with the gold letters F, B, I, emblazoned on it. He had a matching black ball cap with the same markings.

The police supervisor introduced me to the agent, who I now recognized from a previous meeting. On that occasion, he had been wearing cammo tactical gear, and carrying an assault rifle.

We left the supervisor on the stairs and went up into the building.

Ordinarily, you can't get into the Federal building without passing through the metal detectors, and being greeted by uniformed officers. That was not the case today. There were heavily armed officers everywhere, but because members of the general public were not being permitted anywhere near the building, the metal detector was not in use.

The situation in the workroom outside Doug's office was organized chaos. There were FBI agents and others, shouting into telephones and radios. Some were focused on their computer monitors, and people were milling about engaged in who knows what. The agent escorting me knocked on Doug's door and pushed it open.

"Come in John," Doug said.

He was sitting on the edge of his desk facing Jack, who was standing.

Jack McCarthy was clearly there in his capacity as a ranking officer in the Department of Homeland Security. He nodded his greeting.

"What all has happened?" I asked, as I closed the door.

"It's a serious 'Charlie Foxtrot', John. We have a dead DA, in Longview. The Gregg County Sheriff was shot as well, and several pipe bombs were found at the courthouse in Longview." Doug said.

"Was Gary involved?" I asked.

"We don't know any details at this point, but we're pretty damned sure the RAGs did this." Doug said.

I looked at Jack.

"This is what we know so far," he started. "This is a court hearing day in Gregg County and the courthouse was crowded. The Gregg County Sheriff and the District Attorney were standing on the lawn outside the Gregg County courthouse, when a silver SUV stopped in the street. Four armed gunmen got out and opened fire on them. Both men were cut down immediately. Fortunately, the Sheriff was wearing a vest. He was able to return fire, and at least one of the gunmen was hit. The four gunmen retreated to the SUV and escaped. Meanwhile, inside the courthouse when the gunfire started, a sheriff's deputy had just found a backpack containing several pipe bombs. We don't know why none of them were detonated."

"Did the Sheriff or witnesses to the shooting get a good look at the gunmen or the car?"

"Obviously we're working all of that right now, John," Doug said. "We are also examining video from all of the outdoor security cameras in the city of Longview."

"The gunmen were wearing ski masks, John." Jack added.

I considered several different aspects of the information that I had just been given.

"Do we know where Gary or Watkins is, right now?" I asked.

Jack and Doug shot each other a look.

"No, we've been busy with other things. That's why we asked you to come down here. Don't you know where Gary or Watkins is supposed to be working today?"

I nodded in response.

"Gary told me that he would be overseeing a work crew doing demolition of a building in Bullard, south of Tyler. That's in Cherokee County. Watkins was supposed to be managing a bigger crew, building an apartment building outside Chandler. That's in Henderson County. I don't know if that's where they are though."

Doug hit a button on his desk phone.

"Green, get in here," he snapped.

My phone rang. I saw that the call was from Christine, so I answered it.

"Hey, Christine," I said, by way of greeting.

"John, have you seen the news?"

"No, I'm a little busy right now. I'm in the Federal

building, downtown."

"Oh, OK… OH! So you know what's happening…"

"A little bit, yeah. Listen, I need you to try to get Gary on the phone. He's supposed to be on that job site down in Bullard. If you can't get him on the phone, go down there and find him. Pretend to be his girlfriend or something. I need to talk to him right away. Have him call me."

"Have you tried to call him?"

"No, I want him to call me. I'll explain later."

"Ok, I'm on it. Be careful," she added before she broke the connection.

A man came rushing into the room.

"Agent Green, we need to know if a man by the name of Kevin Watkins is presently working on an apartment building construction location outside the city of Chandler. I mean, is he there now, and has he been there all day? I need you to get me that answer, immediately. One other thing, listen now, do not, I repeat, DO NOT attract any attention while you are getting those answers. It is imperative that no one knows that the FBI is trying to locate that man. Got it?" Doug asked.

"Yes sir, I've got it. Kevin…?"

"Watkins. Now get out of here and get me my answers."

Two more men walked into Doug's office. I recognized one of them immediately. He wore a starched and creased white shirt; open at the neck, with no tie, over dark brown pants. He was also wearing a straw cowboy hat. There was a gold star pinned to the shirt. He was Charles Parker, the Sheriff of Smith County.

The other man was similarly dressed, but he wore creased khaki pants, a dark green tie, and his silver badge was smaller. It was just a small star inside a circle that bore a simple message; "Department of Public Safety" scrolled at the top, and "Texas Ranger", at the bottom. There was a single word on the star; Captain.

Both men glanced at me.'

"Sheriff Parker, Captain O'Brian, this is John Wesley Tucker. He is assisting us in our investigation." Doug said, by way of introduction.

"Yeah, I thought I recognized you. I saw you on a crime scene. That child abduction case, and there was all that TV coverage around the trial, last year." The Sheriff said.

"Yes sir. I remember seeing you at that trailer in the woods, while every law enforcement officer in two counties was trying to figure out who had jurisdiction."

He nodded, shaking my hand.

"You can call me Chuck," he said, as he turned to address Doug.

"Agent Booker, we know that this building and the Smith County courthouse are clear. I intend to remove the barricades around the courthouse and the square. What's the progress on the general threat assessment?"

"We are still attempting to gather data. We are analyzing and processing that data as rapidly as we acquire it."

"Yeah, but do you think that there is any kind of imminent danger?"

"We are unable to give you a quantified answer at this time."

"Bullshit. Yes or no, are we expecting to be attacked today, here in Tyler, or not?"

"Sheriff Parker, we just don't know." Doug explained.

"Terrific." Sheriff Parker said, with a frown.

He turned to leave Doug's office, opening the door again.

"We'll alert you the minute we know something, one way or the other." Doug called out to him, as he left the room.

Sheriff Parker did not respond. He walked out of the room leaving the door wide open.

I went over and closed it.

CHAPTER 45

Ranger Captain O'Brian, hadn't left with the Sheriff, and I was wondering why he had stayed in the room.

He seemed to sense my thought.

"The Sheriff was pretty upset to learn his department is being investigated by the Rangers because at least one of his deputies is a white supremacist. He would like to personally pistol whip that guy. Now this thing in Longview... He's mad as hell." He said.

Doug nodded his understanding.

"Doug, I have my associate trying to get in touch with Gary. I don't want to call him, in case someone else answers his phone..." I started.

Gary called me as I was in mid-explanation.

"Hello, this is John. How may I direct your call?" I answered.

"Hey, John, it's me, Gary. Christine said I should call you. What's up?"

"Where are you, right now?"

"I'm here in Bullard, on the demo job."

"Gary, there's been an attack on the Gregg County courthouse in Longview. The District Attorney was killed and the Sheriff is badly wounded."

"No shit? Oh man, that's awful."

"I just wanted to make sure you weren't involved."

"What, why would I… Oh, you think the RAGs did it?"

"Seems likely, don't you think?"

"I don't know anything about it. This is the first I've heard."

"Good, I just wanted to make sure you're OK."

"Yeah, about that… Watkins told me I'm supposed to meet with the other members and leaders this evening."

"When and where?"

"I don't know where. I'm supposed to meet somebody at the place where I buried the body of that black guy, at six o'clock this evening. You know what a remote spot that is. I guess they'll take me to the meeting from there."

"How long have you known about the meeting?"

"… Maybe ten minutes, I'd just gotten off the phone with Watkins, when Christine called me."

"Gary, call me back in a few minutes. I need to discuss this with someone."

"Yeah, I'm pretty worried about it now."

"Don't worry; we've got your back."

"OK, bye," He said, and hung up.

The three men were waiting to hear what I had to say.

"Gary is at the job site in Bullard. He hadn't even heard about the attack in Longview."

"Well, that's a relief. Now we need to know if Watkins had anything to do with it," Doug observed.

"We may be in luck on that score."

"… How?" Jack asked.

"Gary is supposed to be taken to a meeting of the RAGs radicals, tonight."

"When and where?" Doug asked, picking up his phone.

"Hold on, this is an opportunity for him to get further inside the group." Jack said.

"No, we can't afford to wait and see. We'll raid the event and grab up everybody. I need to make an arrest in this attack." Doug responded.

I looked at Jack, who seemed to be thinking the same thing I was.

"Doug, we've just been cleared to have phone taps and surveillance on those guys Gary met out on that logging site. I'm pretty confident we'll gather some useful intel from the intercepted communications, but having Gary inside a meeting could be vital. I think we can tell the press that we are pursuing a number of leads at this point." Jack said.

"I don't care about the press. We've got to stop these guys before they do more harm."

"I think the best way to do that, and be able to make the charges stick, is to gather more intel. We don't have any real evidence that the RAGs even did this. We have to find out who was involved. Gary is in the best position to do that," Jack prompted.

Doug put down the phone.

"Right, I see that. I guess I just got a little bit wound up."

"This is enough to get anybody wound up. I can tell you Gary is plenty wound up himself." I said. "We've got to figure out the best way to manage this situation."

"Well then, I repeat, when and where is Gary supposed to meet these people?"

"This evening, someone is going to meet him in the same place where he buried that body. He thinks they'll take him to the meeting from there."

I was thinking Gary had to be wondering if he might be the next body to be left in a shallow grave out in the sticks.

"OK, we'll set up surveillance just like we did the first time. We'll put a wire on him this time though..." Doug started.

"No, no wire, it's too dangerous" I said.

"You don't get to tell me what I can and can't do.

This is a Federal operation and a matter of national security. I would remind you that you have no official standing, and you're involvement can be terminated at any time." Doug snarled.

"Fine, I'll give Gary a call and tell him to bail out. Good luck with your investigation."

Just then, an agent knocked on the door and stepped in.

"Sir, we think we've figured out why the pipe bombs failed."

Doug took a deep breath.

"Well spit it out, man." He snapped.

"Yes sir, it was the phones."

"What phones? Doug asked.

"It was the cell phones sir; they were using cell phones as the detonators."

Doug made a gesture with both hands.

"And…?"

"… And, this is weird… but it looks like they dialed the wrong number."

"How did you come to that conclusion?" Jack asked.

"The phone records, sir. I'll tell you this, it's a damn good thing that the deputy who found the bombs, pulled the wires away from those phones when he did."

"Slow down, Agent Rogers…" Jack said. "Tell us how you figured this out."

"Yes sir, when we learned that the detonator was a cell phone, we had all the cell towers in and around Gregg County shut down. It was too late of course. It was more than twenty minutes after the bombs were found before we got all the cell service shut down, but then we accessed all of the carrier's call records, from five minutes before, and about five minutes after the shooting, sent to us. We found that there were three calls at about the same time as the shooting, to one specific number that didn't get answered. That would have been at the time that the deputy found the bombs. Those three calls were followed by a fourth call, all four from the same number. That fourth call only had one digit different from the first three calls. It was the number for the detonator phone. If the deputy hadn't pulled those wires when he did, those bombs would have detonated." The agent concluded.

Jack nodded. "Amateurs," he said.

"Yes sir. The deputy told us that immediately after he pulled the wires from that phone, the phone vibrated in his hand."

"I'll bet that they had punched the wrong number into the speed dial. When they finally figured it out, they dialed it one number at a time, but by then it was too late." Jack speculated.

"Thank God," I said.

"Humph! There was no "god" involved. It was just blind luck and their stupidity." Doug responded.

"That was a mighty brave deputy. For all he knew, pulling those wires could have triggered the explosion. Unfortunately he also contaminated the evidence." Jack observed.

"Yes sir, but apparently he has some experience with electronics and explosives. He recognized the threat and was pretty confident when he pulled those wires. I figure he saved a bunch of lives in the process. He didn't handle the pipe bombs, so we may be able to lift some prints." The agent observed.

"Thank you Agent Rogers. Now try to determine who owns the phone that made those outgoing calls" Jack directed the agent.

"We're already on that sir. That number was a prepaid throwaway we believe was sold for cash at a truck stop near Dallas, same as the detonator phone."

When the agent had closed the door, Jack spoke to Doug.

"These guys may be rank amateurs, but we can't hope to get "lucky" again. I also say no to a wire being put on Gary. He's still brand new to the group and they won't take chances with him. They were pretty thorough when they searched him the first time. The important thing is that we follow them to the meeting. That means setting up a perimeter and staging our tracking vehicles."

Doug shrugged, conceding the point.

"We can track his truck, using his transponder for the GPS and emergency services that come standard with the vehicle." He said.

"Sure, if his truck goes to the meeting. Otherwise, we'll have to do it the old fashioned way, with surveillance vehicles. Weather permitting, we'll arrange for a chopper to maintain visual contact as well." Jack said.

His statement gave me an idea.

"That clear cut area is nearly a mile down a logging road from the nearest county road. We won't be able to stage many vehicles anywhere near that area, without them being spotted." I observed.

"Leave it to us, John. We know what we're doing." Doug said.

"I know you do, but you're used to operating in more urban environments. Around here, any time someone sees a helicopter, they check it out. About the only helicopters we see are air ambulances."

"Good point," Jack observed. "We'll use one of those."

"Ok, I'll get the ball rolling," Doug stated.

My phone rang.

It was Gary.

CHAPTER 46

I put Gary on speaker mode.

"Gary, I'm here with Doug and a couple of other guys. I have you on speaker so everyone can participate in the call. We want you to go ahead with the meeting this evening."

"I don't know… this just keeps getting worse."

"Gary, Doug here. We'll have you covered just like we did when you had that first meeting. You go on with them, and we'll have you under surveillance at all times. What we need you to do is try to remember everyone you meet. Learn as much as you can about recent events, and who might have been involved. Don't ask any questions that don't feel right to you, under the circumstances. Do what they tell you to do, and we'll get with you later, to de-brief you. OK?"

"I don't like the idea that they are going to meet me out in the middle of nowhere, and are supposed to carry me to some other location. What if they just kill me instead?"

Everyone in the room exchanged glances.

"Why would they do that, Gary?" I asked.

"I don't know… but what if they do?"

"Gary, listen to me. You are afraid of something that there is no evidence for. It isn't a real threat; it's just your imagination running away with you. We'll all be there to cover you, just like before. If they had some reason to kill you, you would already be dead. Wouldn't you?" I asked him.

"Yeah, I guess so."

"That's right! And we'll follow you to wherever they take you. We won't take our eyes off of you." Doug promised.

"Well, how are you going to do that?"

"We are preparing the plan right now. We'll have surveillance vehicles staged on every road and highway. No matter what direction they take, we'll be right there with you." Doug replied.

"Are you sure about that?"

"Don't even worry about it. We'll have you covered." Doug assured him.

We heard Gary take a deep breath.

"Yeah, OK. Please don't screw this up."

"Just handle it the way you handled that first meeting, and you'll be fine." I added.

When Gary hung up, I turned to Doug.

"He's really scared."

"Yes, I heard that. Like I told you, we know what we're doing. Now, there is something that we need you to do."

"Ok, what's that?"

"Get the hell out of the way." He said, through clenched teeth. "Like I said before, this is a federal investigation and you are not… It's time for you to stand down. From now on, Gary will communicate directly with me and me only. Do you understand what I'm saying?"

I waited a moment to compose myself.

"Yes, Agent Booker, I understand what you're saying. Gary would not be in this position if it weren't for me. You asked me to come down here. So, like I said before, if I'm out, he's out. If he's in, I'm in. I will not stand down and leave his life in your hands. Do you understand what I'm saying?"

"I'll have you arrested for…"

"No, you will not." Jack interjected. "John is right. He has been an essential part of this investigation from the beginning, and we still need him now. Our combined focus has to be on the matters at hand. Gary is the best lead we have at this time. What he learns tonight could be essential. Our job is to keep him safe and gather as much intel and evidence as we can in the process. Doug, I suggest that you start organizing the surveillance teams. I'll arrange for eyes in the sky."

"I would remind you that you are not in charge of this investigation Agent McCarthy. The FBI is the lead agency, not the DHS."

Jack smiled at him, a cold smile that I had seen before. He reached into his pocket and pulled out his phone.

"I would remind you, that in matters of national security, DHS is the coordinating agency. I have the Director of the FBI on speed dial. If I push that button Agent Booker, by six o'clock tonight, you will be on an airplane headed to Pocatello, Idaho, or some other stopping point, on the way to the end of your career. Try me and see."

I thought for a moment that Doug would do just that.

"No, I know that DHS has overall responsibility for these things. I don't mean to deny that, but…"

"Good, then we understand each other. John, will you come with me please?" Jack said, as he opened the door of Doug's office.

Jack didn't say a word as we left the Federal building.

Outside, he said, "Where's your truck? I'll drive you to it."

I didn't argue, the heat had hit us like a hammer when we left the building.

As we drove out of the lot, he spoke up.

"Doug is under a lot of pressure."

I nodded. "So is Gary, we all are."

"Yes, but this is Special Agent in Charge, Doug Booker's, first high profile situation. He has never managed an investigation of this complexity or an emergency situation like this, separately, let alone all at the same time. Tyler is not exactly a primary assignment for a career minded guy like Doug. This is his big break, and he wants to shine."

"I can't afford to have him make a mistake, with Gary's life on the line."

"He may surprise you. He hasn't made any mistakes so far. Sure, he's a little frayed around the edges, and pretty intense, but he's done everything by the book."

We had come to a barricade, and a couple of uniformed officers were moving it aside to let us out.

"I'm not sure that he can handle it." I stated.

Jack looked me in the eye.

"That is not something that you are in control of. Is it?"

And there it was. He was right. Nothing about this situation was mine to control. God alone knew what would happen, and only He could protect Gary.

As we pulled through the gap in the barricade, I sat in silence and contemplated those things.

"You're right. I am not in control of what happens next. No wonder Doug finds me annoying."

Jack smiled at that.

"That's not the real reason he finds you annoying."

"What is it then?"

"You are very open about your belief in God."

"Why is that a problem?"

"You are aware the Righteous Army of God, is supposed to be a group of white Christians?'

"They are not Christians. They're a hate group. There's nothing remotely Christian about hating anyone. They hate people who are not like them, particularly people of color, and pretty much every religion, Jews, Catholics, Hindus, Muslims, and whatever else. Since they aren't any of those, they just figure the only thing left to claim is "Christian". Christianity and the hatred of any person are mutually exclusive. Jesus said, "If anyone says, "I love God," and hates his brother, he is a liar; for he who does not love his brother whom he has seen, cannot love God whom he has not seen". Christians are called to love, even their enemies." I pointed out.

Jack shrugged in indifference.

"Hate is a funny thing. There's usually a reason when someone has a hate problem. What you don't know is that Doug's father was a Pentecostal preacher. I don't know the particulars of how he abused Doug, but he did abuse him, and he said that 'God told him to do it'."

I closed my eyes.

How many people have a distorted view of God as "Our Father in heaven" because of the relationship (or lack of one) that they had with their earthly father?

"The authorities eventually got involved. Doug's mom was a hopeless alcoholic, so Doug was placed in the foster care system. He has worked very hard to get where he is. He worked his way through college. Along the way, he was taught that the most horrific things that have happened in history were because of people's religious beliefs. He graduated with a degree in criminal justice, with a JD. He passed the bar in 2000, and went to work for a prestigious law firm in New York City."

"I guess he thinks he is a self-made man, pulled himself up by his own bootstraps, and all that." I observed.

"On September 11, 2001, his fiancée was working in Tower One of the World Trade Center, when Islamic jihadists attacked us in the name of Allah. She died in the flames and rubble."

I closed my eyes again.

Sometimes, I can't believe I'm such an idiot.

"He joined the FBI pretty much the next day," he concluded.

Jack pulled in behind my truck and stopped.

"Now, at this point in his career, he finds himself in Tyler, Texas, not New York, L.A., Chicago or even Dallas. No, he's in Tyler, Texas. You need to cut him some slack." Jack indicated.

"You're right, I didn't know any of that. I would point out however that you threatening to end his career could hardly be considered as cutting him some slack.

"It saved a lot of talk. We don't have time to waste on gentle suggestions." He replied

"So I can't be open about my relationship with the Creator?" I asked.

"Doug is anti-religion, not just Christianity, he hates all religions, but Christianity and Islam in particular. He's almost an "equal opportunity" hater. He knows a lot more about hate, than he does about love. Try to be sensitive to that."

I nodded, as I climbed out of Jack's car.

"… And, be back in his office by three o'clock." Jack yelled out his window, as he pulled away from the curb.

CHAPTER 47

Christine seldom misses anything. She practically pounced on me, as I walked into our office.

"Is Gary alright?

"Yes. Why do you ask?"

"Duh! I've been watching the news all day. Are you alright? You seem... burdened."

"I have a lot on my mind."

"John, please tell me what's happening with Gary."

"He's supposed to attend a meeting of the Righteous Army of God radicals this evening. We're planning to follow him and provide whatever protection we can."

"Did they kill that D.A. in Longview?"

"We don't know. No one has claimed responsibility."

"Why would they?"

"Whoever did it has an agenda. At some point they'll want the world to know who they are and why they did it."

"I heard some sort of bomb was found in the Gregg County courthouse."

"Yes, pipe bombs, but they failed to detonate. They botched this whole thing. Thank God."

"They killed the D.A."

"Sadly, yes. He was only a target of opportunity. Their planning was very imprecise. They wounded the Sheriff over there, but he is expected to recover and he shot at least one of the attackers. The bombs were crude. The whole thing was sloppy."

"Do you think maybe they learned their lesson and they won't try something like this again?"

"No. I'm pretty sure this was a first strike and the only thing they learned is that they need to do better planning."

"Why? Why are they doing this?"

"There have been several arrests and prosecutions of members of the RAGs in Gregg County. If the RAGs did it, In their minds it's a political statement. They'll make an announcement"

"No, a political statement would be 'I don't like the current administration' or 'I vote for the candidate, not the party'. What they did is murder."

"I understand. I'm just answering your question."

"John, why here? There have been arrests and prosecutions of members of the RAGs all over the country. The jails and prisons are full of white supremacists."

"That's the point. The leadership of the radical wing of the RAGs is right here in East Texas. They've decided they want to punish anyone who has opposed them. They are starting here, but they may be planning a bigger campaign. That's the reason Gary is doing what he's doing. With him inside, we'll learn who their leaders and footmen are and we'll be able to stop them."

"What is going on in this country? Why is there so much anger and open hatred?"

I looked at her.

"Christine, you know why."

She was thoughtful for a moment.

"So many people are frustrated and dissatisfied with the way things are, they lash out at anyone who interferes or seems to oppose their personal beliefs and agendas. We are no longer united by shared values or beliefs. Division is the order of the day."

"Why do suppose that's happened?"

"Maybe because we try to accept so much diversity, we have no core values in common. We no longer teach the Bible in our public schools, not even the Ten Commandments. Most Americans say they believe in God, but they don't attend church and they don't read their Bibles. People who consider themselves sophisticated and erudite reject even the notion of God, any form of deity."

"True, as a nation we have rejected God from our culture, and replaced Him with many gods."

"Do you think He is judging our nation?"

"I believe He has left us to enjoy the consequences of our choices. A nation that does not honor God will not be blessed by God. Without His blessing, grace, mercy and guidance, we are left to our own devices and vices."

"It's getting pretty ugly isn't it?"

"I suspect it's going to get a lot worse, here in this country and many other places. Everyone will do what is right in their own eyes. Under those conditions, anarchy is coming. Where there is anarchy, a strong leader will emerge and some form of order will be imposed, but it will not be God's order. Think Hitler, Stalin or Pol Pot."

"Surely not here in America?"

"Wait and see. Those who do not learn the lessons of history are doomed to re-live them. Those who reject God will be rejected by Him."

"How will we live in a world like that?"

"You'll live each day the same way we do now, by faith. God will always take care of His people, wherever they are. Take care of each other. Continue to be salt and light. Love your neighbors and try to lead them to the light. Continue to be faithful, until that day when he returns or calls us home."

Christine nodded.

"Until that day..."

CHAPTER 48

America's southern forests know no state boundaries. They stretch from Virginia in the East, to Texas in the west and include most of the south-eastern U.S. The city of Tyler is surrounded by forest land and forestry is a major part of the local economy.

By five o'clock that afternoon there were eight men hidden in and around a section of clear-cut timber-land situated on a hillside about eighteen miles east of Tyler. I was there with Doug and six other FBI agents. We were all wearing tactical camo gear and four of the agents were snipers. We had chosen hiding places that afforded a line of sight to where Gary's truck would be parked when he drove in. The land was torn up and littered with piles of brush, limbs and even whole trees that had been left to be burned. This was the same place that Gary had buried the body of a dead, black, drug dealer, in a shallow grave. That had made him look bona fide and been Gary's passport into the radical wing of the Righteous Army of God.

While it was supposed to be at least an hour before Gary showed up, we wanted to be sure we were all in position when the show started. There were FBI agents and Texas Rangers in unmarked vehicles at every road crossing and intersection within three miles of this location. Every vehicle approaching or entering this patch of woodland would be photographed coming and going. The Texas Rangers were helping us because we didn't know who we could trust in local law enforcement. Once Gary was en route to the meeting location, he would be followed by multiple units carefully choreographed to move in and out without attracting suspicion. The problem now was the weather.

The wind had picked up out of the north and the temperature had begun to fall, so had the rain. We drove in on the logging road in blowing dust. The rain started just as we emerged from the vehicles. By the time we had gotten into our hidey holes, the rain had become heavy. The cold front had arrived, eliminating any chance of our having a helicopter overhead. Without any eyes in the sky, we would be relying on surface vehicles to keep Gary in sight while he was being taken to the meeting location. The rain was both good and bad. It reduced visibility, but that worked both ways. While it made it harder to keep a vehicle in sight, it also made it harder to spot the tailing vehicles.

By five thirty, it was nearly dark. The heavy cloud cover and rain had reduced our visibility down to a few hundred yards, and that was fading with the light.

"Man, this is miserable." Doug observed, as he scanned the area with his binoculars.

"I'd think you would be pretty used to rain, coming from Eureka, California." I pointed out.

"Sure, but I didn't spend much time belly down in a cold mud puddle like this."

He was right. We were lying prone in a shallow depression under a snarl of limbs and brush about fifty yards above where Gary would park his truck. The rain was pouring now and our little blind was filling with muddy water. Because of the sound of the wind and rain constantly lashing us, we could barely hear each other speak. I figured the temperature had dropped at least twenty degrees since earlier in the afternoon. In another hour, it would drop at least ten degrees more. The low this morning had been seventy eight. The high had been one hundred and one. The low temperature tomorrow morning was expected to be about fifty degrees, with a high of seventy three. We lay in the mud and tried to stay focused on the reason we were there.

I was wearing an ear bud and it told me I had an in-coming call. It was twenty minutes until six o'clock. I punched the button to make the connection.

"Hello?"

"John, it's me, Gary."

"Hey, Gary, what's up?"

"They've changed the pick-up point. They're worried about getting stuck in the mud at the logging site. They want to pick me up from the old Stuckey's parking lot on the I-20 service road. Do you know where that is?"

"Yes, it's a good twelve or thirteen miles from here. Where are you now?"

"I'm about fifteen minutes away from there."

Doug was paying close attention to my conversation. I muted the phone for a moment and turned to him, yelling.

"They've changed the location where they're going to meet Gary. It's the old Stuckey's parking lot on the I-20 service road. That's at least twelve miles southwest from here, and well outside the perimeter we set up. Can you scramble the surveillance group?"

"I'm on it!" He said.

Doug began sloshing to his feet and keyed his microphone as he started clambering over the limbs and brush that formed our blind.

I took the phone off mute.

"OK, Gary, here's the deal. We're sending units that way, but it will take a while for them to get into position. Don't go directly to the location. Don't drive in there until a few minutes after six o'clock.

They changed the meeting location so they can't expect you to be on time. When you do get there, try to stall for a while. Can you do that?"

"Uh, sure, I guess. You are going to cover me aren't you?"

Yes, but we're in position at the logging site. We've got units headed over there, but it will take a little time to get them set up so you won't be able to spot them or notice them as they're following you. We've got you covered. Just don't get there early."

"OK. But you're sure you'll be there, right?"

"We'll have you covered."

"Ok, bye." He broke the connection with his usual brief adieu.

Doug was down by the edge of the logging road, assembling the agents from their hiding places.

I crawled out of the muddy blind and made my way down to them, in the driving rain.

"I told Gary we would be able to get people into position to cover him. I told him the truth didn't I?" I asked Doug.

"Shit!" He swore. "Yeah, he'll be covered, but we won't be part of it. Every available unit is hauling tail in that direction. Our transport won't be here for several minutes. By the time they get here and haul us out, we won't be able to get there in time to do anything. Where's your God when we need him?"

The other FBI agents fidgeted when they heard him address me that way.

"This is my A-team and these are my only snipers. We don't have any other riflemen in the field. The best we can hope for is to get someone near enough that if things go south, they can rush to Gary's rescue with sirens screaming. Gary isn't wearing a wire, so we won't know who he meets. Somebody will just have to follow whoever picks him up and hope we don't lose them. If they slip by us somehow..."

"Let's not borrow trouble. I told Gary not to go to the new meeting place early. He'll show up there no earlier than six o'clock. Will that be enough time to get some units into position, or not?"

"Yes, barely, but like I said, we won't be there to cover him ourselves. I hate sudden changes I hate this damn rain, and this whole damn mess." Doug indicated, with a wave of his hand.

We were a pretty miserable looking outfit, standing there in the pouring rain with mud slowly being washed down our legs. The snipers had their rifles slung across their chests, muzzle down, under ponchos. There was nothing to do but wait for our evac.

"A good plan seldom goes the way it's expected to. As long as we get people into position to follow Gary to the meeting, we'll still get what we need. The Rangers are pretty well equipped to provide cover for Gary."

"Yeah, maybe, but either way, it's out of our hands now."

"Who knows, maybe when they pick him up, they'll head in our direction."

"Well, the big SUVs with government plates that are coming to get us might be somewhat more noticeable than the unmarked surveillance vehicles, don't you think?"

"Sure, but we don't have to actually take part in the surveillance. We can just sort of trail along and follow them to the meeting place." I suggested.

"I would like that a whole lot. Why don't you ask your god to make it happen for us?" Doug sneered.

CHAPTER 49

Doug's radio eventually informed him there were units in place near each of the on and off ramps along Interstate 20, both east and west of the old abandoned Stuckey's parking lot. There were other units on the county roads that could be accessed from the location. They had managed to get it done by five minutes after six.

Our team had been picked up a few minutes earlier and we were headed directly toward I-20, figuring it would be the fastest route to get to wherever we could do the most good.

"Does anyone have eyes on Gary yet?" I asked Doug.

"Yes, and we have a unit on the other side of I-20, at the gas station there. They have a pretty good view of the Stuckey's lot on the other side of the freeway. They say there is only one pickup truck there and it isn't Gary's. It's too dark and raining too... Hang on..."

Doug was interrupted by the radio breaking in.

We were informed that another set of headlights had just swept into the Stuckey's lot. Another voice informed us it was Gary's truck arriving on the scene. It was one of our surveillance vehicles that had been following Gary.

"Attention, all units! Our asset has just made contact with an unknown number of suspects at the meeting place on the I-20 service road. Stand bye. Agent Carter, can you approach on foot, without being seen?" Doug asked.

"Affirmative, sir." The agent replied.

"Get in there and cover our asset."

I allowed myself a smile. Gary would see the humor in the statement. The agent who was on foot had been dropped off by the unit that had followed Gary to the abandoned Stuckey's.

"All units, be prepared to follow one or more vehicles when they leave the parking lot. I want at least two vehicles prepared to keep eyes on whoever leaves that lot..."

"Sir, our asset has just left his vehicle. He is getting into the other truck. Stand bye. OK. They are swinging around... I had to duck out of sight for a second... They are going north across the overpass, left turn indicator on, down the on-ramp to I-20, headed west."

"Unit nine, we're right behind them sir." Another voice broke in.

"Attention, all units... stand bye, for further instructions." Doug told them.

"Are you thinking what I'm thinking?" I asked him.

"I just want to be sure they don't get off at the next exit, and we can't follow them with the unit behind them. They may be taking steps to spot a tail"

"That was exactly my thought." I observed.

Sure enough, the truck carrying Gary to the meeting did get off at the next exit. The surveillance vehicle designated as 'unit nine' had to stay on the highway headed west. Our agent hidden near the exit watched the suspect vehicle drive across the overpass and go down the on ramp to I-20, now headed east. Another one of our units followed them back onto I-20.

"Stand bye." Doug repeated.

When they got back to the place where they had first gotten onto I-20, they took the off ramp again and our surveillance vehicle had to continue east-bound on the highway.

The suspect vehicle surprised us a little at that point. They drove straight over and across the county road and took the east bound on-ramp, back onto I-20, now just a couple of hundred feet behind the unit that had just been following them.

"Unit seven, take up position behind the suspect vehicle." Doug instructed.

"Now we have a unit in front of them and one behind them. All the suspect can see is tail lights and headlights. Unit seven can clearly see their vehicle. If they stay on I-20 very long, we'll swap out the tailing vehicle from time to time." Doug observed, with a hint of relief evident in his voice. He was studying the illuminated map on the screen of his tablet.

"All units, I want someone at every off ramp ahead of them. If they exit, another unit should be in position to follow the suspect vehicle wherever they go. The command units are approaching Interstate 20 approximately six miles northeast of the suspect vehicle. ETA is five minutes. We will stand-bye to assist as needed. Keep me informed. That is all."

I didn't like being a passenger in the back seat of the SUV. I couldn't see much of anything except what the headlights shone on. From my perspective, that was mostly just falling rain. Doug was sitting next to the driver. He had his headset on and was monitoring the radio. There was nothing for me to do, but sit there in my muddy clothes next to a fully armored, equally muddy, FBI agent. That guy looked like a soldier who was part of futuristic army, ready to invade Afghanistan or possibly Mars.

Once we ran the plates, we knew that the suspect vehicle belonged to Kevin Watkins. The surveillance had indicated that Gary and Watkins were alone in the truck.

I would have given anything to be able to listen in on their conversation. Still, I knew that putting any kind of wire on Gary might have gotten him killed. There had been no opportunity to put a bug inside Watkins truck.

"The subject vehicle is exiting the interstate at exit 575." Unit seven reported.

"Where is that?" Doug snapped.

"The vehicle has left the highway. I've lost visual contact." Unit seven announced.

Doug was looking at the map app on his tablet, trying to figure out where exit 575 might be.

"Unit four, I'm exiting at 575, Unit four... I have his tail lights in sight. Subject vehicle has turned north, repeat north over the highway. He is now northbound on... County Road 3101, repeat northbound on 3101, over..."

"Roger that, you are north bound on 3101. Continue surveillance. We are approaching the interstate on 370, will attempt to intercept you on County Road 1252. ETA..." Doug looked at the driver.

"About two minutes sir."

"... Two minutes, or less." Doug finished informing Unit four, as he shot the driver a meaningful look.

The big SUV's engine roared louder, as the driver pressed on the accelerator.

In a moment we were hurtling through the rain, in the middle of nowhere, in the dark, at seventy five miles an hour.

The rain was stopped for the blink of an eye, as we flew under interstate 20, then it slammed down again like a waterfall on the other side.

"The subject vehicle has turned and is now headed east, I repeat east on 1252. I don't think I should continue..."

"Stay on him. I repeat stay on him, until we relieve you." Doug informed Unit four.

We slewed to a near stop, as we turned east onto County Road 1252. I was afraid the other SUV behind us would slam into us.

"How far?" Doug asked the driver.

"... Half a mile, maybe less. We should see their taillights any minute now."

We sailed across County Road 370 without any concession to the stop sign. I thanked God that there had been no traffic at the intersection.

"It looks like your prayers were answered, Doug. Watkins did come back our way, and we're back in the surveillance." I pointed out.

"What? Hell, we're just damned lucky, if you ask me." He barked.

We could see two sets of taillights ahead of us.

"Break off, Unit four. We have the subject vehicle in sight." Doug instructed.

We saw the turn signal indicating a right turn, blinking on the car ahead of us. That vehicle slowed and turned at a gravel driveway, as we went by it, carefully reducing the distance between us and the subject vehicle ahead.

"Unit nine, I'm stopped on the side of the road, west-bound on 1252. Maybe a mile and a half ahead of you, over..."

"Roger that Unit nine. Stand bye. All units report your locations." Doug ordered.

When everyone had reported in, Doug positioned units at all of the approaches back on to I-20 between our location and the small town of Liberty City.

"Unit nine, turn around and take up a position at the edge of Liberty City. Attention, all units. Stay alert. Units one, two and four, will continue to follow the subject as long as he stays east-bound on 1252. It will get problematic if he goes all the way into Liberty City. We'll converge and redeploy if that becomes apparent. Stand bye. That is all."

CHAPTER 50

It was nearly six thirty now. Most folks had made it home from work, and were sitting down to supper. Out in the backwoods and boonies there was very little traffic in the rain.

Suddenly, the brake lights and the left turn signal flashed in front of us.

"Shit! Doug swore. "Unit four, subject is turning northbound onto County Road 3111, that's Joy Wright Mountain Road. Take over pursuit. "

"Roger that, Unit four, I'll take it from here." Unit four responded.

We had to keep going eastbound. Watkins would have noticed if two big black SUVs had turned to follow him. He probably wouldn't be surprised if a single old pickup truck, the third vehicle on the road, eventually turned onto the same road he was on.

"What do we do now?" I asked Doug.

"We'll pull over right here, study the map for a minute and then follow them up Joy Wright Mountain Road."

"Who is that in Unit four?

"Ranger Sergeant Formby. He's one of the three Texas Rangers in plain clothes, assisting with this surveillance."

We did a U-turn with the other SUV right behind us, turned right onto 3111, and pulled over.

"Man, I wish this rain would let up," Doug said.

And just like that, it slowed to a sprinkle and stopped.

"Another answered prayer." I observed.

Doug ignored me as he studied the satellite imagery on the screen of his tablet.

After a moment, he looked at the driver and said.

"OK, let's go, and don't spare the horses."

We had just pulled up onto the pavement when Unit four reported in."

"Unit one, Unit four, I'm cut off from the subject vehicle. Repeat, I have lost the subject vehicle. Over..."

"What do you mean you're "cut off"?" Doug snapped.

"It's a roadblock, sir. The Sheriff's department has a roadblock up. They told me that I can't go on, because there is a bridge washed out up ahead. They made me turn around."

"What about the subject vehicle?"

"They let them go on through sir, right in front of me."

"Did you ask why?"

"Yes sir, I did. They told me that the subject vehicle was a local and only lived a short distance farther up the road, on this side of the damaged bridge."

Doug was silent for a moment, rage building in him.

"OK, roger that, Unit four. Stay where you are, we'll be there shortly."

The driver was already stepping on the accelerator.

"Did you get the badge numbers?" Doug asked the Ranger.

We were pulled off on the side of the road where the Ranger had waited for us. The north wind had replaced the rain.

"No, Sir, they were wearing plastic raincoats over their uniforms. I did get the license number on their patrol car." Sergeant Formby said, handing Doug a piece of paper.

"Sir, the County Department of Roads and Bridges say they have had no reports of bridge wash outs, not even any flooded roadways." The driver informed Doug.

"No surprise there."

"Agent Booker, under the circumstances I felt that it would have been a bad idea for me to identify myself as law enforcement. Did I make a mistake?" Sergeant Formby asked.

"No. You would have endangered our asset if you had done that. You handled it the only way you could have. This was just something that we didn't anticipate."

"Now what do we do?" I asked.

Doug showed me the satellite image of the area he had pulled up on his tablet.

"The problem is that on just the other side of the creek, the road forks. Even if we could get past the road block, we have no way of knowing which fork Watkins took, and you can see the satellite image shows there are several cross roads and branches on each one of those forks. They could have gone in pretty much any direction. We don't have any Units north of here and no eyes in the sky. That's it. We've lost them." Doug concluded.

"We promised Gary we'd cover him..." I started.

"Yeah, well it didn't work out did it? Apparently you forgot to ask your god to handle the weather and the opposition." Doug sneered.

Before I could respond, my phone vibrated in my pocket. I pulled it out, hoping for some reason that it was Gary calling me.

I saw that the caller was one of my clients.

I put my phone away.

"I repeat, now what do we do?" I said to Doug.

"We wrap it up. If Gary made it to the meeting and lives to tell the tale, he'll probably call you. If he didn't, oh well. It was a nice try."

"Can we at least check out the roadblock? Maybe they really didn't go far past there."

He thought about it for a moment.

"I guess we should. We have to confirm the Sheriff's deputies are either legit or phonies. Sergeant Formby, go back to the roadblock and feed them some kind of story. Maybe you're visiting your sick Uncle or your girlfriend or whatever. See if you can get past the roadblock. Then report in."

"Sir, I tried the girlfriend story already. They didn't buy it…" He saw the look on Doug's face and changed his tone.

"I'm on it."

We waited as Ranger Sergeant Formby's taillights disappeared up the road. A moment later we got the news.

"Unit four reporting, they're gone, Sir. The deputies have removed the barricade and they're gone."

"Wait for us, we'll be right there." Doug responded.

Again, the driver was mashing on the accelerator.

We found Ranger Formby pulled over at the edge of the road, about a half mile farther along. Other than his truck and some car tracks in the mud, there was no sign that anyone else had been out there.

We all got out of the vehicles and conferred for a moment. The wind was gusting at about forty miles an hour.

"OK, they gave us the slip. We're going to go looking for them. When we come to the place where the road forks, Sergeant Formby will go left and we'll go right. We're looking for that Sheriff's department patrol car or any large gathering of vehicles. Look for headlights leaving the road, or any brightly lit building. If anyone spots anything suspicious, we check it out. We have units standing by, so we can call in the cavalry or do whatever we need to do at that point. Any questions...?" He looked around.

"How far do we go, and what do we do when we come to cross roads or intersections?" Sergeant Formby asked.

"Use your best judgment and call it in. We'll do the same."

I had to admit that Doug was doing all he could to find Gary. It wasn't his fault that we had been outsmarted. It wasn't his fault that some local LEOs were involved. The weather had ruined our aerial surveillance which would have covered this contingency. That wasn't his fault either. I could see that he was weighed down by the responsibility, but he wasn't throwing his hands up yet.

It took about forty five minutes of driving around on back roads in the dark, without any indication of where Watkins had taken Gary, before he called it off.

"Attention all units, hold your present positions until further ordered. We'll wait to see if the subject vehicle returns the way it came out here. Unit four, return to the intersection of Joy Wright Mountain Road and County Road 1252. Stand by for further instructions. That is all." Doug informed the other units.

"Let's go meet Unit four at Joy Wright Mountain Road and 1252." He told our driver, dejectedly.

Ten minutes later, both of our big SUVs pulled to the side of the road, southbound on 3111, about a hundred yards away from the intersection with CR 1252. There was no sign of Unit four yet.

"Doug, I don't see much point in sitting out here in the dark for who knows how long, hoping to get a chance to resume surveillance on Watkins. We know that if Gary is still alive and well, he'll be taken back to the parking lot where his truck is parked."

Doug nodded thoughtfully.

"We're not going to stay out here. I'll have Unit two find a spot where they can watch Gary's truck. The other units will stay in position until midnight. You and I will return to base. If we don't hear from Gary or he doesn't make it back to his truck… We'll cross that bridge when we come to it."

He turned to the combat ready agent beside me.

"Agent Sheffield, go climb in with Unit two. Tell them you're to set up back where Gary's truck is parked. If our asset shows up, call it in and provide cover for him until he leaves. Get the license number of whoever drops him off. If he doesn't show, stay with his truck until morning, or until you get further instructions." Doug told him.

"Yes sir," said agent Sheffield, as he exited the vehicle.

CHAPTER 51

Shortly after Unit two had disappeared into the night, a set of headlights appeared behind us, pulled over and cut the lights. Doug got out of our big black SUV with the government plates and walked back to the pickup designated Unit four, driven by Texas Ranger Sergeant Formby.

Looking back, I could just barely see Doug talking quietly with the Ranger.

When Doug came back and climbed into the passenger seat, he told the driver we should head back to Tyler.

"What did you say to Sergeant Formby?" I asked him.

"I just told him losing our subject wasn't his responsibility. There was no way to predict he would be stopped by local Sheriff's deputies. He handled it well, and didn't tip them off that he was following Watkins. He may have saved Gary's life."

"It was a good thing to do, Doug. I'll bet the Ranger really feels bad about how it turned out. I'm sure he appreciates you telling him it wasn't his fault."

He shrugged and said. "Yeah, well the ultimate responsibility rests with me, anyway."

"I still believe it will all work out."

"You would," he mumbled.

"Excuse me?"

"Do you still think you have a direct line to that god of yours? Are you a prophet who can predict what happens next? I don't think so. Nothing has gone according to plan. At the moment, we are up the proverbial creek, without the proverbial paddle."

I didn't bother to respond.

Clearly, SAIC Doug Booker was in no mood to hear the truth.

We drove on in silence for a little while, until Doug spoke up.

"The thing I don't get about you religious types is why you always figure you know some secret that normal, healthy people don't know."

"What do you mean when you say 'normal, healthy people'?" I asked him.

"Well, clearly your belief in some sort of god is irrational, magical thinking, and if it isn't complete insanity, it's certainly delusional."

"Hold on, are you saying you think all people who believe in God are insane?"

"Of course, the evidence is irrefutable. You live in a fantasy world peopled by angels and spirits and who knows what. You think there is some sort of outside force directing the course of world events. You believe there is a higher law than our government or any government. Am I right or wrong?"

"Are you right or are you wrong? That's not a simple question to answer, Doug."

"Oh come on. You people are always pointing out what you think is wrong in our society. You hate homosexuals. You hate people who live any lifestyle you think is libertine. You hate our government for not supporting your twisted religious intolerance. I asked you a simple question. Is what I said about your beliefs accurate or is it completely wrong."

"Why are you attacking me?"

"Oh, do you feel as if you're being attacked? Maybe you should consult with a mental health professional."

"You've made some rather inflammatory statements. You've accused me of hating any number of people. Where is the evidence of that?"

"The thing is this, anybody who has to believe in some kind of imaginary God, who will judge them someday, has to believe in that, in order to have any kind of morality - is a seriously sick and deranged human being. All decent people know the difference between right and wrong. We all have an inherent conscience. You religious types are the ones who are screwed up."

"I'm aware people have a conscience. I believe God has endowed all people with a conscience. But everyone also rationalizes and is subject to self-deceit. Everyone thinks they're right and anyone who disagrees with them is wrong. This leads to pride and resentfulness, rage and hatred, strife, even murder. If the only standard we recognize is one we find within ourselves, we will find ourselves violating even that. We allow all sorts of desires and attitudes to get the best of us. We find ourselves doing and saying things in violation of our own conscience and must therefore judge ourselves as guilty of sin. We can't do the right thing, even if we all agreed on what was right, which we most certainly do not. We all fail and we all fall short. It is the very definition of sin. That's why God sent Jesus to redeem us and give us a new life."

"Your insanity is showing. You really don't get it. We're all just a collection of carbon based molecules. That's it and that's all. You live, you die, and you are forgotten. All that Jesus stuff…? If he ever existed, he was just a guy who claimed he was God, and you people blindly believe the whole mythology. I've got news for you, buddy. The Bible was written by men, a bunch of bigoted-dead-men. You people treat that book like it was literally the word of God. WAKE UP! There is no God, You people have attempted to stop every move our government makes to improve our society into a more integrated and healthy community. You opposed gay marriage. You talk about love and morality. You people are always up on some high horse preaching morality, while you're visiting whores on the side."

I wasn't shocked by his open animosity, but I was offended by his personal accusations.

"You're right, the Bible was written by men, forty of them, over the course of about fifteen hundred years. They wrote it in three different languages, probably on three different continents. Isn't it interesting that not only did they manage to maintain a continuous spiritual narrative and accurately record history, but they also accurately predicted future events?

"That's BS. Silly stories about giants and floods were told by all kinds of ignorant people."

"Hmmm, and that proves, what?"

"It proves the Bible is all a bunch of Jewish fairy tales."

"If I told you someone had written a prophecy; a man would be born in Eureka, California, the son of a Pentecostal preacher and an alcoholic mother. He would attend university and lose his fiancée to terrorists on 9/11, and then become an FBI Special Agent, who would eventually serve in Tyler, Texas. How many people do you know who might fit that prophecy?"

"You son of a bitch! Who told you all that?"

"What makes you think I was talking about you? Those were only six points of prophecy and we arrived at - you. You and you alone, fit the prophetic detail. In the whole world and in all of history only you fit the profile, with six little points of prophecy. In your case, no one ever wrote that prophesy. Jesus fulfilled more than eighty points of written prophecy. That's EIGHTY. Would you like to calculate the odds of that happening randomly or accidentally? Now, try to calculate the odds of one carpenter's son being able to deliberately fulfill all eighty, including his own birth, or of even knowing about those prophecies. I'll bet you don't know very many of the prophecies about the Messiah, and you've had access to everything ever written on the subject."

"Again, how do you know all that?"

"What about the historical accuracy of the Bible."

"Big deal, they got some things right, somebody had to record some of those events. It just happened to be a bunch of Jews who did the writing. Some of it is clearly wrong. You're one of those stupid people who believe the earth is only six thousand years old. You'll believe anything at all. You people are a detriment to world progress. You can't stand the thought that science continues to disprove your myths. You hate people who are smarter than you."

"Doug, I never said I thought the world was only six thousand years old. You are attacking me and generalizing me into a group you refer to as 'you people'. You keep accusing me of hatred. If you're speaking to me about my attitudes and behavior, where is the evidence? I don't hate anyone. I have never said anything to you that was judgmental or unfair. Honestly, Doug, I think you have some animosity you're directing at me without provocation."

He was silent for a moment.

"Maybe, but you're still a religious nut-job," he mumbled.

"Doug, I apologize if I've said something that offended you. Even if I am what you would call a religious nut-job, I really didn't intend any offense."

"Don't worry about it. The day is coming when you people won't even have a voice."

Doug's hatred for people of faith was palpable. I thought about his last statement. While it was chilling, he was partly right and partly wrong.

Doug seemed to think that at some point in the not so distant future, all religious people would be marginalized or even silenced. He was right about the fact that Christians will be removed. What he didn't seem to comprehend was that there are all sorts of religions at work in this world.

Doug didn't realize it, but he was himself a religious person. His was a religion that worshipped intellect and reason, believing he was a superior human being. In effect, Doug was worshipping himself. Other people worship dolphins and deer and the other living things found in nature. Some people worship the planet, mother earth. Others worship science, replacing the Creator with the worship of creation. Some people believe in alien life forms and worship unknown entities in the cosmos. Some worship at the altar of wealth and power, and some worship lady luck and four leaf clovers. Fame and celebrity are worshipped, as are the famous celebrities themselves. Many of the older, darker religions still have practitioners. Everybody practices some kind of religion, even atheists, who are fundamentalists about not believing. Firmly believing there is no God, and putting all their faith, hope and trust in that notion.

What Doug couldn't begin to understand was that all people are religious in some way. Evil has distorted man's natural desire to worship our Creator, and replaced it with a constellation of counterfeits.

Doug was wrong if he thought all religious people would be silenced. Once the Christians are gone, there will still be plenty of religious people on the earth. Evil will have a field day with religious people. Even with people like Doug.

I was hoping to change the subject and get Doug to re-focus on the task at hand

"We sure don't want to underestimate these guys. The RAGs had a good plan to prevent unwanted attention, didn't they? That road block in the middle of nowhere was smart. Watkins did a really good job of trying to ensure he wasn't followed. Don't you think?" I observed.

Doug didn't answer me. He was lost in his own dark thoughts.

It was almost eight o'clock as we came back to Tyler. Doug shook himself and turned around to look at me.

"Do you want to come to my office and wait to hear what has become of Gary, or can we drop you off somewhere?"

"He'll call me the minute he gets an opportunity. Don't you want to hear what he has to say?"

"You're rather optimistic aren't you? We don't even know if he's alive."

"There's no reason to believe he isn't.

"Have it your way." Doug looked over at the driver. "Eugene, take us through a fast food place. We'll get something to hold body and soul together. It could be a long night."

For the first time in the day, I thought I saw FBI agent Eugene Green, smile.

CHAPTER 52

A little after nine o'clock, Unit two reported there was activity at the abandoned Stuckey's parking lot. A pickup truck pulled in and dropped Gary off. A quick check showed it was Watkins.

A couple of minutes later, my phone rang.

"Hey, Gary, I understand Watkins just dropped you off. How did the meeting go?"

"Wow, the Feds are amazing. Even though I knew I was being followed, I could never be sure. Watkins was taking all sorts of precautions, so I was afraid the feds had lost me. I was watching pretty closely but I couldn't spot a tail."

"Yeah, they know what they're doing. I'm here with Doug, I'll put you on speaker and you can tell us about the meeting."

"Hello, Gary, I'm glad things went smoothly for you. Tell us about the meeting." Doug said.

There was a moment of silence before Gary replied.

"I'm guessing y'all got stopped by that roadblock, didn't you?"

Doug and I looked at each other.

"Yes we did, Gary. We couldn't risk trying to get past it. We didn't want to put you in any more danger." Doug replied.

"So, you have no idea where the meeting took place, do you?"

"We searched the area pretty diligently, but unfortunately no, we couldn't find the meeting location. Tell us about it." Doug repeated.

"Well, it was in an old, unoccupied farm house. It's well off the road, down a long dirt driveway. All the vehicles were parked in the empty hay barn and behind the house. You couldn't have seen any of that from the road."

"We had planned to use aerial surveillance, but the weather eliminated the operation." I said.

"No problem. All's well that ends well."

"Tell us about the meeting. Who all was at the meeting, Gary?" Doug asked, pointedly.

"I'm just jerking your chain." Gary chuckled. "You'll be glad to know I'm in. They treated me like a full member of the group. At first there were only nine men there. Everybody but me was wearing those digital camouflage BDUs."

"Who are they, Gary?" Doug was irritated and it showed.

"The three guys I met at the first meeting, you remember that guy, Brown? The other two were Tommy Turner and Hollister, plus me and Watkins, and four others. One of those guys was wounded and had his arm in a sling. They did it, Agent Booker. They talked openly about the shooting in Longview and what went wrong. They talked about the failed bombing and everything." Gary was excited.

"Did you get any more names?" Doug prompted.

"Yeah, but just their first names. The four guys who did the shooting were named Jerry, Jim-Bob, Charlie and Edgar. Those deputies who had the road block set up came along later, so there were eleven of us altogether. The deputies were called Joe and Fred."

"That's it, that's all you got?" Doug asked, somewhat incredulously.

"Hey, that ain't exactly nothing. Besides, we did some planning for the next attack. They asked me a lot of questions about explosives. They all knew I had been a fireman and that I had hazmat training."

"So, they're planning another attack?"

"I just told you that."

"Where and when?" Doug asked intently.

"We'll meet at the same place. They were pretty focused on talking about explosives and being able to acquire the needed components. There was a lot of discussion about incendiary devices as opposed to shrapnel propellants, you know, pros and cons. They were treating me like I was some kind of expert on the subject, which compared to them, I guess I am."

"Did you get any idea about who or what their next target might be?"

"Not really, no. There was some talk about continuing to strike against the government and legal authorities. They are going to make an announcement of some kind, taking credit for the shooting in Longview."

"What kind of announcement. How will they claim responsibility?"

"They are calling our group the "Righteous Patriot's Brigade". There was a lot of heated talk about taking America back from the "mud people". These are some seriously hard core haters. I'm telling you it's scary, man."

"Could you tell who the leader was?"

"The two guys who seemed to be in charge were Hollister and Turner, General Hollister and Colonel Turner. Everyone has a military rank. It was pretty casual at first. Then Brown called us to attention and started addressing people by their rank. It was sergeant this and corporal that. Get this, I'm now a sergeant, because I have specialized skills and I'm supposed to be training them on the use of explosives. Brown is a lieutenant. Watkins is a sergeant, and those deputies are also. Everyone else is a corporal. They consider the ordinary members of the RAGs to be foot soldiers, and I got the impression they have plans to use some of them on operations in the future.

"Did they set a time for the next meeting?"

"Yep, one week from tonight, same time, same place."

"Do you know how to get back to that location?"

"Maybe, not for sure, Watkins made me put a pillowcase over my head when we got to the roadblock. We were on the road for about five minutes before we made a left turn, then a couple of more minutes to a right turn. Then we made a right turn down a twisting, rough road that it turned out was the driveway. That was the place. It couldn't have been more than four or five miles from where the roadblock was. I know the general area."

"Did you have to wear the pillowcase when you came out of there?"

"No, but it was dark and we left by a different route. There were no road signs and all that deep woods looks the same in the dark. The next thing I knew we were coming into Gladewater. Then we went south on 271 to I-20, then back to the Stuckey's lot. I expect they'll have to give me directions to the next meeting."

Doug was studying the satellite image on his tablet, but I could see he wasn't able to pick out the right property. There were too many possible roads, too many farms and the land was too heavily wooded to be able to make out features like the driveway Gary had described.

"Gary, you did a great job tonight. Is there anything else you can tell us that might be useful? Did they have any weapons or explosives stored there" I asked him.

"No. other than some cheap folding chairs and a big RAGs flag on the wall, the building was completely empty. I think pretty much everyone except me was armed, but there weren't any weapons being stored there. They want me to start gathering the materials to put together some explosives. They want me to show them how to build bombs."

"When do they expect you to do that?" Doug asked.

"At the next meeting, that's when I'm supposed to show them how to make explosives."

"How many more people do you think are in this radical group?" I asked him.

"I got the impression there weren't many, if any, other people involved. I think that was the whole core group, but like I say, I got the impression they are planning to draw some others in from the main body of the RAGs."

"Did you get any license numbers from any of the vehicles?" Doug enquired.

"No, there was no way I could have done that without attracting attention."

"OK, you've actually given us several pretty decent leads. Thanks Gary. I know this has not been easy for you." Doug said.

"I'm hoping you'll be able to move on these guys soon. I don't want to teach them anything about creating or using explosives."

"I understand. We'll move as fast as we can. You're aware that once we make arrests, you'll be our primary witness?"

"Fine, I've got no problem taking these guys down, Doug."

"We'll need to meet with you sometime in the next couple of days, to have you look at some photographs and ID some or all of the people who were at that meeting."

"Good, the sooner the better. OK?"

"Yeah, I hear you. We'll be in touch." Doug assured him.

"OK, bye." Gary hung up.

"Doug, how do you plan to get photographs of everyone who was at the meeting?" I asked him.

"We already know the identities of Watkins and the three men Gary first met with. We should be able to identify those sheriff's deputies pretty quickly. We'll snatch up all those guys and put the screws to them. We can make them identify Jerry, Jim-Bob, Charlie and Evan. They have some connection to the others."

"This is coming together. You should be able to make arrests with what you've got right now." I observed.

Doug was thoughtful.

"You have no idea how tempted I am, but I want to talk it over with Jack. I could round up the known suspects tonight and charge them all with conspiracy to commit murder and domestic terrorism. We could charge Watkins for the murder of the Mexican, too. But the opportunity to round them all up at one time, in one place, is even more tempting. I have to weigh all of the potential pros and cons of each option. In the meantime, we've got wire taps and other monitoring on Watkins, Hollister, Turner and Brown. We may gain useful intelligence and evidence from them. I can't wait to nail Brown. He's a ranking officer in the Smith County Sheriff's department."

"You've handled this really well, Doug."

"Thank you. That's the way the FBI rolls. That's what I'm trained for. Still, 'there's many a slip between cup and lip'. This whole thing will go south on me if anyone else gets hurt or killed before we take them down."

"I guess you know my opinion about that."

"What, you have some mythological fairy story about talking unicorns you want to tell me?"

I shook my head and grinned. "God bless you, Doug. I've never even heard of a talking unicorn. Have you heard the one about the guy who had a talking donkey...?"

CHAPTER 53

On my way to the office, the next morning, my truck informed me, Gary was calling.

"Hey, Gary, what's up, any news?"

"I thought the FBI was going to bring me in to look at pictures."

"I believe that's the plan."

"Well, I haven't heard from them."

"I don't think they've had quite enough time to make the identifications yet."

"Will you talk to Doug and find out what's going on?"

"Sure, I'll do it right away. Call me back in ten minutes. Are you still working on the demo job in Bullard?"

"Yeah, call me."

He hung up.

Gary's attitude annoyed me. He knew the FBI was pushing hard to make the identifications. Then I thought about what Gary was going through. And that made me think about how hard all of this was for Doug to manage. I remembered the dead DA and what his family was suffering. I was worried about Gary, and I wanted to see Watkins punished for murdering Eduardo Ruiz. My mind was bouncing from one thing to another like a pinball. Confusion is a weapon often used by our enemy. I took a moment to seek guidance and listen for a still small voice, I realized what my problem was. I was trying to juggle too many chainsaws.

If I continued this way, sooner or later, I would make a mistake.

Sometimes you have to set down one of the chainsaws.

I called Doug.

"Special Agent Booker," was the way he answered the phone.

"Doug, it's John, do you have a minute to talk?"

"Barely, what's up?"

"Our asset is getting pretty desperate to see an end to this thing. How soon do you see arrests being made?"

"We've made some progress in identifying those sheriff's deputies. I have their jackets, with pictures to show him."

"That's good, really good. He's ready to come in."

"Well, I'll meet with him to look over the pictures, but he needs to hang in there till the end."

"He wants it to end now. Again, how soon will you make the arrests?" I pressed.

"I have no idea, certainly not within the next few days," he snapped. "Do you have any idea how hard it is to work out the logistics of this many arrests? If we try to arrest each of them separately, we have to coordinate multiple teams to make simultaneous arrests. If we miss one of them, he will tip off the others and it could become a real nightmare. The suspects will probably be armed, wherever we decide to take them. I'm thinking it would be better if we attempt to take them all in a single raid, on that next meeting. The problem with that is we can't be sure all of them will be there, and it could turn into a pitched gun battle. Either way, I'll have to get our elite tactical team, some local LEOs, and the

Rangers coordinated with air and ground transport. We have to plan for every eventuality. We don't need another screw up." He concluded.

"So, you're still debating when and how to do it?"

"Among other things, we're hoping to gather some decent evidence and further information from our wiretaps. Your friend just needs to take a deep breath. This will all be over soon."

"Can you do me a favor?"

"Maybe, depends on what it is."

"Meet with our asset as soon as you can. Show him the pictures, so he can make the identification and encourage him it's all going to work out."

"I thought that was your job."

"It has been, but I'm in your way and he needs to work this out with you."

"So, you're out of it now?"

"I'm trying to be. He's going to call me in a few minutes. I would like to be able to tell him you have news, and you want to arrange a meeting. Then I'll let you work out the details with him."

"Fine, I'll figure out a way to meet with him, without tipping off the opposition."

"Great. My understanding is that once you make the arrests, he'll go into the witness protection program until it's time to testify at the trials. Is that correct?"

"Yes, John. I've already alerted the Marshal's service. They'll be ready to provide him with protection and move him on a moment's notice."

"OK. Be sure to tell him that, too." I said.

"Are you alright? It sounds like you're struggling with something." Doug asked with some concern evident in his voice.

"This is hard for me. It's hard for me to let go. It's hard for me to trust you."

"Oh ye of little faith', I thought you trusted in God?"

"You know, you're absolutely right. I do. You do the same." I said brightly.

"That'll be the day." He answered, as he hung up the phone.

When Gary called me, I encouraged him as best I could and told him Special Agent Booker was anticipating wrapping the whole thing up within a week. I gave him Doug's direct number and told him he should coordinate with Doug from then on."

"So, is this goodbye? Am I ever going to see you again?" Gary asked me.

"Once you go into witness protection, they will re-locate you and change your identity. No one you have ever known will be able to get in touch with you, and you should never contact any of them."

"... For how long?" Gary asked.

"Gary, Doug explained all this to you. You understood what this would mean when you made the commitment to see it through."

"Yeah, I know... It's just that... Thank you, John. You've been a good friend."

"Listen, Gary, the United States Marshal's service is very good at this. I have every confidence in them, but if you ever need me..."

"I know, man.

"Alright, you hang in there, and God be with you."

"... And with you."

We were both silent for a moment. Then Gary spoke up.

"OK. Bye," he said, as he hung up.

Christine came in and saw the look on my face.

"John, what's wrong? You look like you just lost your best friend."

"Sort of, I just left Gary in the capable hands of the FBI."

"Oh, no!"

"Oh yes. Special Agent in Charge, Doug Booker, now has the responsibility for what happens to Gary."

"Why?"

"They'll have it all wrapped up in a week or so. At this point I'm not much help to either Gary or the FBI. Once they round up the killers and co-conspirators, Gary will go into witness protection with the US Marshal's service."

"Doesn't that mean we won't ever see him again?"

I acknowledged her question with a slow nod.

"Is there any way I can say good bye to him?" Christine asked.

"Yes, if you do it pretty quickly. You could go down there to Bullard and see him on the job site."

"Can I?"

"Sure, but you should have some sort of cover story, especially if you're likely to cry and hug his neck."

"You know me so well."

"I understand how you feel."

"Things are changing awfully fast, aren't they?" She said, sadly.

"Yes, Christine. From our perspective it seems fast. One thing leads to another, as surely as the changing of the seasons."

She was thoughtful for a moment, almost somber, and then she shook it off.

"Speaking of seasons, I'm really looking forward to the holidays. This time of year I think about fires in the fireplace, hot chocolate, Thanksgiving and all the feasting. I think about celebrating the birth of Jesus and all the Christmas cheer." She informed me.

"Will you be going back to the Hill Country for Thanksgiving and Christmas, again this year?"

"Yep, the whole family will be there. You should come with me. Don't spend the holidays by yourself."

I wobbled my head.

"Thanks for the offer, but I hope to have other plans."

She was thoughtful again. I never get used to the way women's emotions can turn on a dime.

After a moment, she smiled and said.

"Hope. That's what keeps us going, isn't it?"

"Sure, we have hope because of our faith."

"We wouldn't have hope without our faith, would we?" She asked, rhetorically.

"Makes you wonder where the atheist finds hope."

"We have hope because we know how much God loves us. That's pretty much all we need, isn't it?" She asked.

"… Faith, hope and love." I answered.

Christine smiled and winked in agreement.

CHAPTER 54

Late in the day, Gary called me.

"Tomorrow night, John, the meeting of the Righteous Patriot's Brigade is set for Friday night. That's tomorrow night."

"OK. Calm down. Have you talked about it with Doug?"

"Yeah, he wants me to go to the meeting."

"Have they made any progress on identifying the men you met?"

"Doug says they've identified all of them and they got everything they need to round them all up. That's his plan, man. They're going to raid the meeting and arrest everyone at once."

"Do you know where the meeting is going to be?"

"Same place as last time. They gave me good directions."

"What do you want me to do?"

"I don't know, John. I'm just kind of freaking out."

"It will all be over soon. All these weeks of fear and sacrifice, I guess you feel like you've been on a roller coaster ride."

"Yeah, that and I'm worried about going to the meeting and then it being raided. These guys won't just surrender."

"Doug has promised to keep you safe."

"I know. It's just…"

"… Scary, you've never been in a situation like this before now, and it scares you."

"That's part of it. Also, I hate having to go and teach these guys how to make Molotov cocktails."

"Is that what they asked you to do?"

"Well, no, not specifically. They want to learn about all kinds of explosives and incendiary devises. I figured to stall them by starting with the easiest and most common to make. I'll point out they can be made pretty much anywhere, from commonly available materials and have tremendous destructive potential. Also, they don't leave any kind of signature or clue that can be traced back. I'll only take about a half-gallon of gasoline with me for demonstration purposes."

"They could practice constructing them with water. That would eliminate the risk and you would need even less gasoline."

"Yeah, I like that idea. It would be safer for everybody involved."

"Good plan, especially since you'll be raided at some point in the process. You don't want somebody dropping a jar of gasoline with a lit wick. There won't be any actual explosives on the property, right?"

"No, they had some black powder, but they used it all in the first attempt with the pipe bombs. They expect me to teach them about other kinds of explosives and how to make them."

"Did Doug ask you to wear a wire?"

"No, he never even mentioned the possibility."

I was glad to hear it. I needed more information before I decided what my course of action should be.

"Tell me everything about the meeting place." I said.

CHAPTER 55

The next morning, I drove my truck to the old farm-house, the meeting place for the "Righteous Patriot's Brigade", the radical arm of the RAGs.

I had been analyzing aerial images most of my life, from the time we had first started taking pictures from the sky. The first aerial pictures were taken by men in balloons, then pilots of single engine air-craft. They were crude by today's standard. Later we used cameras mounted on the aircraft; eventually we learned how to use satellite imagery. Because I had more experience analyzing every kind of aerial images of non-urban land and structures than Doug (or pretty much anyone else) did, I had already iden-tified what I thought was the correct property. I had no trouble following Gary's directions.

I drove right in, down the sloped and snaky driveway that was unpaved and dusty. I parked where it ended beside the old farmhouse, a couple of hundred yards from the road. Other than the house, the only other buildings were an empty hay barn about twenty five yards away, and a sagging pump-house for the water well. The yard was choked with tall grass and weeds, trampled down between the hay barn and the house. I could see where several vehicles had been parked here and in the hay barn.

Since there were no other vehicles parked down there now, and the feel of the place was vacant and little visited, I wasn't too concerned about running in to anyone who might pose a threat. None the less, as I walked around the outside of the house, I called out several times to see if anyone else might be on the property.

As soon as I was confident I was alone and the house was unoccupied, I peeked in the windows. All I saw was empty rooms. I could see into two empty bedrooms without a stick of furniture, a living area that included the kitchen, and other than a shed like back porch, that was all I could see from outside the building. I opened the rusty old screen door and stepped up into the back porch and saw that at one time, the washing machine and perhaps clothes dryer had been enclosed here. I tested the back door and found it locked. Because of the cheap construction, time and my pocket tools made slipping the lock the simple task of only a moment.

I had already determined there was no alarm system. Although the house was supplied with electricity, running from a power pole in the yard, there was enough light inside that I didn't need to turn on any of the overhead fixtures. A quick tour revealed that the only furniture in the house was a table, shoved into a corner of the kitchen/living area, a ratty old couch, and a bunch of folding chairs leaning against a wall. There was a single, rather dirty bathroom between the two empty bedrooms. The only adornment in the house was a blood red flag, nailed to a wall. The flag had a black cross on it. A cross with a big "R" at the top, a big "A" on the left side with a little "o" in the middle, and a big G on the right. It was the flag of the Righteous Army of God.

I opened the refrigerator and found it was packed full of light beer in cans, a few bottles of water, and nothing else. I grabbed a paper towel from a roll on the counter and wiped my prints off the refrigerator door handle. Better safe than sorry. There was an empty trashcan under the sink, but I put the paper towel in my pocket.

There was nothing else to be seen in the house. It only took me about five minutes to photograph everything inside the house.

Outside, I scouted around a little until I found a well-worn trail that wandered off into the woods. It was too narrow for a car or truck, and had the tracks of all-terrain vehicles. I decided to go for a hike.

The trail meandered through the woods and although there were places where it branched off, I stuck to the main and most worn part of it. After about twenty minutes, and a little more than three quarters of a mile of walking, I came to a small clearing. There was evidence here that the clearing had been used as a parking lot. It appeared to be a place where people came to unload their ATVs to go for a ride in the woods, or maybe hunters headed out to their blinds. There were several trails converging here.

I could see where the cars and trucks had come in off the county road and I followed the tracks up to the fence line. There was no real gate, just a gap, with a wire gate, and a twisted wire to keep it closed.

I opened it and walked out onto the pavement. I needed to identify some landmarks, so I could easily find this gap again. The gap in the fence appeared to be the first worn spot past the driveway to the old farm house. That property was just around a curve and about a half a mile as the crow flies, down-hill from this spot on the road. The clearing in the woods was perfect for my needs.

I pulled the wire gate aside. Then I walked back down the trail through the woods, to the farm house where my truck was parked. Five minutes later, I was parked in the clearing, with the wire gate closed behind me. I pulled the tarp off the things I had covered in the bed of my pickup.

I spent the next few hours testing and practicing with my multi-rotor, remote control aircraft. I had spent several thousand dollars on this baby. Most of that money had been invested in the cameras and gimbals that provided stable and brilliant images to my monitor. The battery powered aircraft was high tech enough that it could be programed to fly a particular pattern, or I could control it with a joystick, out to about three quarters of a mile.

It had another limitation though; it only had a flight time of about twenty minutes before it would need new batteries. The thing was so smart, if it sensed the batteries were getting low, it would return to the launch point and land itself. I had brought extra batteries and a charger that was plugged into my diesel pickup. I had custom painted the little aircraft and disabled the running lights, so it would be very difficult to see, day or night.

I soon learned that the programed flight was what I needed in this situation. It could fly down to the farm house in about one minute and circle at a given distance and altitude, for about fifteen minutes, and then fly back and land beside my truck. I found that an altitude of about one hundred feet made it virtually impossible to see or hear from the ground, and provided excellent video to my monitor. The primary video camera was capable of low light photography and it had an excellent zoom lens. The other camera did thermal image, and/or "night vision," video photography. The multi rotor drone aircraft had been reasonably priced; the cameras had cost a fortune.

Once I had the program worked out and had tested it a couple of times, I had pretty well used up all the batteries I'd brought with me, so I packed up and headed into the town of Gladewater, to get more batteries and something to eat. A body needs to recharge too.

By four o'clock that afternoon, re-stocked with batteries and other essentials, I was headed back to the clearing. The meeting at the farmhouse wasn't scheduled to start till six o'clock, but when I drove down into the clearing in the woods, there was a truck parked there. The tailgate was down and a folding ramp leaned against it. I recognized the truck. It belonged to Kevin Watkins.

I shut off the big diesel and got out to look for Watkins. It was evident he had unloaded an ATV and gone for a ride. I couldn't hear a motor running anywhere, so I suspected he had gone to the farm house. I decided to sneak on down there and have a look. Then I remembered why I had brought the multi rotor aircraft.

Ten minutes later, the multi-rotor was circling about a hundred and fifty feet above the farm house. There was no immediate sign of the ATV. I decided to see if I could lower the aircraft to look into the hay barn. I knew this would be risky. If the drone was anywhere near the farmhouse or the hay barn when it lowered out of the sky it could be spotted by Watkins. Using the joystick, I took a minute to circle it out away from the back of the hay barn and slowly lower it. I was sweating now, partly because of the afternoon heat and humidity in the woods, but mostly because of apprehension.

I was able to point the camera straight down as I lowered the aircraft. This gave me a good view directly below the aircraft, which helped prevent me from flying it into a tree, fencepost, or some other object sticking up from the surface of the abandoned hay meadow. Once it was about six feet above the hay meadow, I reoriented the camera, focused on the hay barn and sent the aircraft slowly in that direction. I watched my monitor carefully. By the time the drone was about a hundred feet from the hay barn, I could see into it. I used the zoom for the first time and I was able to fill the screen with an image of the ATV that Watkins had parked there. I could also read the license plate on the SUV that it was parked beside. Someone else had come to the meeting more than an hour early. I hit the record button.

Five minutes after that, I had successfully brought the multi-rotor back to the clearing. I took all my gear and eased back into the woods, out of sight of anyone else who might show up early for the meeting, intending to park in the clearing. This possibility was fraught with danger. If someone did show up in the clearing and they saw my truck, a truck that didn't belong there. I would be in trouble. I had to risk it because anywhere else I could park the truck would be too far away to operate the aircraft.

This was the place I had to be.

CHAPTER 56

From my hiding position back in the woods, I considered the way Doug had told Gary things were going to go down. Gary told me Doug had assembled an elite team of FBI agents. Once the meeting started, there would be road blocks on the county road to prevent anyone from approaching or leaving the site. These road blocks would be manned by Texas Rangers. The FBI strike team would arrive in five SUVs and there would be a helicopter providing eyes in the sky. The FBI agents would quietly surround the farm house while the meeting was in progress and hit hard in a coordinated assault, using flash-bang grenades and teargas. Everyone at the meeting would be arrested, and anyone who resisted or attempted to fight would be shot. Gary was to drop to the ground the moment the assault started. In that way, he would be out of the line of fire, if any gunfire broke out, which after the stun grenades and teargas, was highly unlikely. Once the arrests were made, Gary could be handed over to the Marshal's service for protective custody, until it was time for him to testify at the trials. When the trials were completed and the felons locked away, Gary would live the rest of his life with a new name in a different location.

It was a pretty good plan. I was concerned about all the things that could go wrong. What if there was another roadblock using the same local LEOs? I knew Doug would have already considered that and had a plan of action. He had spent several days planning the raid and would have spent some time considering every imaginable scenario. This was the kind of thing the FBI knew how to do. They had learned the hard way. I couldn't help remembering the FBI raid on the Branch Davidian compound in Waco that left 74 people dead, including 20 children. On the other hand, the old farmhouse was not a compound. There were only about a dozen men, and no children. The men inside were not prepared for some sort of government raid. I figured I could count on the FBI. Surely, the mistakes of the past would be remembered and avoided in the present.

I remembered Doug had handled the unexpected changes in the first attempt at finding the meeting location, with confidence and care. This time there would be air support and the meeting location was already known. I wondered if the FBI helicopter would be able to spot my multi-rotor aircraft. I doubted it. My little flyer would be very difficult to spot against the forest land below, much lower than the FBI chopper would be flying, and when I heard it coming, I could move the multi-rotor away from the area entirely.

By a quarter to six, no other vehicle had showed up in the clearing. I moved out of my hiding place and got my high-tech little aircraft ready to fly. At about five minutes to six, my multi-rotor was circling over the farmhouse and I was able to recognize Gary's truck as it came down the driveway. In another five minutes, I had managed to photograph every vehicle parked outside, some in the hay barn and a couple of men who were smoking cigarettes in the yard. A little after six, I had to bring the aircraft back for fresh batteries.

Six fifteen found my multi-rotor circling the farmhouse again, but everyone was indoors and there was nothing to see. I rotated the aircraft to get a look at the county road in the distance. As I did so, five black federal SUVs in a line, eased to the side of the road and cruised to a stop. They could not have been seen from down at the farmhouse, even if sentries had been posted.

The sun was low in the sky now and the light was fading. I saw about twenty FBI agents deploy from the vehicles, but they didn't go down the hill toward the farmhouse. They had their weapons ready and they spread out along the side of the road, but it appeared they were awaiting orders to move in. I took a moment to zoom in and try to spot Doug, but the men were all in heavy, black combat gear and the helmets, ski masks and goggles or face shields obstructed my view.

I had to bring the aircraft back for fresh batteries. As I prepared for the next flight, I became aware of the sound of a helicopter, a quick search of the sky showed a distant chopper circling high above the farmhouse, the low light of the setting sun showing it to be a black speck. I pulled my binoculars out of the truck and studied the chopper for a moment. It was an unmarked Sikorsky UH 60M Blackhawk, without the stubby wings or weapons pods that attack helicopters typically carried. I figured there were probably eight or ten additional FBI tactical agents on board.

I sent my multi-rotor back to the farmhouse. A little after six thirty, and still no movement from the FBI agents on the ground, it was nearly dark now. I was proud of my camera. Even in the low light it was sending perfectly clear images to my monitor.

By seven fifteen. It was fully dark and all the lights were on in the farmhouse. The helicopter was no longer visible overhead, having no running lights, I couldn't see it. I could barely hear it, somewhere in the area. I lowered my aircraft, now hovering only fifty feet above the farmhouse, to just a few feet above ground and zoomed in on a window, to get a glimpse of what was going on inside the building. It appeared everyone was gathered around the table which had been moved to a more central point in the room. I couldn't make out Gary or anyone else in particular because the men nearest the window were blocking my view.

By a quarter to eight, I was on my next to last set of batteries. I had just put the multi-rotor back into its circling program over the farm house. I was watching the monitor as some of the men came out the front door. My camera could see them fairly clearly standing in the yard in the light that spilled out through the windows and the open door. I zoomed in and saw that one of the men was Gary. The men in the group appeared to be talking and relaxed, They were drinking beer and chatting; unaware there were twenty FBI agents just a couple of hundred yards away, an un-marked helicopter and a remote control aircraft circling overhead. More men started to come out of the farmhouse. I panned back out to get a look at the whole scene.

There was a sudden streak of light and instantly my monitor was overwhelmed with a flash of white light. At the same time, I heard the roar of an explosion. I looked away from the monitor and saw a ball of fire over in the direction of the farm house. I looked back at the monitor and saw that my aircraft had lost the image of the farmhouse and was being buffeted by turbulence, the picture jerky and pixelated. I thought surely it would go down. Somehow, the multi-rotor got itself back under control, as it circled away from the worst of the super-heated air.

I switched to manual control and got the aircraft and camera pointed at the place where I thought the FBI agents would still be standing out by the road. I couldn't see anything out there but the reflected light of the burning building, the glare of the fire flickering and rolling over the trees and brush between the house and the road.

I remembered my thermal imaging camera also had night vision capability, and in a moment I had switched it over. I saw on my monitor many glowing images of men moving fast away from the road and down toward the burning farmhouse. That was the FBI agents moving in. I switched back to the other camera and rotated the vehicle to put the focus back on the men in the yard. Just then, a bright light lit up the yard and I realized the helicopter had arrived on the scene. I had been vaguely aware of the sound of the chopper approaching, but too intent on what I was seeing to have paid it any attention. The Blackhawk was hovering with its spotlight illuminating the men in the yard.

The force of the explosion had hit the men in the yard, throwing them to the ground. As the FBI agents arrived at the burning farmhouse they began shooting the half a dozen men who were struggling to get away from the burning building. There was no return fire from the men who had just come out of the RAG meeting. I could clearly see Gary where he lay on the ground, staying down and still, just as he had been instructed to do. I saw an FBI agent stand over him and shoot him in the head, more than once.

I was frozen, stunned by what I had seen and in a state of shock. What had just happened? What had caused the explosion? Why did the FBI shoot everyone? Why did they shoot Gary? Were there any survivors?

CHAPTER 57

I managed to get my mind and body working again. My aircraft only had a few minutes of battery life left. I circled the multi-rotor up and away from the carnage and switched to thermal imaging, looking for movement away from the scene of destruction. In a moment I saw something on the ground moving fast in my general direction. It was moving too fast to be a person. I could see it was someone on an ATV, traveling without headlights, up the trail away from the mayhem. I brought the multi-rotor back to the truck and was waiting as the ATV eased into the clearing.

The ATV had some sort of specialized muffler, making it surprisingly quiet. It merely puttered as it approached. When it was about twenty yards from my truck, I switched on the headlights and lit it up.

Watkins was blinded by my headlights. He stopped the ATV.

"Throw your hands up, Watkins," I yelled.

I had the front sight of my .45 centered on his chest. He had no trouble hearing me, but he couldn't see me because I was behind the truck's headlights.

I could see him thinking about reaching for the gun he had somewhere on his person, but he was just smart enough to know he was probably outgunned.

The engine on the ATV stopped puttering, and Watkins put his hands up high.

"Keep your hands up and step off that thing." I instructed him.

He did, and as I approached him with my .45 centered on him, he stood next to the ATV, as still as if he were frozen.

"Who are you and how do you know me?" he asked.

My answer was sharp and filled with rage.

"I'm John Wesley Tucker. Gary Babcock was my friend and because of you, he's dead."

Watkins just stood there, with his hands up, about six from me. I had both my hands extended, keeping the .45 motionless; my sights fixed, center mass, my finger on the trigger.

"Reach very slowly with one hand and toss your gun off to the side. If you make one wrong move, I'll blow a hole through you where your heart used to be." I told him.

I was aware of the sound of the Blackhawk, still hovering somewhere in the distance.

Watkins slowly lowered his right hand and gently pulled a revolver from a holster on his right hip. He carefully tossed it aside. A revolver can discharge, if there is a shell under the hammer when it hits the ground, but that didn't happen. It landed softly in the tall grass on the other side of the ATV.

"Put both hands on the seat of the ATV and spread your legs, you know the drill."

I intended to pat him down and bind his hands behind him with a cable tie I'd tucked into my belt. I was certain Watkins was the only survivor of the raid on the meeting. I needed him alive.

As I stepped toward him he twisted suddenly and something hit my hands, knocking them numb and my gun fell away. He moved to swing again and I realized he had a telescoping ASP in his right hand. I stepped straight into him, inside the swing, and as I slammed down on his extended forearm at the wrist, with my left hand, I simultaneously drove my open right hand up against his elbow. He screamed as I heard the crunch and snap of his elbow joint being destroyed in the violent hyper-extension, the ligaments and tendons breaking away, the meniscus tearing. Even as he dropped the telescoping baton, I brought my right elbow back in a strike to the side of his face, then I stepped to the side and kicked him on the outside of the knee of the leg that held most of his weight. It popped and gave way under him. He fell to the ground, moaning. I knelt on his back then and pulled both his hands behind him, tightening the cable tie around his wrists. His right forearm was twisted, pulling on the elbow joint. When I pulled that arm up behind him he screamed again. With two major joints badly damaged and his hands bound behind him, Watkins was completely debilitated. I knew the pain would be excruciating. I had a hard time caring. Surgery and time would eventually repair most of the damage.

I was thinking of Gary, whose body was lying dead, next to a burning building.

It only took a moment to find my .45 where it had landed after the stinging blow to my hands from Watkins' ASP knocked it away. I examined my handgun and found it undamaged. I holstered it. In the process, discovering while my left hand and right wrist were bruised, they were otherwise unimpaired.

Watkins didn't even try to get up. I don't think it would have been possible. I found his ASP in the grass a couple of feet away. I picked it up, telescoped it closed and slid it under my belt. I found his revolver on the other side of the ATV. It was a .357 magnum, loaded with hollow points. I put it in my waistband, in the small of my back. When I patted him down, I found a large folding knife in his right front pants pocket. It had an eagle and snake motif on each side, showing through the clear plastic handle. It was exactly as Gary had described it to me. I put it back in his pocket.

Watkins could neither stand nor walk, so I grabbed him by the waist band and belt, and half-dragged/half-carried him to the passenger side of my truck. He was in horrible pain.

I dropped him, and left him there on the ground while I secured my things in the bed of the truck. It took some effort to get him into the truck on the passenger side, but I did it and fastened the seat belt around his waist. With his hands bound behind him, Watkins was forced to lean forward. He couldn't stand the weight of his body pressing back against his crippled elbow.

As I loaded my gear and my passenger into the truck, I'd been watching for the FBI helicopter. From the sound, I figured the big Sikorsky had landed in the hay field over by the burning farmhouse. I'd expected it to suddenly come flying over the forest to this clearing and hit us with the spotlight, but I thanked God it hadn't happened.

I was confident with the chopper on the ground and all the activity around the burning farmhouse, the sound of my diesel engine would not be heard or particularly noticed, as I drove out of the clearing. Diesel trucks are ubiquitous in farm and ranch country. Because the FBI vehicles were parked around a curve and more than a half mile down the hill from where I came out onto the county road, I would not be observed driving away. I kept my headlights turned off anyway. Better safe than sorry.

I knew I was headed toward a roadblock. Doug's roadblocks were the provision he had put in place to prevent anyone from leaving the scene of the raid.

I drove north about three quarters of a mile before I came to the roadblock in this direction. There were four or five vehicles behind a barricade, with their blue and red lights flashing. I flashed my headlights as I approached, reducing my speed. I slowed to a stop, with spotlights and headlights blinding me. I could see indistinct shapes approaching my truck from all sides. I knew there were probably several rifles and shotguns trained on me by half a dozen Texas Rangers. I sat very still, with my hands clearly visible on top of my steering wheel. Watkins was looking around, trying to see past the blinding lights. He looked emaciated in the glaring illumination.

Both the passenger side door and the door on my side were pulled open at the same time.

"Hello John, Fancy meeting you here," a familiar voice said.

I turned my head and looked into the face of Texas Ranger Captain, Luke O'Brian.

"Hey, Luke, you're a sight for sore eyes. This guy is Kevin Watkins. A few months ago, he murdered a Mexican national named Eduardo Ruiz. He has the murder weapon in his right front pants pocket. If you talk to Lieutenant Tony Escalante of the Tyler, PD, he'll fill you in on all the details. After what's happened tonight, I believe Watkins may also be the only living member of the Righteous Patriot's Brigade. He's all yours."

I got out of the truck and stretched. A couple of Rangers were taking Watson out of my truck. He was groaning with the effort.

"What the hell happened down there, John? We saw a streak from something, then a huge explosion. Did those RAGs blow the place up?" Captain O'Brian asked me.

"Luke, tell me about the streak you mentioned. Tell me exactly what you saw from here."

He nodded and thought for a moment.

"We're probably a mile and a half from the farmhouse. We can't see it from here because of the woods and hills between here and there, and it's dark. We were keeping a sharp eye out for any approaching vehicles. We saw something. A flash or streak of light, then BOOM! It was like a rocket hit something. What was it?"

"I'll tell you in a minute. Could you see the helicopter from here?"

"Yeah, well no, not really. We saw it in daylight, and then later, we saw the spotlight sweeping the ground, you know, like they do. We figured it was the same chopper, lighting up the scene. There weren't any running lights though. All we could see was the spotlight."

"That helicopter was lighting the scene so the FBI agents would have an easier time killing the survivors of the explosion."

"What did you just say?"

"I saw it, Luke. The FBI tactical strike team came in and systematically shot everyone who survived the explosion, including my friend Gary."

"No, I don't believe that."

"I have it all recorded. You should look this over very carefully." I handed him a thumb drive. "Keep it hidden and be very careful who you show it to."

"What about the explosion. What was it, John? What caused that explosion?"

"I think it was a hellfire missile." I said.

Luke grabbed my arm. "Do you know what you're saying?" He asked me, intently.

I nodded and said, "Yes, Luke. Think about what you saw. I believe the FBI used a drone to attack the RAGs meeting. I got a good look at it and there isn't any kind of rocket launcher on that helo. If I'm right..."

"... The FBI, using a drone to kill American citizens on American soil? I can't believe it." Luke shook his head.

"We'll see. It's all there on that thumb drive. It all needs to be analyzed by someone who knows what to look for, but I'm pretty sure they hit that meeting with a hellfire missile. Listen, Luke, I need to get out of here. I don't want the FBI to know I was ever here. You need to keep Watkins under wraps for a few days, too. He's the only other person who knows what happened down there, and the only person who can tell us what happened in that meeting. He's going to need some medical attention. Keep him hidden."

"Yeah, I'll do that. How did you get a recording of what happened down there?" Luke asked.

"Providence." I answered, pointing to the sky.

Luke studied me for a moment, and then he arrived at a decision.

"If you say so," He turned to the men at the barricade.

"Boys, get the barricade out of the way. This gentleman needs to be on his way and, LISTEN UP, he was never here. Now, to be clear, THAT'S AN ORDER. Get the lead out!"

CHAPTER 58

I had barely left the roadblock behind me when the call came in. I checked the caller ID before I pushed the button to answer the call.

"Hey, Jack, what's up?" I asked wearily, by way of greeting.

"What the hell are you playing at?" said Jack.

"Excuse me?"

"Don't act stupid with me. I know you've spent the whole day in the vicinity of that farmhouse. You're not supposed to be interfering in an FBI operation."

"You really are keeping tabs on me aren't you? Let me guess. You're tracking me using the GPS in my truck. Is that about right?"

"How I do my job, doesn't matter. Why were you there, and what did you see?"

"Do you really want to talk about this on an open phone line?"

He was silent for a second.

"I nearly had you picked up. I probably should have sent someone to get you. Hell, I should have come after you myself."

"How do you want to handle this?"

"Meet me in the usual place, as soon as you get back to Tyler. It should take about fifty minutes from your present location."

"Sure, Jack. I'll meet you there."

So that was it. Jack knew exactly where I had been, but not specifically what I had been doing. I wondered if Jack had told Doug I was in the area. Considering what I had seen and recorded, I doubted it. If Doug had known I was there, he would have done something about it. This was a mess of historic proportions. The FBI could not have gotten a drone attack authorized without the DHS and someone in the DOD knowing about it. The Attorney General of the United States would have had to sign off on it. Jack's friendship with me would only protect me so far.

What were they thinking? Did they really think they could kill American citizens without even giving them a trial? Clearly, they did think so. Was this the due process of the future? Welcome to the bold new America, where no warrants, arrests, or trials were needed, An America where a man could risk his life in service to his fellow citizens and be murdered for his trouble.

Not on my watch.

I was late to my meeting with Jack. I had to unload some equipment, copy some files and send some e-mails before I met him on the top level of the parking structure.

"What have you done?" Were the first words out of his mouth.

"... My patriotic duty." I replied, wearily.

"I thought you were above all that. I thought all you cared about was what you believe God wants you to do. Now, all of a sudden you go back to being a, a... I don't know what you are."

"Did you know what was going to happen out there tonight?" I asked him.

"What did happen out there? What did you see?"

"Oh come on, Jack. You seem to know everything about everything. Are you telling me you didn't know what was going to happen?"

"Are you asking me if I knew a group of anti-American domestic terrorists, who had attacked and killed a public servant and was conspiring to kill other government personnel, was going to be the subject of a police action? Did I know the FBI was going to take them down? I knew the leadership of the Righteous Patriots Brigade was not going to get the chance to do any recruiting in prison. I knew they wouldn't get the chance to spew anymore of their hate speech. And, I knew those animals were not going to get the chance to kill anyone else. We saved the American people, all of the American people, untold misery, terror and expense in bypassing the judicial process. I don't approve of the method, but I approve of the action. It was in the best interests of national security."

"Really, you approve of the cold blooded murder of men who were never even accused of a crime? You approve of the murder of my friend, Gary?"

"What? No. What are you talking about? What happened to Gary?"

"I saw an FBI agent shoot him in the head, while Gary was lying on the ground, just exactly as he had been instructed to do."

"My God, there must have been some mistake!"

"... Mistake, Jack? The Attorney General of the United States authorized a drone strike on American soil, specifically to kill American citizens, and you think there must have been some mistake!"

"Now see here, John. You don't want to go around making statements like that without any proof."

For a moment, I stared out at the lights of the city, twinkling through the trees. I took a deep breath and scrubbed my face with my hands.

"No, Jack, you're right. Without any proof, I would be wasting my breath. Nothing good could come from me running my mouth about something I can't prove."

"That's right! Now, you let me handle this. I'll look into what happened to Gary.

I nodded dully, in response.

"John, you're upset. That's perfectly understandable. I can't imagine how horrible it must have been for you. Try to put all this behind you. You have another mission don't you? Concentrate on the next thing you need to do. Can you do that?"

I looked Jack in the eye. "I'm all about my mission." I replied.

"Good man. I knew I could count on you."

I had learned a couple of useful things from Jack. He hadn't denied that a drone had been used. He and I both knew a Hellfire missile could not have been fired from the FBI helicopter. The other thing was that Jack did have prior knowledge of what was going to happen. It meant there was more than one federal agency involved.

I thought about all those things for a moment. Then I made the phone call.

"Hello, John, I was just about to call you." Special Agent in Charge, Doug Booker said.

"Hey, Doug. Yeah, I thought I should call. I knew I wouldn't hear anything from Gary. He told me you were going to take down the meeting tonight. I know you put him straight into protective custody, so he can't contact anyone. I just wanted to know how the raid went."

"John, I'm afraid I have bad news. Gary was killed tonight. At the present time, it appears he was shot by someone in the Righteous Patriot's Brigade. Apparently they saw or heard us coming. They shot Gary and engaged our agents with gunfire. About that time someone inside the building touched off the explosives and… You can imagine. We have a big job on our hands sorting through the rubble and identifying the remains. I'm sorry to have to tell you about Gary. I know you were close."

I waited a moment and considered my response.

"Are you sure? Maybe he got away…"

"John, I'm so sorry. Gary's body was found just outside the farmhouse. We've made a positive ID. Again, I'm sorry."

"I can't believe it…"

"I know. It's a shock. We didn't anticipate they would choose to fight and die rather than be captured."

"Did you get all of them?"

"Yes, John, we did."

"How many did you arrest?"

"John, they were all killed, most of them in the explosion."

"There were no survivors, Doug?"

"No, John, I'm sorry. I have to go. I'm still on the scene, and, as I said, there's a lot of work to do."

"Ok. I still can't believe it."

"I understand how you feel. Good bye, John."

I had learned three things from our conversation.

Doug Booker had taken part in the massacre, he had no idea that Kevin Watkins was in the custody of the Texas Rangers, and he had no idea I'd ever been in the area.

CHAPTER 59

The next morning, Christine, Tony, and I were sitting in the reception area of my office, watching the story of the FBI raid now being broadcast on every television news channel in the country.

Christine was crying, holding a ball of tissue clutched in her hand, so tightly her knuckles were white. Tony sat beside her with his arms around her.

"John, do you think there's any chance the FBI made up the story about Gary being killed, to make keeping him safe, easier? Maybe they have him in protective custody somewhere and he will be starting a new life..." She suggested, plaintively.

"No, Christine. Gary is gone. He has started a new life, but not here in this world."

She sobbed at that, and Tony wrapped her more tightly in his arms.

We sat and watched the story unfold.

The FBI had provided footage of what we were told was the inside of the farm house, supposedly taken by an undercover agent, just hours before the explosion. The unidentified undercover agent would have had to be Gary. How he was supposed to have done the photography and provided the video footage wasn't mentioned.

The video showed rooms filled with automatic weapons, ammunition, RPGs, various types of military equipment and an assortment of explosives. I could tell the video had not been shot in that farmhouse, but how could the ordinary viewer know it was a ruse?

The scene cut to a live shot of the reporter standing a few dozen yards from the smoldering ruins of the farmhouse, wisps of smoke drifting in the light breeze.

"I'm here with the FBI's, Special Agent in Charge, Douglas Booker. Agent Booker, I understand you led the raid on the terrorist compound last night. Is that correct?"

Doug was dressed in black combat fatigues.

"Yes, Tawny, I was in command of the FBI's special tactical unit which raided this property at zero nineteen hundred and forty five minutes, last night. As you have reported, we had positively identified the persons on the property as being members of the domestic Christian terrorist group known as the Righteous Patriots Brigade, which is a splinter group of the Righteous Army of God. These were the same people responsible for the attack which caused the death of the Federal Prosecutor and the wounding of the Gregg County Sheriff, at the courthouse in Longview, just days ago."

"When you say "domestic", Agent Booker, are you indicating that this Christian terrorist group was made up of American citizens?"

"That is correct, Tawny. We are seeing a rise in religious extremism in this country. These people are irrational and dangerous. They believe in some unseen presence they call 'god', that directs them to do these horrible things. These religious hate groups are anti-government and they are becoming an ever increasing threat to national security and the safety of the American people."

"After the shooting in Longview, where they killed the prosecutor, how did you know where to find them?"

"The FBI immediately employed every tool at our disposal, to identify and locate the perpetrators. We had an informant within the terrorist sect. He was instrumental in locating the meeting place and in providing valuable information about the plans and preparations the group was making."

"My understanding is your informant was killed by the terrorists. Is that correct?"

"Our informant was killed just before we arrived on the scene."

"Can you tell us who the perpetrators were?

"I am not at liberty to comment on that, Tawny. This is an on-going Federal investigation."

"So there you have it folks..." The network anchor cut in. "At seven forty five, Central time, last night, the FBI raided a domestic terrorist compound in East Texas. A gun battle ensued and the terrorists detonated explosives, leveling the building where they were holed up. We have heard possibly as many as fifteen terrorists may have died in the raid; most of them were killed by the explosion itself. None of the dead have been identified at this... Correction; I've just been informed the man who was working as an informant for the FBI, the man killed on the scene by the terrorists, was named Gary Babcock. Mr. Babcock was a resident of Tyler, Texas, a town about forty miles from the scene of the horror visited on the region last night. Mr. Babcock was a retired firefighter for the city of Tyler..."

A picture of Gary in his Tyler Fire Department dress uniform was shown on the screen.

Christine began sobbing in earnest, her body wracked and her breathing ragged.

My phone rang and the caller ID prompted me to take the call.

"John, have you seen the television news coverage

of the raid?" Texas Ranger Captain, O'Brian asked me.

"We're watching it now, Luke."

"I watched the video you gave me."

"All four hours of it?"

"… Pretty much, yeah. This is a cover-up, John. The FBI is trying to make out like they didn't set out to kill everyone at that meeting."

"Listen, Luke. I don't want to talk about this right now."

"Huh? Oh yeah, I get it,"

"We should meet sometime soon and discuss the various ramifications and possible course of action which might be most pertinent."

"If you mean, figure out what happens next, you've got that right." Luke said.

"I assume you've made sure everything I gave you is accounted for and secure?"

"Yes, and it has proven to be a source of valuable information."

"That's the only good news I've heard all morning."

"Give me a call, when you're ready to meet." Luke hung up on his end.

"Tony, can I see you in my office? Christine, will you excuse us for a little while?"

When I had closed the door behind us, I brought Tony up to speed.

"Tony, I was there at that farmhouse last night. It didn't go down the way the FBI is presenting it."

Tony stared at me for a moment.

"What are you telling me, J.W.?"

"I have photos of everything inside that house. Photos I took just a few hours before the raid. I have aerial images of the entire property, including that farmhouse from every angle. The video we saw on the news, showing all those weapons and equipment was not shot inside the farmhouse. It doesn't even resemble it. I also have video of the FBI systematically shooting and killing the few men who escaped the blast, including Gary."

"Hold on, J.W. Are you suggesting the FBI gunned down unarmed men?"

"I don't know whether they were armed or not. They probably had handguns, but they offered no resistance. They were crawling and staggering away from the burning farmhouse that had just been blown to bits."

"Can you prove it?"

I told you, Tony. I have it all on film. Well, not really film, but you know what I mean."

"J.W., are you telling me you were there, shooting video, while FBI agents killed Gary?"

"Yes and no, Tony, I was about a half mile away, using a remote control aircraft to get the video."

"You have it all, the explosion, the shooting, everything?"

I nodded, solemnly.

"Show me." He said.

CHAPTER 60

Tony and I watched the most pertinent segments of the images I had recorded the previous night.

"As you can see, Tony, none of those guys are expecting any trouble. They're just talking and…"

"Run it back, J.W. Did you see the flash, just before the explosion?"

I ran the images back and started again, from the point where some of the men began to emerge from the farmhouse.

"There! Did you see that?" Tony asked, about forty five seconds later, as the picture went to white and was broken up by the explosion.

"I did, Tony, and so did at least a half dozen Texas Rangers who were about a mile and a half away. There may have been other witnesses as well."

"Can you run it back and then play it in slow motion?" Tony asked.

"No, Tony, I don't know how to do slow motion on my computer. But the Texas Rangers have a copy of this, so does a guy who works for the local ABC affiliate. There are people in Washington D.C. who are looking at this right now. They can do all kinds of things to enhance the image and look at it frame by frame."

"J.W., that looked like an incoming missile strike."

I nodded in agreement. "It was what caused the explosion, Tony. There were no explosives inside the farmhouse."

Tony was scrubbing his face with his hands.

"This is completely... unacceptable." He struggled for the word.

"It may be even worse than what you've just seen, Tony."

"I don't see how it could be any worse."

Tony was almost incapable of imagining that any fellow law enforcement officer could be capable of horrendous crime. He had seen some things before, but he was so committed to his own personal integrity, he had a difficult time thinking another cop might be crooked.

"Tony, where did the missile come from, and why did they use it?"

Tony closed his eyes and shook his head.

The image now was the wide shot of the area, showing the FBI agents arriving on the scene, the helicopter spotlighting the action. Watching it again was even harder for me, because I knew what I was about to see. The picture was clear and there was no doubt about it, the heavily armed and armored FBI agents were shooting down the survivors of the explosion, without any provocation. We saw one of the agents standing over Gary, shooting him repeatedly with an assault rifle.

Tony groaned.

I stopped the video.

"That was a carefully planned execution. They never intended to arrest anyone." Tony noted.

"... Exactly." I responded. "It's why they killed Gary. They couldn't have him contradicting their version of the events."

"They intended from the beginning there would be no witnesses and no survivors." Tony observed.

"They failed, on both counts." I answered

"What? Who survived?"

"One of the men who had been in the meeting, I hauled him out of there and turned him over to a trusted friend. Are you getting this, Jack?"

Tony looked at me, clearly confused.

"Tony, say hello to our friendly DHS agent, Jack McCarthy. I expect he and his cronies are, or will be, listening to this entire conversation."

Tony's face got red.

"Here's the thing, Jack. By now, there are at least a dozen people who know what really happened last night. Today, from here to Washington D.C., there are people watching and analyzing all the evidence I've provided them. Within hours, this will all go public. If anything happens to me, or anyone I know, it will come back on you. You might want to get busy figuring out how to save yourself."

Tony looked at me.

"Nice speech, J.W. Do you really think he's listening to any of it?

"I don't know for sure, Tony, but he does like to do that sort of thing. I'll tell you something else."

"Yeah, what is it?"

"That was all the warning he's going to get."

A little more than an hour later, FBI Special Agent in Charge, Doug Booker, still dressed in his black fatigues, arrived at my office. Tony had gone back into the reception area to watch the ongoing TV news coverage with the Christine. Doug walked in to my office without any interference from either Tony or Christine. He carefully closed the door behind him.

"Hello Doug, have a seat. Evidently someone gave you the news."

He sat down and took a deep breath.

"So, you were there. I guess I shouldn't be surprised. Look, I'm sorry about Gary. One of my men saw a man on the ground, reaching for a handgun and he panicked. There was a lot of shooting going on, the building had just exploded and he panicked. He shot Gary before I could stop him."

"Doug, did you come by here to try to lie your way out of this thing?"

The muscles of Doug's prominent jaw bunched up.

"Are you calling me a liar?" He growled.

"You may recall you promised me you would personally do everything in your power to keep Gary safe. For all I know, you shot Gary yourself. So, yes, Doug, in my opinion you're a liar, a bigot, and a coward."

"Stand up, you son of a bitch." Doug spat, rising to his feet.

"What, you want to fight me? Nothing good would come of that. Sit down, Doug. You came here presumably to talk, let's talk."

Doug continued to stand. He pointed his finger at me.

"You're trying to ruin me. You've been out to get me from the moment we met."

I studied him for a moment.

"No, Doug. You've probably ruined yourself, but I had nothing to do with it."

"You religious hypocrite, you've taken it upon yourself to punish me." He said.

"No, Doug. If I had taken it upon myself to punish you, you would already be dead." I said, looking him in the eye.

Agent Booker stiffened and blinked several times. I sighed.

"Believe me, Doug. I mean you no harm. It's not my place to punish you. There is a judge you will answer to, but it isn't me. On the contrary, I forgive you, Doug. I'm a guy who has screwed up and deserves nothing more than hell and horror, myself. I'm just thankful that God, who is rich in mercy, has forgiven me my sin, and He will do the same for you."

"Sin, what sin? I've only done what needed to be done. Everything I do serves the best interests of my country." Doug said, indignantly, with a wave of his hand.

I studied him some more.

"Doug, you're lying to yourself. You organized an execution. You denied justice to those men because of your own hatred towards them."

He shook his head.

"I provided a service to my country in the routine course of my duty."

"I don't think the country will see it that way, once the evidence is made public."

Doug crossed his arms and looked down at me where I was seated.

"I don't know what you've got, but it won't be enough. I'm not alone. I have friends in high places. Whatever you have, or think you have, you can't touch me."

"I'm not even going to try, Doug. I'm sorry, so very sorry. I wish you could see the light. I'll pray for you."

Doug moved toward the door. "Pray for yourself. You're one of the lunatics who believe in that shit. One of these days, the shoe will be on the other foot. Something about you doesn't fit. We're looking into that. If you ever see me again, it will be when I come to get you."

As Doug stormed out through the reception area, Tony and Christine watched him go.

On the television the news anchor was announcing they had just received word there was some question as to the actual events which had occurred at the farmhouse in East Texas. It had been reported there was going to be an announcement from the Justice Department. The rumor was that several witnesses and some video footage had come forward, casting the raid in a completely different light.

My mission is all about the light.

EPILOGUE

Most people lead lives of solitary anxiety, solitary, because they don't talk about their fears with anyone. They don't even want to admit they have them.

They don't know who they are, or why they are on the earth.

Introspection only brings more doubts and fears, so they seek solace from science.

Science tells them they are just biological organisms, evolved from muck, eking out a brief existence, at the expense of a doomed planet. Science tells them life is random, meaningless and pointless. Take another pill, and try not to think about it.

The clock is ticking.

Many wander through life, aimlessly waiting for the clock to run out. Some are seeking to find something that makes them feel as if their life matters in some way. They mostly want to "do the right thing," but violently disagree on what "right" is, because, "Every way of a man is right, in his own eyes."

The clock is ticking.

People know that from the moment of birth, they

are doomed. They know life is short and uncertain. It may end at any time. The best of them ask "why"?

Why do we exist? Why are we the way we are? Why do bad things happen? Why is there suffering and death? What happens after we die, do we just cease to exist? When we die, will it be as if we had never existed at all?

The world offers many different and conflicting answers. Most of them are lies.

So, most people everywhere, in every walk of life, are as lost as sheep without a shepherd, stumbling blindly through however many days that remain to them, silently screaming in desperation.

The clock is ticking.

I know why I get up in the morning. I know what I'm supposed to do and how I should do it. I live to serve, but I don't serve the planet earth, the government, or myself.

I serve the holy God; the creator of all things. I am appointed as one of His ambassadors in this place.

I serve The Good Shepherd.

He alone is perfect.

His sheep are imperfect, but His sheep know His voice when they hear it.

Other sheep wander around lost, following whatever voice sounds most pleasant to them at the moment, even the voices that lead them to slaughter.

Sheep without a shepherd are helpless against the predators.

I am appointed as a Shepherd of His sheep, to seek the lost sheep, and to stand against the wolves.

We who serve as Shepherds are also imperfect, but we are empowered and equipped for service.

I have the sword of Truth, the message of glorious hope.

I have work to do.

I wish I were a better Shepherd.

The clock is ticking.

ACKNOWLEDGEMENTS

I'd like to thank all the major news organizations who daily bring us their well-honed stories of horror, tragedy, and the corrupt condition of this present world. It makes the work of writing fiction so much easier. All any fiction writer need do is expand on the news of the day.

You can't make this stuff up.

****

"These three remain; faith, hope and love. The greatest of these is love."

A LOOK AT: THE TICKING CLOCK

(ANGELS & IMPERFECTION 3)

**IS THE VIOLENCE IN HIS PAST INTERFERING
IN HIS RELATIONSHIP WITH GOD?**
When private detective John Wesley Tucker meets Hafsah Bashir, his world and his mission are turned inside out. She's searching for a missing family member and the fate of millions hangs in the balance.

Since the fall of ISIS, radicalized recruits from the internet have been ineffective at bringing mass casualty terror back to America. The Islamic State recognizes they need leadership and training. The caliphate has just the right man for the job; they've sent him to America. Before he begins organizing a network, his first group of home-grown muja-hedeen will strike in East Texas. DHS Agent Jack McCarthy enlists John's aid in stopping them...

Coming May 2020

ABOUT THE AUTHOR

Born in Bakersfield, California and abandoned by his parents in Seattle, Washington. After living in the foster care system for some years, Dan Arnold was eventually adopted. He's traveled internationally, lived in Idaho, Washington, California, Virginia, and now makes his home in Texas with his wife Lora. They have four grown children and three grandchildren of whom they are justifiably proud, not because they are such good parents, but because God is good.

A Member of the Association of Christian Fiction Writers, and Western Writers of America, in 2015, writing under the name Daniel Roland Banks, his book Angels & Imperfections was selected as a finalist in Christian Fiction in the Reader's Favorite International Book awards.

Find more great titles by Dan Arnold and Christian Kindle News at https://christiankindlenews. com/our-authors/dan-arnold/